# WHERE I'M SUPPOSED TO BE

## H.K. CHRISTIE

*For Kiki*

# LATE SUMMER

# CHAPTER 1

CASEY KNELT down to meet the eager stare of the black and tan Rottweiler trapped behind the bars of his shelter cage. The canine, sporting a red bandana, bent his head to the left as Casey cooed. "Hi there, fella." She studied the name on the cage and grinned. "Espresso Bean. Aren't you adorable?"

The dog wagged his tail as he kept his chocolate brown eyes fixed on her.

In spite of the musty stench of the cells filled with lonely animals, Casey's insides glowed. She pivoted toward her coworkers with eyes wide and declared. "I have to have him! Did you see his eyes? And that bandana!" She placed her hand across her chest.

Javier approached and chuckled. "Interesting choice. He's a little big, don't you think? There are a few Chihuahuas that might be better suited for you."

Casey shook her head. "Nah." She inched closer to the cage. "Look at him."

"Oh, honey," Javier sighed, setting a hand on his hip. "I'm not sure Jason will share your sentiment. I shudder at what he'll do to me at the next couples dinner when he finds out it was me who dragged you to a shelter during our lunch break."

Casey rolled her cornflower blue eyes. If she wanted a dog, she'd get a dog.

She peered over at Dana. "Dana, what do you think? Is he a keeper, or what?"

Dana pushed back her wire-rimmed glasses and gritted her teeth. "I'm gonna have to agree with Javier. He's a little big for you—especially since you've never had a dog before." Dana cocked her head. "I didn't even know you wanted a pet."

Casey hunched into her shoulders. "I didn't...not until now. Now that I've met Espresso Bean." She exaggerated the word bean and eyed her friends. "This is both of your faults! It was your idea to come here."

It was true. She hadn't considered getting a pet until now. She didn't have pets growing up with the exception of a few goldfish and an ill-fated hamster. She never thought a pet was something she wanted, but now, standing in the humane society, she felt an overwhelming force telling her this wasn't what she wanted, it was something she needed.

"What about you, Javi? You find one?"

"There are a few I could snuggle and cuddle all day, but I need to bring Ben to meet them first."

Ben, Javi's latest boyfriend, was pushing for a commitment that included a fur baby.

He continued. "We should head back. We don't want to be late to the research meeting. You know how *he* gets if you're late to one of his riveting lectures on the latest in protein purification techniques."

At the mention of their lab director—aptly nicknamed 'he who shall not be named'—they shared a laugh. His superior attitude and boring lectures were more of a challenge for the lab personnel to stay awake than a form of education as they were sure he intended.

On the drive back to work, Casey stared out the window imagining Espresso Bean frolicking at the dog park, playing fetch, and greeting her when she got home from work. The smile creeping up her face fell when she realized Javier was probably right. It would be more than a little challenging to convince her new husband to allow her to bring Espresso Bean home.

---

CASEY PULLED into their two-car garage and parked her new Corolla next to Jason's black Acura coupe. She thought, *Of course he's home.* Where else would he be? School? Not likely. Who knew graduate school required so little attendance?

She entered their home through the 90s-inspired kitchen with its outdated white-tiled counters and yellowing laminate cabinets and made her way through the living room. She hopped up the stairs to Jason's office.

When they'd rented the townhouse, he'd insisted he needed his own room since he was a graduate student and needed to study. Casey couldn't recall the last time she'd seen him study. It was odd, because when they'd met during their second year of college through a mutual friend from high school, he'd been on the fast track to get his bachelor's degree a semester early. She would've never predicted his lackadaisical attitude toward graduate school. Maybe since he, a doted-on youngest child, had never had to work a day in his life, he'd decided to slow down and go at his own pace? She didn't know. Casey had grown up as one of five children to a single mother and had been working and going to school since she was fifteen. It wasn't until after graduating from college she understood the luxury of having only one job. How had she ended up marrying her polar opposite?

She shimmied off the thought and knocked while opening the door.

Jason swiveled his head toward her and took off his headset. "Hey."

Casey made herself comfortable in the club chair next to his massive desk. "Hey. How are things?" She glanced at the screen and saw he'd been playing video games. Surprise, surprise.

Jason ran his fingers through his chestnut hair. "Good. Got a little work done. I was just playing GTA. How was your day?"

Casey sat up straight. "Great actually!" She went on to tell him about her outing to the humane society and the desire to adopt Espresso Bean.

Jason squished up his face. "That's ridiculous. You're joking, right?"

"Why would I joke about that? His name is Espresso Bean, and I love coffee—it was meant to be!"

He pursed his lips and shook his head. "It's a stupid idea."

Casey scowled at him, willing her fingers not to curl into fists, using all of her energy to keep her cool. His condescending looks of disapproval had become all too familiar. His constant criticisms made her feel like she was never good enough. She had also grown tired of him trying to dictate what she could do or could have. They were both twenty-five, yet since they got married last year, he'd been acting more like a father than a husband.

She spat back, "It's not a stupid idea."

"Calm down. There's no reason to get excited."

Casey shut her eyes and breathed through her nostrils. Of course they couldn't get excited about things. He never got excited about anything other than video games or the stock market. He was certainly uninterested in anything having to do with her or their supposed life together. She was finding it more and more difficult to have a civil conversation with him. She forced herself to remain seated and not to storm out of his office.

Jason sighed. "Okay, fine. The idea of a dog isn't stupid. I just think a dog that size won't work for us. This place isn't big enough. We don't even have a back yard."

She glanced around the room while processing his words. She hated to admit it, but he was right. They didn't have the room Espresso Bean deserved. Maybe they could move? Not likely or practical. She couldn't have Espresso Bean. She deflated into the chair. She needed a dog.

She refocused her attention on Jason. "What if we found a more size-appropriate dog?"

He smirked. "Since when do you want a dog? This is probably just another one of your whims."

She remained straight-faced. "It's not a whim."

It wasn't. She knew deep down, she wanted and needed a dog. She wouldn't stop until she got one, but she didn't want to bring a dog home without Jason onboard with the idea. They didn't need any new reasons to argue, and she wanted her marriage to work. They'd taken vows, in a church. To God. To their families. To their friends. She had to do all she could to make it work.

Jason sunk back into his executive desk chair. "Okay. I'll make you a deal. If in two weeks you still want a dog, we can research the right breed for us. Deal?"

She knew in her heart she wasn't going to change her mind. What was two more weeks? She extended her hand. "Deal."

They shook.

Jason gave a half-hearted grin. "Pizza?"

Casey eyed him. "Sure. I'll call for delivery."

"Sounds good."

Casey brightened. "Oh, and I was thinking, maybe we can go out to the movies this weekend or maybe a hike? We're supposed to have nice weather." They hadn't gone on a date in ages. She hoped since he was showing signs of openness toward a dog maybe he'd finally be open to spending time with her.

Jason deflected. "Oh, I don't know. I'll think about it."

She didn't want to fight. "Okay."

She went back downstairs with her laptop and began researching dog ownership and different breeds for small spaces.

Despite her irritation over her conversation with Jason, she was ecstatic about the idea of a possible addition to their family.

THE FOLLOWING WEEK, Casey paused near Jason's door when she thought she'd seen a pack of dogs flutter across his computer screen. The two weeks weren't up for another few days. Was he already researching dogs? Was it possible he actually wanted one too? Delighted, Casey entered the room. "What's that? Is that a dog? Are you looking up dogs?"

Jason playfully said, "Guilty."

Casey's eyes lit up and she squealed. "Does this mean we can get a dog?"

He glanced over at the screen. "I did find some really cute ones." He waved her over. "Look at that."

Casey leaned in to study the small creature that looked as if it was made of cotton balls. "Oh. My. God. That is the cutest thing I've ever seen. What kind of dog is that?"

"A Shih Poo." He explained.

"A Shih Poo. What the heck is a Shih Poo?"

"It's a cross between a Shih Tzu and a Poodle. There are a whole bunch of mixed breeds great for small spaces, and they are adorable. The hardest part is picking which one to get."

Casey couldn't believe what she was hearing. She was getting a dog! They were getting a dog. They actually agreed on something—something big.

She told him she'd be right back. She jogged downstairs, grabbed her laptop, and made her way back up to his room. She plopped herself back on the club chair and searched on her computer alongside Jason. They joked and laughed as they compared their results.

It dawned on Casey how much fun they were having. It seemed like ages since they'd actually enjoyed each other's company. Maybe they weren't doomed to become part of the 50 percent of marriages that ended in divorce?

Casey sat back and studied the images of black and white fur on her screen. "You know the Shih Tzu by itself is pretty darn cute. Look at these puppies!" She handed Jason her computer.

His amber eyes lit up. "My gosh. You're right. So freakin' adorable."

"Maybe we should get a Shih Tzu? According to this website, they are known for their wonderful temperament. Clever, playful, lovable, intelligent, spunky and..." She giggled. "Clownlike."

Jason threw his hands in the air. "Let's do it!"

Casey jumped up and hugged him and gave him a peck on the lips. "I'm so excited!"

She couldn't remember the last time they'd hugged. She shrugged off the revelation and jumped back into the chair. "I'll search for rescues."

Jason squirmed. "Really? A rescue? I kind of wanted a puppy. Says here you can get one as young as twelve weeks. They're so tiny!"

Casey searched the Shih Tzu rescue site. She didn't find any puppies but did find a few that were one to two years old. She explained to Jason that a one-year-old was almost a puppy.

He hesitated and said, "What about this one. I found an ad on Craigslist that says the litter wasn't planned. It's their family dog that accidentally mated before they could get her spayed. I know it's not a rescue, but it's not from one of those awful puppy mills either."

Casey considered it. Was her desire for a rescue dog worth a fight with Jason? And, she had to admit, she would love to have a four-pound ball of fluff. She exclaimed, "Okay, I'm in. Let's call."

She sat at the edge of her seat as Jason dialed the number listed on the advertisement. He put the phone to his ear.

He whispered. "It's ringing."

After what seemed like an eternity of Jason saying, "uh-huh

and okay," he hung up. "Okay, they have a few black-and-white males and females left. We have an appointment tomorrow at eleven to meet them."

Casey leaped out of her chair. "I can't wait!"

For the first time since their wedding day, Casey was excited about their future together.

# FALL

# CHAPTER 2

THEY STROLLED up the driveway and waved to an older gentleman wearing dirty overalls in the two-car garage, standing at a work bench with a black-and-white Shih Tzu lying three feet away. The dog lay on its belly, its eyes following every movement of Casey and Jason.

Jason said, "We're here to see the puppies."

Casey had to suppress a giggle as a mental image of Cruella de Vil popped into her head.

The man waved toward the front door of the sea foam green house. "Go ahead and knock on the front door. Marion will help you out."

Jason said, "Thanks."

The dog redirected its attention to the yellow lab walking past the driveway with its owner. The Shih Tzu remained on its belly. Casey turned to Jason and said, "I'm surprised the dog just lays there. Shih Tzus must be really obedient."

Jason shrugged. "I guess so."

They knocked on the door and a middle-aged woman with tan skin and dark eyes answered. "Hi! You must be here for the puppies."

Jason said, "Yes, I'm Jason, and this is my wife, Casey."

"I'm Marion. Nice to meet you. Please come on in."

Casey and Jason followed her inside and sat on one of the two sofas separated by an oval coffee table. The home smelled of fresh flowers and clean linens.

Marion said over her shoulder, "I'll be back in a moment with the puppies."

She left without another word. The house was silent. Casey and Jason exchanged glances and leaned back against the cushions.

A minute later, Marion returned from the hallway to the right. Puppies followed behind. Casey's eyes widened as flashes of black and white fur dizzied her senses. The pint-sized puppies sprinted and hopped in all directions around the room. She jumped when one of the fluffy creatures landed on her lap. She gazed into the wide, brown eyes as the puppy planted itself on her thighs. The pup had a face full of mostly black fur with a spike of white centered above her eyes.

The puppy stared up at her, panting, with its pink tongue curled up high enough to touch her snout. Casey wasn't sure what to do. It had been years since she'd held a dog, and she couldn't remember ever playing with one so small. Was it breakable? She apprehensively extended her hand to stroke the back of the precocious pup.

Jason joked, "Looks like you've been claimed!"

Casey smiled nervously, "I suppose I have."

Jason called over to Marion who stood in the hallway, "Which ones are still available?"

Marion strolled back into the room and gave a warm smile. "The males over there are, but she's the last female." Marion pointed to the creature sitting on Casey. "She had been reserved, but it fell through. I think she likes you."

Casey grinned as the dog remained planted on her lap. She glanced down at the puppy and paused as her heart melted. She turned her head to make eye contact with Jason. "I think she's the one."

As if the decision was theirs to make.

Jason chuckled. "I think so." He stood and approached Marion. "Well, it's decided. When can we take her home?"

Casey remained sitting since her new best friend had curled up on her lap. Casey continued to stroke her fur and gaze into her curious eyes.

Marion said, "Not for another week. She's not quite old enough, so I'll need a deposit to hold her. Although I have little doubt about whether or not you'll be back."

Jason pulled out his checkbook, scribbled, and handed it to Marion. He faced Casey. "Are you ready to go?"

Casey knew that 'no' wasn't the appropriate answer. She gave the puppy one last pet and placed her on the carpet. She stood and nodded.

They said their goodbyes and stepped out of the door. Casey glanced over her shoulder and paused for one last glimpse of those big brown eyes before heading toward Jason's coupe.

Casey climbed into the car and braced herself on the open door while her chest constricted as if a part of her was being ripped away. It was her. It was that ball of black and white fluff. She'd gotten into Casey's heart so fast it was as if she'd always been there.

On the drive home, Jason suggested they stop for lunch to celebrate meeting their newest member of the family. Casey was surprised he'd initiated spending time together. It seemed like ages since they'd been on a date.

They settled on a tiny Italian bistro near their townhouse. They walked in and inhaled the scent of tomato sauce and garlic bread. The hostess sat them at one of eight tables covered in red-and-white-checkered tablecloths and were approached by a potbellied man of about fifty with fair skin and a thin mustache. "What can I get you two?"

Jason pointed to the menu. "I'll have the tortellini with marinara."

"And you, miss?"

Casey replied, "I'll have the ravioli with pesto."

"Very well. Be right back with bread."

The waiter collected their menus and headed toward the back of the restaurant.

Jason leaned forward. "What are we gonna name her?"

Casey twisted her mouth. "I don't know. She's got a personality, that's for sure. It should fit her. Like Diva or Superstar."

Jason chortled. "Ha! This is our dog, Superstar. No seriously, a little too kitschy, but I agree. She's got spunk and confidence to spare. She's got moxie!"

Casey stiffened, and her eyes widened. " Roxie! Roxie with lots of moxie!"

Jason's mouth gaped open. "I like it. Roxie. Roxie, with lots of moxie. Roxie it is!"

Over their carbohydrate-loaded lunch they continued to talk about Roxie with a new light in their eyes that Casey thought had burned out long ago.

***

DURING THE NEXT WEEK, Casey thought of nothing but Roxie. The pull toward the fluffy creature was beyond reason. The only way to remain sane was to focus on preparing for Roxie's arrival. She and Jason conducted extensive research on the internet to figure out what they would need for her. A bed, water dish, training pads, food, treats, harness, leash, and a pen.

Casey wasn't much of a crafter, but she made it her mission to sew Roxie a matching set of pillows and blankets to accompany her new bed, which she personalized with prominent lettering spelling out her name with a little flower she'd ironed on. The blanket and pillows made of pastel-flowered fleece weren't perfect. The seams were crooked and the pillows an odd shape, but she knew Roxie wouldn't mind.

They researched how best to train a Shih Tzu. They decided they would follow all the rules. No sleeping in the bed. No people food. A strict potty-training routine. Roxie would be a perfectly trained puppy. Friday evening before the weekend they were to pick up Roxie, they set up her four-by-six-foot pen made of black wiring in the living room next to the fire place. They'd placed a piece of linoleum underneath and filled it with toys, her bed and pillows, water dish, and a training pad. They were sure Roxie would love it.

Saturday morning, Casey and Jason stood on the porch of the sea-foam green house once more. Casey clutched Roxie's blanket as she pressed the doorbell. The sound of dogs barking filled her ears and warmed her insides. She glanced at Jason and a wide grin stretched across his face, too.

The door opened, and Marion greeted them with a smile. "Hello! Come on in. I was just giving her a bath."

Casey asked, "Does she like taking baths?"

Marion hesitated. "Yeah. Let me get her dried off. Take a seat on the sofa."

They sat and fidgeted while awaiting their new fur baby. Jason said, "So we're really doing this!"

Casey shrugged. "Looks like it." She set the blanket on her lap.

Marion returned with a freshly bathed Roxie and handed her over to Casey. Casey sat her down on her lap and gazed into her eyes. "Hi there, Roxie. So happy to see you."

Jason bent to be eye level with Roxie and said, "Hi Roxie. How do you like that name? I definitely think you're a Roxie."

Casey squeezed Roxie to her chest.

Jason faced Marion and extended his digital camera to her. "Can you take a photo of us?"

She chuckled. "First family photo! Of course."

Jason sat back while Casey straightened and adjusted Roxie to face forward. Marion exclaimed, "Say cheese." They grinned with shining eyes.

Post-photo, Casey wrapped Roxie in her new blanket like a black and white furry burrito and headed toward the car. They settled into their seats, and Jason took more pictures of their precious cargo in Casey's lap. Roxie shook. Casey understood the shaking to mean that Roxie was cold and held her tight to her chest the remainder of the ride home.

Casey stepped into the kitchen with Roxie in her arms and said, "Welcome home little Roxie!" They went through the kitchen and into the living room to show Roxie her new pen. Casey opened the gate and set her down inside. Roxie stared at her as if asking, "What am I supposed to do now?"

Jason picked up a yellow stuffed duck in an attempt to get her attention. Roxie inched back to Casey. Casey stroked the fur on her back and spoke softly. "It's okay. It's just a toy." Casey placed a water dish in front of Roxie's paws. The pup sniffed before lapping up the water for nearly fifteen seconds.

Jason and Casey glanced at each other. Jason said, "Guess she was thirsty."

"Guess so."

Hydrated, Roxie began to explore the pen. She climbed up into her blue fleece bed as if she knew it was hers. After exploring the pillows and crevices, she hopped out and began investigating the letters on the front. She pawed at the *R*. Pawing turned into chewing. Jason stiffened and pushed her back. "Stop that, Roxie!"

Casey's mouth widened. "Don't yell at her! She's just a puppy."

"We have to teach her."

"Marion said she was teething. It's not her fault. Jeez. Temper much?"

Jason stood up and shook his head. "I'll get the baby carrots before she tears apart the house."

Casey picked up Roxie, held her close, and told her not to worry. Why would he yell at a puppy? Who does that?

Jason returned with a bag of baby carrots. He extended one to Roxie. "Here you go, yummy carrots."

Roxie sniffed and retreated back to Casey.

Jason pleaded. "C'mon girl. Carrots are good." He took a bite and gave a reassuring nod. "See?"

Roxie inched back over and sniffed Jason's half-eaten carrot before prancing back to Casey.

Jason shook his head. "She won't even try it. I thought dogs were supposed to love carrots?"

Casey shrugged.

Over the course of the weekend, not only did they learn Roxie didn't like carrots, but it was soon apparent she wasn't a fan of any of the rules they tried to implement. Her aversion to kibble could only be explained by her thinking it was poisoned, and she cried during the night as if her pen was a Guantanamo Bay for puppies.

By Sunday night, the only letters remaining on her bed were the *X* and *E*.

---

MONDAY MORNING, Javier and Dana flanked Casey's desk in the lab. Javier combed his dark hair with his fingers and studied Casey. "Girl, you look terrible."

Dana playfully swatted at Javier's shoulder. "That's not nice."

Casey arched her eye brow and pursed her lips. "Thanks. Didn't get much sleep. Roxie cried all night. It's pretty safe to say she hates her pen." She laughed and continued, "This is pretty much all your fault. If you hadn't insisted we go to the Human Society last month I'd be sleeping through the night!"

Javier clapped his hands together. "I totally forgot you got

Roxie this weekend! We must see pictures. You have pictures, right?"

Casey faced her computer. "Of course. Let me pull them up." She went into her email to retrieve the photos Jason sent.

Dana sat on the edge of her desk. "How's Jason with Roxie?"

Casey shook her head. "Not great. He likes her, but he has zero patience. He expects her to understand all his commands right away. He doesn't get that it takes time."

Javier and Dana exchanged knowing glances.

Casey shook off the thoughts of Jason and opened the files. She straightened her monitor and said, "There she is, Miss Roxie."

Dana and Javier said, "awww," in unison.

Javier placed his hands on his cheeks. "She's adorable. Oh my god. So precious."

Dana agreed.

Casey continued scrolling and stopped on the family photo. She chuckled. "And here is our first family portrait. Aren't we just the most perfect little family?"

Javier and Dana burst into laughter. They knew Casey and Jason's relationship was far from perfect.

# CHAPTER 3

A WEEK LATER, Casey climbed into bed and tucked her head under the pillow. Jason nudged her, "What are you doing?"

Casey pulled her head out and sat up. "I can't take it. She's cried every night this week. It breaks my heart. Not to mention, I'm not getting any sleep."

"You just have to be strong."

Casey shook her head. "I am strong, but I'm not heartless, and I can't function without sleep."

Jason smirked. "The article I read says it will stop eventually."

"How long is eventually?"

"It didn't say."

Casey jumped out of bed in a huff and grabbed her pillow.

Jason asked, "What are you doing?"

Casey stood with a scowl on her face. "I'm sleeping next to her to see if it will calm her down."

"You're going to sleep on the floor?"

"Yep." Casey strutted out of the room and downstairs. She reached the pen where Roxie lay crying. Roxie sat up and pounced on the wall of the pen when she spotted Casey.

Casey leaned over and picked her up. "Hi, girl. Why are you so sad? Did you miss me while I was at work?"

The puppy cocked her head to the side.

"That's it, huh? I hate it too. I'm not lucky enough to stay home all day with you like Dad." She snuggled her and said, "You have to stay in your bed, but I'll be right here." She gave her a squeeze and a kiss on the top of her head and placed her back in her fluffy, blue bed.

Casey situated her pillow next to the pen, pulled the blanket over her, and put her head down. Within moments Roxie was next to the wire wall pawing at her. Casey willed herself to stay strong. She could handle a little pawing. At least Roxie wasn't crying anymore. Eventually, she settled down and lay on the floor next to the wall in an attempt to be as close to Casey as possible.

THE FOLLOWING WEEK, Jason stepped up to the pen in his pajamas holding a Superman mug full of hot coffee. With one hand he picked up Roxie from the pen as Casey stirred awake. She pushed the blanket off and sat up, letting out a groan. She pushed her shoulders back and surveyed the scene. "Morning."

Jason smirked. "Morning. Looks comfortable."

"Not even a little. It's been a week. Maybe she's settled. I think tonight I'm going try sleeping upstairs again. If I keep this up, I'll need to start going to a chiropractor." She stood and rubbed Roxie on the head. "Morning, little one." She proceeded to the kitchen and grabbed the glass carafe and let the coffee drip into her favorite mug, a glass beaker with a handle. She stood and watched Roxie playing with Jason, hoping Roxie was acclimated to her pen. Sleeping on the floor was the pits.

LATER THAT NIGHT, Roxie stared through the gaps in the wire pen as if in disbelief that Casey and Jason would head upstairs without her. Casey kept her head down as she climbed the steps. She couldn't meet the sad little pup's gaze. She climbed into bed and lay her head down.

Fifteen seconds.

Thirty seconds.

Thirty-four seconds. High-pitched cries echoed up the stairs. Casey exhaled. "I can't do this. She's just going to cry all night."

Jason lay on his side, facing her. "You can't sleep on the floor forever."

"I know. What if we brought her bed up and put it right there. She'd be able to see us." Casey motioned to the adjacent wall that had a three-tiered bookshelf and a space next to it big enough for Roxie's bed.

Jason shook his head. "I guess we can give it a try."

Casey hopped out of bed and jogged downstairs to the crying puppy who instantly stopped when she saw Casey. Casey picked up Roxie, her fluffy tail wagging, with one arm and grabbed her bed in the other. She hugged her and received a lick on her nose in return.

Casey chuckled. "Yes, Roxie, you win."

Back upstairs, Casey placed Roxie's bed along the wall and plopped her in. Roxie's eyes followed Casey as Casey climbed into her and Jason's bed. Casey turned to Jason. "Here goes."

He replied. "Fingers crossed."

They lay down, and within seconds the sound of small paws clawing at the side of Casey and Jason's bed began.

Jason said, "Boy, she is determined, I'll give her that."

Casey sighed. "Well we did name her Roxie with all the moxie." She paused and sat up. "What if we let her in the bed, just for one night. Maybe it won't be so bad?"

Jason sat up. "I don't know. Everything I've read says don't let them in—not even once."

"What do you suggest? I don't know how much more I can take."

Jason nodded. "I know. I don't know how much I can take either."

They exchanged knowing glances. Casey got up and picked up the black and white fur ball trying to get into the bed. She eyed her. "You've really won, haven't you?"

Roxie's tail swayed back and forth before she jumped between Casey and Jason. She curled up and went to sleep as they giggled softly, realizing they'd been beaten by a five-pound Shih Tzu.

***

THE NEXT MORNING Casey woke with a puppy perched on her chest staring at her. Casey chuckled. "You're happy this morning, aren't you?" Roxie responded with more licks to Casey's nose, from which Casey recoiled. She laughed. "I love you little dog, but I'm not a fan of your kissing style."

She glanced at Jason's empty side of the bed, surprised he was up before her. She realized it wasn't bad having Roxie in the bed between them. It wasn't like she had extinguished the romantic flame that lived in their bedroom. There hadn't been any flames between her and Jason for quite some time. Why had they resisted having Roxie in the bed in the first place? This solution seemed like a win-win.

She climbed out of bed with Roxie in her arm and headed downstairs to let her out on the patio.

Back in the house, Casey started in on their breakfast routine. She called out, "Hey Roxie, time for breakfast." Roxie hopped over as Casey meticulously placed a single kibble into a snake design leading up to her food dish. Roxie was a picky eater, and Casey had to play games with her to get her to eat. Roxie watched while Casey finished the design she was making on the floor out of kibble.

Casey glanced over at her. "Okay, Roxie, go at it."

Roxie ate each bit one at a time until she reached her dish. When she was done, she sat up and stared at Casey for her well-deserved treat.

"Good girl Roxie! Be right back." But Roxie followed her to the kitchen where Casey cut up a baked chicken breast and a cup of spiral wheat pasta. When she was done chopping, she mixed it together and stuck it in the microwave.

Jason entered the kitchen and sat at the island. "Hey, look at that, you can cook!"

"Haha. Very funny."

Jason placed his hand on his chest and pretended to have a heart attack. "No, really, I'm shocked."

"You knew I wasn't exactly Martha Stewart when you married me."

"Yeah, but I thought you'd learn at some point."

Casey ignored him and scooped Roxie's chicken treat into her bowl.

After Roxie devoured it, she ran over to the carpet in front of her pen and wiped her face. Now clean, she grabbed her yellow duck in her teeth and pranced over to Casey.

Casey grinned. "Oh, I see it's playtime." She sat on the ground cross-legged, and Roxie hopped into her lap and chewed on her duck while Casey rubbed her fur.

She looked over at Jason. "Don't forget my mom and sisters are coming over later to meet Roxie."

Jason said, "Don't worry. I'll make myself scarce."

"You know you don't have to. My family wants to visit with you too."

"I have work to do."

Casey rolled her eyes. "Sure you do."

"What, now I'm a liar?"

"You know they're your family too."

He shrugged. "I guess."

"You guess? Ignoring them won't make them go away."

He smirked. "Don't I know it."

He returned his focus to his laptop and didn't say another word.

Casey shook her head and returned her attention to Roxie who was content playing with her duck in Casey's lap. She couldn't believe she thought Roxie would make their relationship better. Sure, they both loved Roxie, but it didn't change anything between them. If anything, it caused more issues or at least brought up the old ones. Like Jason thinking he was better than her family. How did he not get that when you marry someone you marry their whole family?

---

CASEY OPENED the door with Roxie in her arm. The three visitors said, "Hey!" in perfect harmony. It was as if everywhere they went, they were their own cheering section. They cooed and awed over the little fur ball in Casey's arms.

"C'mon in, guys."

She led her mother and sisters into the living room and sat on the floor and let Roxie meet Anna, Cara, and Agatha on her own terms. Roxie pranced around sniffing each one but was most interested in Cara's purple and silver magician's cape, which she attempted to bite. Cara giggled as she tried to pull the cape away from her. She said, "Roxie's so funny!"

Casey nodded. "You have no idea! She's definitely got a mind of her own."

Anna kneeled next to Roxie with a stuffed taco and tried to get her attention by saying, "Hey Roxie, I've got your taco!" Roxie hopped over to Anna and fought her for the toy and won. Roxie, clearly proud of herself, went down panting with the stuffed toy in her mouth.

Roxie calmed down and lay her head on the floor as her eyes followed the visitors' movements.

Casey faced Anna, who wore her straight, dark hair pulled back in a long ponytail and had on ripped jeans with a matching jacket. Casey asked, "What's new, Anna? I believe someone is turning sixteen pretty soon."

Anna batted her mascara-clad eyelashes. "Yes, thank you. Thank you. I'm studying for my driver's test, but Mom," she paused to glare at Agatha, "freaks out every time we go driving. I'm not getting enough hours. Can you take me?"

Agatha put her hand on her sun-kissed cheek and shook her head. "It's just so scary."

Cara and Casey chuckled as Anna's eyes widened and she said, "See what I have to deal with?"

Casey regained her composure. "Of course. I've got your back. We'll have to make a date, okay?"

Anna gave a sly grin. "Fo' sure. Thanks."

"Cara, what's new with you? How's the fourth grade?"

Cara brushed her strawberry-blonde hair behind her ear. "It's good. I'm getting all A's so far."

Casey high-fived her baby sister. "Good job, Cara! How's soccer?"

Cara pursed her lips and tipped her head. "First game of the seasons is in a few weeks. You have to come!"

Casey said, "I wouldn't miss it. Maybe I can bring Roxie. She only has a few more vaccinations left and she can be out exploring."

Cara grinned. "Cool." And she returned her attention to Roxie.

"How about you, Mom? How are things?"

Agatha folded her arms across her lap. "Well, I thought you'd never ask. We actually have some pretty big news."

Anna and Cara sat up straight and nodded enthusiastically. Agatha continued. "I bought a condo! No more apartment living!"

Casey's mouth dropped open. "That's awesome! Where at? Tell me all the details!"

Agatha went on to explain it was close to where they lived in Walnut Creek, and escrow would close in three weeks. Anna said it was cool, but she still had to share a room with Cara which was, like, the worst.

Casey retorted, "At least it's only the two of you! Remember when all of us had to share a room? That was the pits." They erupted into laughter. Casey felt it comforting that they now could laugh at the darker times in their past. It seemed a lifetime ago.

Casey faced Agatha. "Have you talked to Kelly? I was supposed to see all of them, but then Roxie happened." Casey didn't want to give the real reason, which was that Jason couldn't handle when her sister, Kelly, and her three kids came over. Casey had made excuses, delaying Kelly from visiting often.

Agatha answered, "Yes, I talked to her, and they're doing good. Brie isn't much of a sleeper, which is hard on Kelly. I think Paul has been helping, but you know that situation is a bit messy. Angelina and Olivia now have to share a room, which neither is happy about. But what are you going to do, really?"

Anna jumped in. "You know he's still married, right?" Anna referred to Paul, Kelly's boyfriend and father to six-month-old Brie. It was another reason Jason had issue with Kelly's visits. Paul was technically still married but had been separated for a while. It didn't seem quite long enough to have had a baby with someone other than his wife, but a while, none the less.

The group continued to discuss the tricky situation and the drama around the relationship not only within their family, but with Paul's family too. It was unanimous that nobody was a fan of Kelly and Paul's union. A thud came from the ceiling. Agatha paused mid-gossip. "What was that noise upstairs?"

Casey stared upward. "Oh, that. It's Jason in his study."

Agatha's mouth gaped open. "He's here?"

Casey nodded.

"Well we should go up and say hi, don't you think?"

Casey suspected Agatha hadn't missed Jason's not-so-subtle clues over the last five years that indicated he didn't enjoy Casey's family visits. "Sure."

Agatha stood. "Let's go, ladies." She led the charge up the staircase to Jason's room. Casey, Anna, and Cara followed suit. Agatha stood in the doorframe and chimed, "knock knock."

Jason displayed a too wide smile. "Hey! The whole gang's here!"

Agatha strode into the office and bent to embrace him in a hug while he remained seated. Anna and Cara followed. They stood back as Casey entered with Roxie and a Stepford-Wife smile. "They wanted to say hello."

Jason nodded. "Great. Anna, Cara what's new?" He paused and studied her cape. "That's a cool cape."

Cara put a hand on her hip. "Thanks. I just got it. It's a wizard cape."

Anna rolled her eyes. "She's obsessed with *Harry Potter*."

Cara squished up her face. "Am not. *Harry Potter* is really cool. Have you read it?"

Jason shook his head. "Can't say that I have."

"You totally should. It's not just for kids, you know."

Despite his prejudice against Casey's mother and older sister for their less-than-perfect marital and relationship status, he'd always been friendly and kind to Cara and Anna. Although, it was difficult to not like those two girls. Not to mention, there was no escaping them if Jason or any man were to be with Casey. She and her sisters were a package deal.

Agatha interrupted Cara's long-winded explanation of the first book in the *Harry Potter* series. "Sorry, Jason. You probably need to study. We should go. We'll have to plan a visit for when you aren't so busy." Agatha exaggerated the word "so."

Casey suppressed laughter. She knew her mother well enough to know when she was being facetious.

Jason waved his wrist. "It's no problem. I can take a little break." He leaned over to pick up Roxie as she tried to jump on his chair. "Hi there, Roxie."

Roxie greeted him with a lick to the lips.

"Have your parents come by to meet Roxie yet?" Agatha inquired.

"Not yet. They're stopping by tomorrow."

Agatha placed her hand on her chest. "What? I got to meet the little bundle of joy first? I'm shocked!"

Jason said. "They've been out of town. My mom is dying to meet her."

Agatha said, "I bet."

Agatha eyed Casey from across the room. Casey sighed. Like Casey with Anna and Cara, Jason and his parents were a package deal. A package that made frequent visits and deliveries.

---

THE NEXT MORNING, Casey woke to what was her new morning scene. A furry-faced rascal three inches from her face. "Good morning, Roxie." Casey scratched her head and sat up before Roxie could get a lick in.

Jason turned on his side to give Roxie her morning belly rub. "Boy, you're a happy puppy now that you've weaseled your way into the bed." Roxie responded with a hop and slobber to his nose. He lifted his wrist. "We should get up. My parents said they'd be here at ten."

"What time is it?"

"Nine."

"Wow. I guess we're catching up on all that lost sleep." She slid out of bed and reached out her arms for Roxie. "Come on girl, time for potty."

While they were finishing up their morning routine the familiar sound of the doorbell rang out. *Bing bong.* Jason rushed to the door as Casey remained on the floor with Roxie and her kibble maze.

Betty entered wearing a stylish beige pantsuit and a hairstyle resembling a blonde helmet that didn't move.

She squealed. "Oh my goodness!" She hurried to the living room floor where Roxie was already on her way to investigate the visitors.

Frank stood in the blue tiled entry conversing with Jason while holding a large plastic shopping bag. Frank stepped into the living room when he saw the flash of black and white fur across the beige carpet. He joined Betty, now sitting on the floor, trying to get Roxie to play with a green plastic frog half the size of the pooch.

Betty placed the frog in front of her, and Roxie jumped back. She lunged at the frog and then jumped back again while growling. They all giggled at the sight of Roxie's newly developed aggressive side.

Frank, wearing Bermuda shorts and a button-down Hawaiian shirt, lay on his back near the pen. Roxie seemed to take this as her cue to climb onto his chest and give him wet kisses on his nose and mouth before hopping down to roll around in his thick silver hair. Frank chuckled, and his eyes lit up at Roxie's antics.

Casey said, "She's really warmed up to you both!"

Betty grinned from ear to ear. "She is just precious. We bought a few presents for her." She pulled out a half a dozen toys ranging from plush animals to Nylabones.

It wasn't surprising. Betty and Frank were known for what seemed to be endless generosity.

Betty continued, "Also, we grabbed her a harness for when she visits. I got an extra small, will it fit?"

Casey nodded. "That's what we she wears now."

"Oh good. We also arranged a little set-up at our place for when she visits. We got a bed, water dish, and of course, treats."

Jason sat down next to Betty. "I'm glad you're up for puppy sitting. We've learned the hard way this little one doesn't like to be alone. Even if we're upstairs—it's too far away!" He went on to explain the sleeping situation.

Frank continued to rub Roxie's belly and replied. "No problem. She can visit Grandma and Grandpa anytime."

Casey glanced at Betty and Frank. It hadn't occurred to her they would treat Roxie as if she were their human grandchild.

# CHAPTER 4

CASEY PULLED her coat tighter around her chest to shield herself from the chilled air as she hurried down Telegraph Avenue in Berkeley. She wished she'd brought a scarf to cover her mouth and nose to avoid the stench of garbage outlining her path to the restaurant where she was meeting Rachel.

She arrived at Golden China and pushed open the glass door that jingled as she entered. She spotted Rachel sitting near the back of the crowded restaurant decorated in a black and gold theme throughout. Rachel waved her slender arm above her head and stood. She wore a cream-colored sweater and a chunky turquoise necklace matched with a pair of black skinny jeans. Her copper hair was pulled back into a low ponytail. Rachel extended her arms to hug Casey. "Hi!"

"Have you been waiting long?"

Rachel shook her head and sat. "Nah. Just got here." She grinned at her friend. "It's so good to see you. I don't think I've seen you since your birthday—a few months back."

Casey studied the menu. "I think you're right."

She'd consciously been avoiding Rachel over the last few months knowing she'd have to talk about her deteriorating relationship with Jason. Rachel knew her too well to accept an "everything is fine" response from her. They'd met during their first year of college and since then had spent a fair amount of time sharing adventures, their feelings, and their dreams for the future.

A petite woman wearing a black apron around her waist approached. "Hello ladies. What can I get you?"

Casey eyed Rachel. "You know what you want?"

"Yep, I'll get the lemon chicken and combo chow mien." Rachel handed her menu to the waitress.

Casey quickly glanced at the menu and back up. "I will have the broccoli beef and shrimp fried rice." She paused. "Rachel, you wanna share the potstickers?"

"Sounds good to me!"

Casey continued. "And the potstickers."

The waitress took her menu and left them to themselves.

Rachel clasped her hands together. "What's new?"

Casey glanced up and grinned. "We got a puppy!"

Rachel's lime green eyes widened. "A puppy? What brought that on? You have pictures, right?"

Casey explained the origins of their new addition and shared printed photos she pulled from her purse. Rachel handed the pictures back to Casey. "Does this mean things are getting better between you and Jason?"

Casey paused. "Not really. But we both love Roxie, and we take care of her together. So we finally have something in common. Go figure. Other than that—no change."

Rachel's expression turned to compassion. "I'm sorry."

It was a look Casey hated above all others. Rachel had been in their wedding party and knew every detail of the devastating news Casey had received three weeks before the wedding. Casey remembered it like it was yesterday.

CASEY HAD STUMBLED through the front door of her and Jason's townhouse, after a night of club hopping for her bachelorette party. She flicked on the staircase light and tip-toed up the steps attempting to be quiet to not wake Jason if he was already home. They had agreed to have their bachelor and bachelorette parties on the same night. She'd been a little surprised at the sight of their empty bed at two in the morning, but she didn't think much of it. She climbed into bed and passed out.

The next morning, she woke to the sound of the front door opening. She stood at the top of the stairs and watched as Jason locked the front door behind him. She grinned and ran down the steps. She threw her arms around him and whispered, "Morning fiancé," in his ear. He hugged her for a moment and gently pushed her back. He mumbled, "crazy night," and lugged himself upstairs.

She followed him up. "How was your party? Did you guys venture into San Francisco?"

He kept his head down. "Oh, uh. At first."

"Did you have fun?"

He groaned. "Drank too much."

"Oh. Where did you guys go?"

"Uh. I don't remember. I'm gonna take a shower."

She watched him. He wouldn't look at her. Why wouldn't he look at her? She couldn't shake the feeling something was off.

She headed downstairs to make coffee and prepare breakfast. Over a bowl of cereal, she heard the water turn off upstairs. He didn't come down until she'd finished her bowl. He entered the kitchen and gave a sheepish grin, "Sorry if I was short earlier. I'm pretty hungover. How was your party?"

"It was super fun. We stayed mostly in Walnut Creek and danced all night. The girls all wore matching sparkling tops with pink feather boas. I had a tiara! Kelly tried to get me to play a weird scavenger hunt, but I was not into it. Why would I want some gross stranger eating a candy necklace off of me? Other than it was a blast. How about you?"

Jason stared at the ground. "I need to tell you something."

A pit formed in Casey's stomach.

He continued to avert her gaze. "I drank way too much last night. Too much."

Her heart raced, and her body shook. "Is that what you wanted to tell me?"

He exited the kitchen and sat down on the couch.

She followed him and stood staring at him. "What is it?"

He glanced up at her. "I drank a lot. They kept giving me shots. We were at Smith's and they had these dancers and some of the old high school crew." He paused. "I don't really know what happened exactly. I was dancing with one of the girls, and she pulled me into a bedroom." His voice cracked. "I was so drunk."

A wave of nausea washed over her. She leaned against the wall to prevent herself from collapsing.

His face was red, and tears formed in his eyes. He croaked, "We slept together."

Casey felt like she'd been punched in the stomach. With the little energy she had, she asked, "You slept with a prostitute?"

He waved his hands in protest. "No. No, nothing like that. It was someone we went to high school with—a friend of Smith's." He pleaded, "I swear to you, I was so drunk."

She studied him. Did he think that knowing the woman he slept with was better than if it were a prostitute? Her blood began to boil. "So your excuse for having sex with another woman three weeks before our wedding is that you were drunk?"

He pleaded again, "I'm so sorry."

Something inside Casey snapped. She screamed, "Are you kidding me? Seriously? You're blaming being drunk? Seriously?" She swirled around and picked up a framed photo of the two of them. "So you gave us up because of alcohol? It was all the alcohol, nothing else?" She chucked the picture frame across the hall into the dining room. It landed with a bang and the sound of broken glass.

Jason's mouth dropped open.

Casey shook as she stood with her hands balled into fists by her sides.

His eyes widened. "I'm sorry. I don't know what else to say. I understand if you hate me or want to call off the wedding."

She shook her head as the tears flowed freely. "What? You want to call off the wedding?" She braced herself on the wall once more.

"No. I was just saying if you wanted to, I'd understand. What I did was awful. I hate myself for it. If you let me, I'll spend the rest of my life making it up to you. I'm so sorry."

He was saying he was sorry and he'd make it up to her? If he loved her and wanted to marry her why would he cheat on her? Was he trying to end their engagement? Is that why? Part of her didn't believe he cheated because he was drunk, but then why would he say he'd make it up to her if he wasn't sorry? She didn't know what to do or what to say. She felt like the earth below had opened up and she was being dragged down into a dark place she didn't recognize.

She wiped her tears. "I need you to leave."

She remained frozen as he gathered his keys and wallet and left out the front door. That day she cried like she'd never cried before. The pain she felt in her chest was like she had been beaten by a prize fighter. Rachel had called several times before Casey had the strength to pick up the phone. Rachel had listened as Casey told her everything.

---

CASEY COULDN'T SUGARCOAT her and Jason's relationship to Rachel, like she did with most people. Rachel knew too much.

Casey shrugged. "It is what it is."

"Any hope it will get better?"

Her nostrils tingled as tears began to form. She took several deep breaths before answering. "I don't know."

"It's that bad? Are you fighting a lot?"

"Not really. Only if we talk about real things like spending time together or him hiding out in his room. Other than that, we just kind of exist like roommates. We don't talk or spend much time together other than taking care of Roxie."

Rachel spoke softly. "Sounds lonely."

Casey pushed a potsticker around with her chopsticks not acknowledging Rachel's astute observation. Of course it was lonely. She'd never felt more alone. It wasn't like she had any close friends who were married she could talk to about it. Not that her friends weren't there for her, but they couldn't possibly understand what she was going through.

"Casey, it's been well over a year. What are you going to do?"

The waitress arrived with their dinners, giving Casey a bit of breathing room. She had no idea what she was going to do about Jason. She feared they'd never make it to their two-year anniversary. She picked up her chopsticks and said. "Mmm. Bon appetite!"

Rachel did the same, and they ate their dinner silently. Rachel put her chopsticks down. "Casey. I'm sorry. I just worry about you. I know you're still hurt, and it isn't getting better. Sounds like he's still shutting you out. You're only twenty-five. You can't possibly be okay with this for the rest of your life."

Casey kept her focus on her rice. "I just don't know what to do." She picked up the tiny plastic cup filled with water and sipped until she'd calmed herself. "Ugh. This is so depressing. Can we talk about something happier? You just got back from India. You have to tell me everything. How was Raul's wedding?" Casey prayed Rachel would drop it.

Rachel hesitated. "India was amazing, and so was the

wedding. Oh my gosh..." Throughout the rest of their meal, Rachel continued telling Casey about all the exotic things she ate and saw.

When the check came, Rachel said. "Hey, one other thing I've been wanting to do ever since I got back was to get my cartilage pierced. You wanna come with me?"

Casey cocked her head. "Right now?"

Rachel threw her hands in the air. "We're on Telegraph. There is no shortage of piercing shops. There's actually a good one right across the street. Why not?"

Casey loved Rachel's spontaneity and her ability to always put her in a better mood. She shouldn't be avoiding her. She needed her now more than ever. She said. "Sure. Let's do it. Maybe I'll get one too!"

They exited the restaurant and jogged across the busy street to the largest of the piercing studios. They laughed nervously when they made it to the other side of the street without getting killed. Before entering, Casey gritted her teeth and said, "Here goes."

They hurried to the counter. A woman with a purple mohawk and tattooed arms said, "How can I help you?"

Rachel charged forward. "We want to get our cartilage pierced. Do you have any open appointments?

The woman surveyed her computer screen. "Yep, we can take you both right now."

Rachel replied. "Awesome!"

The woman requested the fee, processed the transaction, and said, "Give us a couple of minutes to get ready. You can browse if you want. We'll get you when we're ready."

Rachel and Casey linked arms as they wandered around the brightly lit store. It was set up more like a bookstore selling tchotchkes than a piercing studio. Within minutes Purple Mohawk approached them, "We're ready."

They followed her to a row of white pleather recliners that

reminded Casey of dentist's chairs. Casey climbed on and laid back and watched as Rachel did the same, in the chair in front of her. The seat was cold and smelled of rubbing alcohol. Rachel peeked over the top and gave her a thumbs up.

A bald, heavily tattooed man approached Casey. "Hi, I'm Mike."

Casey extended her hand. "Casey."

"Says here you want your cartilage pierced. Which ear?"

Casey hadn't thought of which ear. She yelled out to Rachel. "Hey, Rachel, which ear are you doing?"

Rachel called back, "Left!"

Casey turned to the massive man and proclaimed, "Left it is."

He nodded. A minute later she was staring into a hand mirror admiring the silver ring dangling from the top of her left ear. She carefully stepped out of the chair and made her way over to Rachel.

"What do you think?"

Rachel bobbed her head. "Oh yeah. Love it. Do you love it?"

Casey's eyes sparkled. "I do. I love it! Let me see yours." Casey leaned in. "Very cool."

They strolled out into the brisk air and hugged their good-byes. Casey felt thankful for Rachel who not only supported her in the good and bad times, but also had the uncanny ability to brighten her darkest days.

---

CASEY BOBBED her head and sang along to the music blaring from the car speakers as she drove home from her night out with Rachel. When she pulled into the garage, she waited to shut off the engine until J. Lo finished singing about how real she is. Casey hopped out of the car and stepped into the kitchen where Jason stood leaning against the island with a glass of red wine in his hand.

Casey chirped. "Hi!"

Jason remained straight-faced. "Hey."

Casey looked around the kitchen not quite understanding what she just entered into. Where did the wine come from? There was an odd feel to the air. The sound of claws on the tile brought a smile to her face. She bent over and picked up Roxie. "Hi there, sweetheart!" She pulled the puppy close to her chest. Roxie rested her head on Casey's shoulder but then popped it up to stare into her eyes. Casey whispered. "Thank you, honey. Your hugs are the best." And Casey gave her another squeeze.

On her way to the living room she heard, "Where have you been?"

She turned back. "What do you mean, where have I been? I told you I was out with Rachel."

He sipped his wine and put a hand on his hip. "What were you doing?"

Casey squinted. "What was I doing? We had dinner and then got pierced." She extended her neck to show off her new jewelry. "See? Cool, huh?"

Jason scrunched his face. "Oh, really. Where did you go to get that done?"

"Rachel and I went to Lifestyles after dinner. Why?"

Jason shook his head back and forth. "Oh, I know about Lifestyles. What's next? Tattoos? Drugs?"

Casey stared at him. She didn't understand how he'd deduced that after one gets an earring they start doing drugs. It was odd, even for him. Especially knowing her family history and her aversion to illicit drugs. What was his deal?

Bewildered, she replied, "I don't know what is going on with you, but you're acting insane."

Jason squinted and spat, "Am I? You go out all the time. Now, you're getting pierced. When will you settle down and grow up? What will you do when we have kids? You can't even cook!" Jason raised his voice. He rarely raised his voice.

Casey's face twisted. "Are you kidding? You're a video-game-obsessed Peter Pan who hides behind a graduate student designation." Jason stepped back but Casey didn't stop. "I'm the one with a career, friends, family, and a social life. All you ever do is lock yourself away in your office or visit your parents!" Kids? Oh heck, no. Not with him.

She took a breath.

Jason stood frozen, wine glass in hand.

Casey crossed her arms and softened her voice. "I don't know what's with you. I'm the same person you dated and married. What do you expect from me?"

Jason placed his glass down and stepped forward. "I expected you to change."

Casey froze. There it was. He'd expected her to be different than the person he married. He didn't want her. He wanted someone he thought he could turn her into.

She avoided his gaze and moved into the living room. She sat and set Roxie free to pick a toy to play with. Roxie pranced back a few moments later with her yellow duck between her teeth. She climbed into Casey's lap and chewed while Casey scratched her belly.

Jason sat on the sofa across from Casey and Roxie and stared with a scowl on his face. Casey eyed him. "Why don't you just leave me and my dog alone?" She returned her attention to Roxie content on her lap.

He shook his head. "Oh no, she's my dog. Isn't that right, Roxie?"

Casey thought, *He's kidding, right?* She glared up at him and declared. "She's my dog."

"Whatever."

"Whatever? I don't get you. You say you want me to change? What if I don't? I have no intention of becoming someone else. Not for you or anyone. What do you want from me?"

He shrugged. "I don't know anymore."

She felt like she'd been stabbed through the heart. Neither looked at the other, and finally Jason scurried out of the living room and up the stairs to his office. His heavy footsteps sounded through the ceiling.

Her mind directed her back to two and a half weeks before their wedding. It was the night he'd come back to the house after she'd kicked him out after his confession that he'd slept with another woman. Before he came back, he'd phoned every day begging her for forgiveness, and after three days, she gave in and let him come home.

He'd walked into the living room while Casey sat on the sofa. He said, "Hey."

Casey glanced up. "Hi."

"Can we talk?"

Casey nodded.

He approached the sofa and sat down and faced her. "I'm so sorry. What I did was horrible. Unforgivable. But if you can, somehow, forgive me, I promise to make it up to you for the rest of our lives. We can get married and put all of this behind us. If not, I understand. It's totally up to you."

Casey watched him. She still couldn't believe he'd betrayed her. He was the one thing in her life she thought she could count on. The one person she thought would never hurt her. He had made her believe she could have a happy marriage and a happy family. A normal life. He had no way of knowing how much his actions destroyed her. He didn't understand what it was like growing up in a turbulent, dysfunctional family. He didn't know what it took for her to trust him wholeheartedly. She felt utterly shattered. She didn't know if she could ever trust him again or forgive him.

She spoke softly. "I don't know."

"You don't know what? If you want to get married still?"

She studied him. He was calm. He was confident. Shouldn't he be terrified that she'd want to call off the wedding? Shouldn't he be at least a little sad? Shouldn't he be begging her not to go? Shouldn't he have brought flowers? Or something? He said he was sorry, but the tears from three days ago seemed long gone.

She stared at the floor. "I don't know what to do."

He sank back into the cushion. "Look. I'm sorry, but I can't spend all my time apologizing. I need to know what you want to do about the wedding. My mom says she has to give the restaurant the final deposit for the rehearsal dinner by tomorrow."

She closed her eyes and opened them slowly. "The rehearsal dinner? That's what you're concerned about?"

He shook his head. "Well, we do have two hundred guests who plan to attend our wedding. I think we need to make a decision soon. Don't you? If you aren't sure, maybe we should call it off."

He still didn't seem upset. He was still calm and still confident. She knew what she should do, but she didn't know if she could. She wiped the tears streaming down her cheeks. "If we call it off, I don't know if I could face everyone."

He sighed. "I can do it. My mom can help make the calls. I can send the gifts back."

Casey glanced over at the dining room that had a few stacks of early wedding gifts sent by their family and friends. "I can't do it. I can't face everyone." She hated herself for not being stronger. She stared at him. "What do you want?"

He shrugged. "We could still get married. What's the worst thing that could happen? We get divorced?"

Casey wiped the remainder of her tears with the back of her hand. "I guess."

"So, we're still on?"

She nodded. "Yeah. Still on."

How had she ever thought things would get better between them?

# CHAPTER 5

A FEW WEEKS LATER, Casey entered the coffee house and paused to inhale the scent of freshly ground beans. She stepped into the line to order. The perky cashier sporting a green apron asked, "What can I get you today?"

Casey replied, "I'll have a grande coffee."

"No problem!" The cashier completed the transaction and spun around to prepare Casey's drink. The sound of the espresso machine overpowered the classical music playing through the sound system. The barista slid Casey her order across the counter and said, "Have a great day!"

Casey thanked the highly caffeinated woman, grabbed her paper cup, and surveyed the half-empty coffee house for a quiet spot. She headed toward the corner and sat at a table designed for two. She plopped in the metal chair, pleased to have found a table and to be out of her and Jason's house. The two of them hadn't spoken more than a few necessary words over the last two weeks since their explosive argument. She was definitely ready for her coffee date with Kat.

She pulled off her scarf and placed it in her tote. She stared at her phone on the table and sipped her coffee while waiting.

She watched the other patrons deep in conversation or sitting contently alone reading the newspaper. She thought of Jason who had told her he'd never go to a restaurant or sit at a coffee house by himself because he didn't want people to think he was a loser. Casey never had an issue being out by herself. She thought it was nice to have a meal or coffee or any time, really, to oneself. You didn't have arguments or have to entertain anyone. It was a time for peace and quiet.

Casey jumped at the sound of the vibration of her phone on the metal table. She picked it up and grinned. "Hey Kat!"

Kat, or Katherine as her parents called her, had been Casey's best friend since before they'd graduated from the chemistry department at St. Mary's College in the San Francisco Bay Area. When Kat had been accepted into the University of Washington for graduate school, Casey was thrilled for her but sad she wouldn't get to see and talk to her every day.

A love, or what some might call an addiction, of coffee was something they enthusiastically shared. After Kat moved, they decided to continue their coffee dates over the phone. Casey would go to a local coffee house and so would Kat, and they'd act as if the other sat across from them. With Kat's demanding graduate school schedule, a stark contrast to Jason's, they usually could only meet up every two to three weeks. Casey wished it were more often, but she tried to make it up by flying up to Seattle during Kat's school breaks. It had given her much needed girl time and space from Jason.

Casey asked, "How is school—and more importantly—how are things with Glenn?"

They chuckled.

Kat replied, "School's same old—busy, busy. Things are going well with Glenn." She paused. "He started talking about us moving in together."

Casey's mouth dropped open. "What? Oh my gosh. That is so

exciting! Have you talked about when and where and all the details?"

Kat said, "We're thinking when our current apartment leases are up—at the end of the school year—which isn't for a while, but we spend almost every day at each other's places. I think he's it, like the one." She emphasized "the one."

Casey was not surprised. When she and Kat had gone to Whistler earlier in the year, Kat and Glenn had talked on the phone every night. She hadn't called Jason once.

Casey asked, "Any talk of other serious things?" Her voice trailed off, insinuating marriage talk.

Kat took a few seconds to answer. "Well. He did ask what cut I like!"

Casey nearly jumped out of her seat. "Holy moly! That's huge!" Casey would've given anything to be with her in that moment to give her a massive hug and participate in a celebratory dance, the kind the two of them were famous for.

They continued their discussion of diamonds and rings and all fun things associated with a wedding. Kat stopped and said, "Enough about me. How's Roxie?" She paused. "And you and Jason?"

Casey deflated. "Roxie's great. Adorable. The only happy thing at home, really."

Kat asked, "Things aren't any better?"

Casey sighed. "Not even a little." She went on to explain his latest disclosure of how he wanted her to change who she was and that they hadn't spoken in nearly two weeks. Casey was at the end of her rope.

Kat interjected. "Have you considered counseling?"

Casey stared at her empty cup. "Not really. I guess it couldn't hurt. Only one way for us to go—up! How's that for a positive attitude?"

They chatted a bit more about Jason before Casey strategically moved the conversation back to Kat and Glenn. She was tired of being the downer in every conversation. She was tired of being miserable. She was tired of pretending she was living her happily-ever-after.

---

CASEY APPROACHED the living room and heard a familiar thumping of tiny paws descending the stairs. She picked up Roxie. "Hi, girl! I missed you, too!" She brought her over to the carpet and played fetch with the stuffed taco until Roxie climbed into Casey's lap for belly scratches.

She glanced at the ceiling at the sound of an office chair rolling overhead. She contemplated starting a conversation with Jason about counseling. Could counseling fix their marriage? They'd been happy at one time. It seemed like a long time ago, but they were. She was.

When they got engaged, she thought she was getting everything she had always wanted: a husband, a house, normal in-laws, and—one day—children. She had a family of her own that was expected to grow by two humans according to her and Jason's plans. She would stay at home and raise them. They'd be a happy and whole family.

When Jason and she had discussed marriage, they had agreed on everything they wanted together. They were sure it would last and both touted they didn't believe in divorce. Divorce was for people who gave up. Quitters. They were going to do it right. They'd felt fortunate they'd found their other halves at such a young age. They wouldn't have to be desperately single into their late twenties, gasp, or, god forbid, their thirties. They had it all figured out.

Casey picked up Roxie and went up to Jason's office. She silently entered and sat on the chair next to his desk.

She focused on him. "We need to talk."

He swiveled to face her. "Yeah. I think so. I'm sorry about

what I said. I know you'll be a great mother one day. I see how you are with Roxie and your sisters. I'm sorry. I don't want to fight with you."

Casey flinched. He knew she'd be a great mother. Back in college, in one of the literature courses she was forced to take, they had discussed why people get married. The professor said, "You want to know why someone decided to get married? Ask them for three reasons why." The class had erupted into a discussion about why they thought people married. Many hypothesized love and shared goals were likely the most common reasons. Casey had taken the cue to go home and ask her then fiancé, Jason, the three reason he wanted to marry her. He had quickly replied. "You're smart. We have similar values. And you'd make a great mother."

At the time, she'd felt as if the wind had been knocked out of her. He hadn't said he wanted to marry her because he loved her. It had been four years since he'd given his reasons. A little over a year since they'd been married. It still haunted her.

She gazed down at Roxie resting in her lap. She'd never tire of Roxie's spunk, affection, and unconditional love. She swallowed and refocused her attention on Jason. "I don't want to fight either. We both know things aren't going well—haven't been for a long time. Maybe counseling will help? I was talking to Kat and she suggested it. A counselor could help us move forward. What do you think?"

She'd wondered if she could ever really move forward with him. The day he'd confessed he'd spent the night with another woman he'd begged her for forgiveness. He'd said he was drunk. He'd said he was sorry. He'd said he'd spend the rest of his life making it up to her. Part of her had believed him. Part of her knew he didn't love her. Part of her knew he had hoped she'd cancel the wedding.

She doubted he knew how often she'd broken down and cried since that day. She'd never told him or anyone her misery. She'd smiled and laughed at all the right times in front of everyone. The only people who knew what he'd done were Rachel and Kat. She was too ashamed to tell anyone else she'd been too weak to leave him. She couldn't remember the last time she'd taken a shower without falling to pieces. He'd broken her heart, and now she was living a lie.

He nodded. "I think it's a good idea. We should try to make this work."

"Yeah?"

He tilted his head. "Yeah. I can research marriage counselors that take our insurance."

Casey was surprised by his quick decision. "That would be great."

She wondered if Jason thought there was hope for their marriage or if he was just trying to hold on to his baby-maker. Or maybe he thought if they went to marriage counseling they could say they tried everything before calling it quits. It struck Casey, she now believed in divorce. How about that? Was it possible Jason now did too?

Jason half-laughed. "Man. We're going to be 'those people' going to marriage counseling."

Jason was always concerned about what other people thought. Their marriage, his car, or his status in school. It was only good enough if other people thought it was good enough. Was that why he agreed to counseling, so they wouldn't get divorced and he wouldn't be a loser divorcee?

Casey shrugged. "Guess so."

Jason said, "Hey, you want to try that new Mexican place that just opened up? We could go for lunch?"

Casey was shocked at his suggestion. "Sure. I'm getting hungry. You wanna go now?"

"Sure. Let's go."

Casey put Roxie in her pen, despite the scratching at the gate and a pleading look that could only mean she felt both surprised and betrayed by their departure. It left an ache in Casey's heart each time she left her, but she figured—scratch that—hoped Roxie would eventually be okay with occasionally being left alone for a few hours.

Casey sat across from Jason in the boldly colored restaurant. He gave a weak smile. "How are things at work?"

Was he actually trying to have a conversation about something other than Roxie? Maybe things were really looking up. She gave a reassuring nod. "Good actually. I've been cross-training with the purification team. Javier has been teaching me how to use the new protein purification system. It's super high-tech. It's kind of like an HPLC but much bigger. I like the idea that I purify the protein and analyze it, versus just getting the samples from Javier. I feel like I have a better understanding of my analytical results now. It's cool. And of course, working with Javier's a riot. The purification group is much livelier than our little analytical team. Not to say Dana isn't great, but Javier keeps us in stitches."

"That's great."

"How's school?" She hoped the question wouldn't turn the conversation south.

"It's going. Slowly."

Casey refrained from comment and opted to change topics. "Cara said that the *Harry Potter* movie is coming out in a few weeks. According to critics it's going to be good."

"I think I read about it. It's supposed to be huge."

Casey nodded. "Cara keeps asking if I've read the book yet. She loaned it to me a while ago, but I haven't yet. Maybe I should, before I see the movie." Casey wondered if she should suggest they see it together, or if it would be pushing her luck. The conversation had been pleasant, and she didn't want to ruin it.

"Yeah." He paused as the waiter approached with their entrees. "Looks great."

Casey agreed.

Jason chuckled. "It's kind of nice to be able to eat without a little fur ball jumping up or whining at you. She acts like we starve her!"

Casey giggled. "Oh, I know! That dog." She shook her head. "I was eating an apple the other day, and she practically attacked me to lick it! It was hilarious."

They continued to chat like old friends about TV and movies they wanted to see, and they laughed over Roxie and her silly antics. It was pleasant. It was platonic, but pleasant.

Before they got married, they'd never had an issue with having a good time. Whether it was going out to eat, watching movies, or traveling, they usually enjoyed each other's company. She'd always thought that because they were friends first, it would be a lasting relationship. Isn't that what *they* always said?

Over the last few years, not only had their intimacy faded, but also their friendship. Jason hadn't wanted to do anything with her except to go out to eat. Mostly because neither of them wanted to cook. He certainly hadn't kept his promise to spend the rest of his life "making it up to her." He'd done nothing but shut her out. He didn't even come out of his office when she got home from work. If she brought it up, he told her she needed to get over it already, because he had.

Sitting across from him, it dawned on her that it wasn't just her he didn't want to do anything with. He'd stopped going to the gym and school and stopped seeing his friends. He spent all of his time in his office. If his mother didn't force him to visit, he'd probably never leave his lair. Maybe it wasn't just her? But if it wasn't just her, why did it feel so personal?

# CHAPTER 6

A FEW WEEKS LATER, Jason twisted the doorknob to the counselor's office and pushed. He glanced back at Casey with a sheepish grin and arch of his eyebrows. A tall, dark-skinned man wearing khaki trousers and a striped polo shirt greeted them with a bright smile. "Hello! You must be Jason and Casey. I'm Malcom Johnson." He shook Jason's hand.

Jason responded. "Nice to meet you."

Casey did the same.

Malcom motioned them toward a beige sofa with corduroy fabric, no doubt a remnant from the 1970's, in the center of the cramped, musty-smelling room. It had a window over a rectangular desk, a fake ficus tree in the corner, and a large chair in front of the couch. The only artwork on the wall was a watercolor of a field of amber-colored grass.

Malcom said, "Please sit down. You can call me Malcom or MJ if you'd prefer."

Jason sat at one end of the sofa with his hands clasped in his lap, and Casey sat stiffly on the other side. Malcom sat on the large chair facing them with a yellow notepad in his hands.

"Okay," he said. "Who wants to tell me what brought you here today?" He gave a reassuring smile.

Jason and Casey exchanged glances. Casey shrugged and began. "Jason and I got married almost a year and a half ago. Things have been strained since then."

Jason interrupted. "Things were strained before that."

Malcom lifted his hand out as a sign for them to stop. "Okay, so you've been married for a little while, things aren't great. That's good for me to know. Before we get too far into that, I'd like to learn a little more about each of you. I feel it helps me understand communication styles and point-of-view a little better. Okay?"

They nodded.

"Casey, why don't we start with you. Tell me about what growing up was like in your family."

Casey thought, *Oh great. My favorite topic.* She hoped the session wouldn't be a repeat of their pre-marital retreat required by the Catholic church before they'd been married. Each of them had been required to fill out lengthy questionnaires about their family and family roles. It catapulted a huge fight between Jason and Casey when they'd been asked to share with their retreat counselor. Jason had criticized her family and Casey criticized his. To say their childhoods were different was a massive under-statement.

Casey took a few breaths. "Well, I am one of five children ranging from twenty-eight to ten years old and was raised mostly by a single mom."

Malcom intertwined his fingers, tapping the pointer fingers together like she was a puzzle for him to figure out. "That's a good start. Any family history of drug abuse?"

Casey chuckled. "It would be faster to tell you who in my family didn't have a problem with drugs or alcohol. My mom and dad divorced when I was a baby. A few years later Mom met my heroin-addict step-dad. They divorced after my sister was done with chemo—when I was in junior high. After that it was pretty much just Mom, my little sisters—they're now fifteen and ten—and me. My older siblings moved in with my biological father around that time. They've both wrestled with drugs. A few of my mom's siblings have had an addiction to narcotics and alcohol too."

Malcom's chocolate colored eyes dimmed a bit. "Have you ever had a problem or dabbled with drugs or alcohol?"

This time Jason chuckled. It was a source of tension between them that Casey wouldn't allow alcohol in their house on a regular basis. Special occasions only.

She answered. "No. I've never tried drugs—not even cigarettes." She shook her head. "I rarely drink."

Casey eyed Jason whose leg was now twitching. A sign he was either agitated or bored.

Malcom asked. "Tell me about your relationship with your mom and sisters. And your dad and older siblings. Do you have contact with your step-father at all?"

"I see my little sisters a lot. We're close. I'm like a second mom to Cara—that's the ten-year-old. I helped raised them after my step-dad left. I don't see him at all. Ever. Anna, my sister—his daughter—she's the one that had cancer. She sees him on occasion. I don't see my dad very often or my brother. My brother is still finding his way, I think, and my sister Kelly, I see her, but not as often. Her life is very different than mine. She has three kids and hangs with a different crowd."

Malcom bobbed his head slowly and paused. "What do you do for a living?"

Casey's eyes brightened. "I work for a biotech company doing analytical method development."

Malcom studied her like she was an alien. "So, you're a scientist. You have a degree in?"

"Chemistry."

Malcom grinned like he'd just discovered a new species. "Remarkable. You're a survivor." He stared intently at her.

Casey sat back and melted into the cushion. She'd never been called a survivor. She didn't know what to make of it or how to respond. Thankfully, Malcom seemed satisfied enough with her background and finally turned to Jason. "Jason, tell me about your family."

"I assure you, my story isn't quite so colorful." He chuckled arrogantly. "I grew up with both parents—still married. I have an older brother in the Air Force. We see each other whenever he's on leave. No drugs or alcohol problems in my family. I'm a full-time graduate student at Stanford. That's pretty much it. Boring little family."

Malcom shook his head and scribbled on his notepad. "It sounds like the two of you had quite the opposite upbringings."

They nodded. It wasn't a new revelation for them.

Malcom let out a cleansing breath. "Okay, I feel like I know you a little better. Let's revisit why we're here. Jason, why don't you get us going?"

Jason began. "Well, we've not been happy. We just go through the motions. She hasn't forgiven me. It's like she can't move on. She always brings up..."

Malcom interrupted. "What hasn't she forgiven you for?"

"I cheated. Just once, a little while before the wedding. I haven't since."

Malcom shifted his seat. "Casey, is it true you haven't forgiven him?"

Casey stared at the ground. "I guess not, but it's because he's not sorry. He said he'd spend the rest of our lives making it up to me. He's done nothing. He just stays in his office all day and night. He never wants to do anything. He doesn't even come out of his office when I get home from work. He rarely leaves the house."

Malcom tapped his number two pencil on his chin. "Jason. How are you feeling about what happened?"

Jason inched closer to the arm of the sofa. "I'm over it. It's her who isn't."

"Jason, is it true you don't feel like going out or doing things?"

Jason stared at the ceiling. "Yeah."

"Why do you think that is?"

He shifted in his seat. "I don't know. I'm just sad."

Casey watched a tear form in the corner of his eye. She put her hand to her chest. Could it be he was as broken up about their relationship as she was? Were her insecurities around their relationship all in her head? Maybe he did love her?

Malcom asked. "Why are you sad, Jason?"

Jason dotted the corner of his eye with his pointer finger. "I think about Ian. All the time." He paused to compose himself. "Ian was a close friend who passed away four years ago. A freak accident while in Mexico."

Malcom passed a box of tissues to Jason. "I'm so sorry for your loss." He paused to allow time for Jason to dab his eyes with the tissues.

Casey stiffened. She knew he'd been devastated by the loss of his good friend, but she had no idea it was something he actively thought about. Here she had been so wrapped up in her own grief over their relationship, she hadn't seen his, for Ian.

Malcom lowered his voice and asked Jason to elaborate on his feelings and motivations on a daily basis. Jason soon poured his heart out to this stranger they'd just met. He'd never shared any of it with Casey. They'd both coped in their own separate ways. Instead of turning to each other for comfort, they'd pushed the other away. Malcom gave him a few more minutes before refocusing the conversation on the two of them. He said, "Thank you for sharing that with me. Now, we only have a few more minutes. Before we go, I'd like to bring our conversation back to the two of you. You're quite different from each other, no?"

They nodded and smirked in unison.

Malcom gave a small grin. "I'd like to ask you, what made you choose each other? Jason, why did you decide to marry Casey?"

Jason responded exactly as he had four years earlier.

Malcom lifted an eyebrow. "And because you love her?"

Jason's face remained serious. "Yeah."

The pit in Casey's stomach deepened.

"And you, Casey? Why did you marry Jason?"

She shrugged. "Because I love him, have fun with him—well, we used to have fun—and we have similar goals."

Malcom's face was neutral. Casey thought his expression was a far cry from the ear to ear grin from forty-five minutes earlier.

He said. "Great. I can tell there is love here, and I think we can make some good progress. Let's do this. Between now and our next appointment, I'm giving you some homework. Okay?"

Both of them nodded once again.

"I want you to choose one night this next week where you get out and do something fun. Maybe mini golf or a hike. Whatever it is you like to do—outside of the house. Do you think you can do that?"

More nodding.

"Okay, I'll see you two in a few weeks. Be well."

Jason and Casey each shook his hand as they exited the office. Casey couldn't help but feel a little sorry for Malcom. She certainly wouldn't want to be tasked with trying to fix the unfixable.

They strolled silently to Jason's car. Buckled up and on the road, Casey asked, "What did you think? Should we keep going?"

Jason kept focused on the road. "Yeah. Definitely. I think it was okay."

Casey stared ahead. "I'm sorry about Ian. I didn't know you were still grieving."

Jason was silent.

"You know you can talk to me?"

Silence.

Casey didn't know what his silence meant. Was he mad? He didn't want to talk about it? He didn't want to talk to her? She kept quiet the rest of the drive, hoping both of their sufferings would end soon.

# CHAPTER 7

THE NEXT WEEK AFTER WORK, Casey jogged up the stairs to Jason's room. He was intently watching the car-chase action on his screen. Casey picked up Roxie and said, "Hello, girl!"

Jason glanced over his shoulder. "Hey."

Casey took a seat. "How was your day?"

"Fine. Did some work, now relaxing. You?"

Casey doubted the accuracy of his statement but wanted to play nice. "Day was okay. Found out Dana is leaving. Gave her two weeks' notice. Which is a bummer."

Dana was one her best work buddies. They weren't terribly close outside of work, but when Casey had missed several days of work due to crisis around her and Jason's relationship shortly before the wedding, Dana and Javier had covered for her. They had continued to support her even though they didn't know all the details. Dana and Javier knew Casey's home life wasn't great, but they were kind enough not to ask too many questions.

"Where's she going?"

"To some start-up in Fremont. She's pretty stoked."

"That sucks. I'm sorry."

"Yeah, what are you gonna do. Hey, I was thinking about our homework. What if we went for a hike this weekend? It'll be chilly, which is perfect hiking weather."

Jason refocused on his screen. "I don't know. I thought I heard it might rain."

His lack of interest in the subject didn't escape her. "Well, if it rains, maybe we can go play pool and eat pizza at that place downtown?"

Jason muttered, "I'll think about it."

Casey felt fire soar through her veins. "What do you mean you'll think about it?"

Jason shook his head and scrunched his face. "Can we not talk about this right now?"

Casey stood. "What do you mean not right now? You're not doing anything! Just playing video games. It's like you don't even care about our relationship."

Jason swiveled around and threw his hands in the air. "Oh, here we go again. I must not care about our relationship because I'm not doing exactly what Casey wants right this very second!"

Casey wanted to punch his smug face. "Are you kidding? It's always the same with you. I try to talk about us, and it's not a good time. I try to get you to go out. You don't feel like it. I try to have a simple conversation, and I'm just an intrusion. You never want to talk. You never want to be with me. Why the hell did you even marry me?" Her whole body was shaking. "Oh, that's right. Because I'll be a great mother to your future perfect children. What a fucking joke." She stood with her hands on her hips and what felt like steam coming out of her ears.

Jason smirked. "A fucking joke is right. That's the perfect way to describe this."

"How do you expect our marriage to work if you don't plan to participate in it?"

Jason pivoted back toward his computer.

Casey yelled. "That's really fucking great. You're a real grown-up, Jason!" She stormed out, and Roxie shivered in her arms.

She ran downstairs and locked herself in the bathroom. She sat on the floor and cried until there weren't any tears left. She peered over at Roxie whimpering next to her. "I'm sorry, sweetheart. You don't like it when we fight. I'm sorry. Come here." She picked her up and held her tight. "Let's get you a toy."

Eyes dried, Casey sat on the living room floor stroking Roxie while the little dog snuggled in her lap and chewed on her stuffed turkey. Casey contemplated how scary it must be for Roxie to hear all the yelling. The poor pup had been shaking. It made her feel guilty and like a bad dog mom. She could only imagine how traumatizing it would be for a human child. She shuddered and then thought, *Note to self. Don't have kids with Jason.*

THE FOLLOWING WEEK, Casey sat at the end of the outdated sofa trying to pinpoint the moldy odor filling her senses. She deduced the recent rains were likely the cause of the new smell. She crossed her leg and scooted closer to the arm. She couldn't get far enough away from Jason where he sat contently at the other end of the couch.

Malcom sat in his usual chair with notepad in his hand and grin on his face. "Alright. Let's get started, shall we?" He read their straight faces and continued. "How were these last two weeks? Where did you decide to go for your homework?" He chuckled at the last part.

Casey assumed his other clients must be much more cooperative for him to have such a cheerful disposition. She widened her eyes. "No homework this week."

Malcom's mouth straightened. "Do you want to tell me more about that?"

Casey sighed. "Sure. I asked Jason if he wanted to go play pool or hike. He said he had to think about it. And now we're here."

Jason sat shaking his head back and forth. "Sure, it's all my fault."

Malcom fanned his hands down. "No. There is no blame here. Let's just talk about what happened. Jason, is it true you said you had to think about it?"

"Yeah."

Malcom's face remained soft. "What did you have to think about? Did you not feel like going out? Were you not feeling well?"

"I didn't feel like it."

Casey forced her lips shut and closed her eyes. She opened them and focused on Malcom. "This is basically just one example of how our entire marriage has been. He says he doesn't feel like it. That's what I get. All the time." She threw her hands in the air.

Malcom spoke softly. "Casey, I can tell you're frustrated. Let's hear more from Jason about why he doesn't feel like it."

Casey sat back into the sofa while Malcom questioned Jason on his lack of motivation to do things with and without Casey. She couldn't believe this was her life now.

Malcom asked, "Casey, how do you feel when Jason doesn't want to spend time with you? What about intimacy? Is there intimacy?"

Casey snorted. "No on the intimacy. Not even kissing. Apparently, he now says he doesn't like kissing."

"How does that make you feel?"

How the heck does he think it makes her feel? Great! Super. She replied, "Not good."

"Jason is that true?"

"Yep."

Malcom pursed his lips. "The not wanting to do things together, not wanting to kiss. Jason, I think you are angry with Casey. Are you angry with Casey?"

"Yeah."

"Why are you angry with Casey?"

"I don't know. I guess. She just pushes until she gets what she wants. All the time. I'm tired of it."

Malcom glanced at the floor and back at them. Casey was amazed at Malcom's capacity for patience and calm.

He asked Jason, "What does she push for?"

Jason rolled his eyes. "Talking, going out, dog—just everything."

He said, "I hear you. I'm not sure these things you say Casey is pushing you to do are unreasonable. Do you?"

Jason shrugged a shoulder.

"Hmm. I've been reviewing my notes. Jason, your lack of motivation with school, going out, socializing with and without Casey. I think you're depressed. Have you ever been treated for depression?"

"No."

Malcom gave a sympathetic grin to each of them. "Jason, I think you are going through a lot. I would recommend you seek counseling on your own. I'm not sure marriage counseling will be fruitful unless you're also receiving help. And maybe get a little time apart. Some separation to allow you to work through things. Jason, I'm going to give you the names of some great therapists I think can help." Malcom ruffled through the papers in his notepad and handed a sheet of paper to Jason. Jason begrudgingly took it. "Does that sound like a plan?"

Casey tried to process what she was hearing. She hadn't realized Jason was depressed. Then again, she didn't know much about depression.

Both of them nodded silently.

"Great. Only homework this time is for Jason to start with his new therapist. Maybe some time apart. Casey, give Jason some space, okay?"

She nodded, and Malcom grinned.

"I look forward to our next session," he said.

Casey thought, *There is that never-ending optimism again.*

Malcom stood near the exit and bellowed, "Be well," as they exited.

On the way to the car, a mixture of thoughts swirled around in Casey's mind. Depression. Jason needing a therapist. Separation. She felt as if she were trapped inside of a vortex of emotion.

On the road, Casey asked, "What did you think about what Malcom said—about getting help?"

Jason's eyes remained facing forward. "I don't know."

"What do you mean, you don't know? He just said he didn't think there was a point to marriage counseling if you didn't get help?"

Jason glared at her and shouted. "Yeah. That's right. Everything is my fault. Everything is always my fault!"

"That's not what he said. He just said we can't fix this if you don't get help."

Jason spat. "Oh, I bet you just loved that. I really fucking hate you sometimes."

Casey froze. He'd never said he hated her before. She shook her head and laughed bitterly. "Well that's fucking great. I think counseling is definitely working!"

Casey sat with her arms crossed, staring out the window the remainder of the ride home. How had things gotten so bad between them? She honestly thought things couldn't get worse and that counseling could only help. How could she have been so wrong—about everything?

———

THE NEXT WEEK, with a clear head, she made her way up to Jason's room. She knocked on the door. "Hey."

He was hunched over his desk. "Hey."

"Can we talk?"

Casey had been instructed to give him space, but it had been over a week since they'd spoken, so she figured it would be okay. Also, she thought Jason would like what she had to say.

"Sure."

"Wanna go downstairs?" She gave him a sheepish grin. "Maybe have a glass a wine? I bought a bottle." It was her peace offering.

Jason sat up straight. "Okay."

Casey leaned against one side of the island while Jason perched himself on a bar stool. She poured a glass and handed it to him. It was an occasion for her to have one as well. She took a sip, and another, before placing it down onto the counter.

She said, "I've been thinking about what Malcom said. About getting some time apart. A separation. What if we did a separation?"

Jason's eyes brightened. "Like not living together anymore?"

"Right. I figure I could find an apartment closer to work. You could stay here. What do you think?"

Casey watched as Jason looked happy for the first time in— she couldn't remember how long it had been.

He nodded and gave a half grin. "I think it could be good for us. I think we should do it."

Casey smiled warmly. "Me too." She felt a huge weight lifted from her shoulders and from the looks of Jason, he did too.

Jason chuckled. "Poor Roxie, she'll be from a broken home."

Casey picked her up and giggled. "Oh, I think she'll be alright in our new apartment. Won't you girl?"

Jason teased. "No, Roxie's staying with me. Aren't you?"

Casey's smile faded. "No seriously, she's coming with me."

Jason slouched. "What if she stayed here with me during the week while you're at work and then you can pick her up for the weekends? Just temporarily until things get settled?"

Casey glanced up and nodded. "Yeah, I think that could work." She nuzzled Roxie. "What do you think? I know you hate being by yourself!"

Jason laughed. "That she does."

They continued to sort out the details of how they'd tell their respective families and when the separation would start. They laughed and joked as they launched into planning mode. They had both agreed there was no time like the present.

# CHAPTER 8

TWO WEEKS LATER, Casey sat on her respective spot on the counseling couch waiting for the session to begin. When they'd
entered, Malcom pulled Jason aside to discuss a matter in private.
Casey assumed it had to do with his homework assignment. She
tapped the cushions and surveyed the room as they chatted.

She watched from across the room at Jason and Malcom
nodding, and then Malcom gave Jason a slap on the back. She
straightened in preparation for their approach.

Malcom sat and gave a quick grin. "Thank you for waiting.
Let's begin." He folded over a sheet in his notebook and poised
his pencil to write. "How have things been? Jason, do you want to
start? How was the homework?"

Jason casually shrugged. "It was pretty good. I didn't feel
smothered and," he paused, "although I haven't made an appointment with the counselor yet, I plan to call tomorrow." He gave a
genuine smile. "Promise!"

"Great. Great. How about you, Casey? How have things been
with you?"

"Good. I tried to give Jason his space."

Jason interrupted. "She did. I can attest. Thank you, Casey."

She nodded. "Sure."

Malcom's eyes brightened. "Well, you both seem to be in a better mood. From what I can see. That's great. Any other updates before we get started?"

Jason and Casey exchanged glances and a crisp nod. Casey shook her head and continued. "We have some news. We decided to take your advice and separate. I've started looking at apartments closer to work, and we've come up with an arrangement for Roxie. Feeling pretty good about it. Jason?"

Malcom tilted his head to the right.

Jason enthusiastically replied, "Yeah. I'm gonna stay in our townhouse and keep on with school and everything. Feeling good about it."

Malcom's eyes blinked rapidly as he raised his right hand. "Okay. So for the record, I did not suggest for you to separate. What I said was to have some space. For example, Casey letting Jason come to you if he wants to talk. And for Jason, taking the time you need to cope. I didn't in any way mean to imply you should separate."

Jason and Casey glanced at each other. Casey thought, *Oops. Guess we just heard what we wanted to.* She said, "Well I think we both agree it's what we think is best. I apologize, Jason, I don't want to speak for you." Casey thought, *Good job. Let him have his own voice. You don't have to be in control all of the time.*

Jason said, "Absolutely agree this is best for us." He chuckled. "It's one of the few things we've agreed upon during our marriage."

Malcom nodded. "If this is what you both want, can I assume you still want to work on the relationship?"

Jason quickly said. "Of course."

Casey agreed, "Yeah."

Malcom scribbled on his notepad and stared out the window

for more than a few moments. Casey and Jason exchanged sheepish expressions. Casey couldn't help but wonder if they'd stumped their counselor after only three sessions.

Poised, Malcom spoke. "Here is what we need to do. You need to have regularly scheduled visits. Dates. If this is going to work, you must follow the schedule. It is critical. Let's discuss frequency and thoughts around this. Casey?"

She scratched her neck and said, "Sounds fine. I don't know. Once a week? Jason?"

Jason nodded. "Once a week is perfect."

Malcom hesitated. "Once a week it is. Now, let's set up the ground rules."

Malcom continued speaking about the rules, but all Casey could focus on was the relief that washed over her. She was excited about the possibilities the separation could bring. Maybe space would restore what they used to have, back when they were just dating. Back when things were light and fun. No hurt or anger or feeling like she was the only person in their relationship. Things used to be good between them. At one time. A time that seemed so long ago. It dawned on her at that moment, she wasn't ready to give up. She just needed a little breather.

THE NEXT NIGHT, they shared a glass of wine around the island as they discussed their latest marriage counseling. Casey sipped and waved her hands in the air. "I heard him say he suggested we separate. You heard that too, right?"

Jason poured himself another glass. "Totally. I don't get why he'd now say he never said that. What are the chances that both of us misunderstood? Not likely."

"Oh, I know, right?"

Jason sipped and asked, "Any luck with apartment hunting?"

She gave an exaggerated head bob. "Yeah, actually. I found this totally cool apartment online. It has a washer and dryer inside, and they allow dogs. They have a gym and a pool, and it's not far from work. Fifteen minutes max. It's really nice. I plan to check it out this weekend and maybe sign a lease."

Jason gave an encouraging nod. "Sounds awesome."

This newfound ritual of wine chats in the kitchen were pleasant. It reminded her of their early days when they sat and talked for hours on end. It was as if they'd never run out of things to talk about. It warmed her heart they could still chat and joke with each other. She had been certain they wouldn't make it to their next anniversary. Now, she was optimistic.

She laughed at an impression Jason made of a flustered Malcom. She glanced over at Roxie pacing between them. She picked up the bottle of wine and her glass and motioned for Jason to move their party to the living room.

She sat cross-legged with Roxie in her lap as she drank. She was feeling woozy, but in a good way. She didn't feel worried or alone. She felt breezy and light. She giggled. "Truth or dare?"

"I'm probably too tipsy for a dare! Definitely truth."

She grinned, remembering all the nights they'd played truth or dare. It usually ended with them either rolling around on the floor laughing hysterically or rolling around the floor doing much naughtier things.

She controlled her giggles. "Okay. Here goes. What's worse: being divorced, or having to tell people you're divorced?"

He chuckled. "Oh, definitely having to tell people I'm divorced. Talk about sounding like a loser!"

She finished off her second glass as her heart hardened once more. "Yeah, totally."

She poured the wine into her glass until the bottle was empty. She knew she would get drunk, but she didn't care. She wanted to be numb. She didn't want to have her emotions in continuous flip-flop mode. One minute she thought there was hope that she and Jason could rekindle their love and that her fears were simply her own insecurities. The next minute she believed there was no hope for the two of them and she would soon be free from the burden of trying to salvage the unsalvageable.

She pushed aside her emotions and asked, "How are we gonna divide up the stuff? We've got lots of stuff."

Jason climbed off the couch and sat on the floor. He picked up Roxie's duck and said, "Hey, girl!" Roxie hopped over to play. He cocked his head. "Huh. That's a good question. We both take what we brought into our relationship, but for our shared stuff, we could make a list and decide, and if we can't decide or agree, flip a coin?" His eyes widened. "Hey ,we could make it fun. You know how my parents got us that gift certificate to that fancy restaurant in the city?"

Casey nodded. Yes, she remembered their anniversary gift they'd never used because Jason hadn't felt like it.

"Well, we could go there and over a five-course meal decide who gets what. It'll be like a celebration. No reason it needs to become messy, right?"

"I totally agree." She slurred the totally but didn't pay any mind. Why would their separation and crumbling marriage need to be messy?

Casey's head spun. Maybe that third glass had been a mistake? She winced. "Oh, jeez."

"What?"

"Celebrations. The holidays. Christmas is next month. Ugh. What do we do? Will we still go to each other's family celebrations?"

Jason's face paled. "Shit. You're right. I hadn't thought about the timing. My parents will be devastated." He scratched the side of his head. "What if—okay. This might sound crazy. What if we waited to tell them until after the holidays?"

"But what if I don't live here anymore? The apartment I was

WHERE I'M SUPPOSED TO BE

looking at is available as early as next week." Casey tried to focus on the fireplace to ease the spinning.

Jason said, "Hmm. Well we just won't host any parties. People don't need to know you've got your own place. We can wait until after the New Year. It's not technically lying—not really. We just don't say anything,"

Casey contemplated his proposal. Boy, did he have an answer for everything when it came to their separation, as if he'd been thinking about it for quite some time. She stared at him. He looked like a different person, more confident than before. "It could work. Yeah. Let's do it. I mean it's only for a month or so that we'll have to keep it under wraps from our families. We play along until January?"

Jason said. "Yeah. Totally doable."

Casey thought about having to keep this enormous secret to herself for a month. She'd been living the lie that she'd been in a happy marriage for so long, could she really handle this one too? She contemplated her options.

She glanced at Jason, contently rubbing Roxie's fur. "One exception. Make that two." She lifted two fingers. "I can't keep it a total secret. I mean, I'm moving. It's easier for you. You aren't going anywhere. I have to do a change of address and all that jazz. I have to be able to tell at least Kat and Javier. They don't talk with our families or your friends. I'll tell'm to keep it hush-hush. Is that cool?"

Casey realized she didn't need his permission. They were her support team, and she needed them, but probably for the sake of her and Jason's relationship it was best to go full disclosure.

Jason bobbed his head. "Not an issue. It's cool. I just don't want it to be a thing during the holidays."

"Great."

He said, "Oh, and I'll make a reservation for this weekend, since you'll need to pack pretty soon."

Casey thought, *Boy, he just can't get me out fast enough!*

She gave her best, believable grin. "Sounds great!"

Casey couldn't help but consider the irony that she and Jason had to communicate, compromise, and work together for their secret separation scheme. If only the rest of their relationship could have included such stellar examples of teamwork, she imagined how different things could have been.

# WINTER

# CHAPTER 9

CASEY SLUGGED toward her car after a challenging morning cardio kick-boxing class. She reached for the door handle when she heard the muffled ring of her cellphone hidden in her gym bag. She leaned on the door, looked at the screen. She answered, "Hey Kat!"

Kat screeched, "Hey!"

Casey replied, "Awesome, I just got out of a class and was going to call you when I got home. But hey, now's good."

She'd been dying to talk to Kat about the covert operation she and Jason were running. She had too many emotions and thoughts to keep to herself. It had been eating her up inside. Would their separation lead to divorce or a rekindled marriage? It was all happening so fast, like she was on a roller-coaster with her hands in the air screaming at the top of her lungs. Kat was a great sounding board and calming force in her life. Right now, she needed her more than ever.

Kat replied. "I have news! Glenn and I are engaged!"

Casey felt like she'd just taken a roundhouse kick to her chest. She gathered every bit of strength inside of her to exclaim, "Congratulations! You have to tell me everything."

As Kat launched into the story, Casey pulled open her car door and slunk into the driver's seat. She did her best to silence her sobs as tears flowed. She couldn't ruin Kat's moment. She couldn't tell her about the separation and all she was going through. How one minute she'd feel elated to be free and the next she'd break down because her marriage and relationship with Jason had failed. That her deepest fears were coming to fruition. She couldn't talk to her. She couldn't talk to anyone.

"And of course, you know you'll be my matron-of-honor, right?"

Casey stared at her steering wheel. Of course. Of course, she was going to be in a wedding the year her marriage fell apart. She eeked out, "I'm so excited. I can't wait. Have you thought about dates yet?" Thank goodness she'd just burned off some of her anxiety with fifty minutes of cardio. If she hadn't, she wasn't sure she would've made it through the phone call.

Kat replied, "We're talking about the summer after Glenn graduates. I can't wait. I'm so happy. I don't think I've ever been this happy in my life! I should go though, Glenn's parents drove up to take us out to celebrate. I didn't want to go another day without telling you though. Talk soon, okay?"

Casey held her breath and exhaled. "Absolutely. Tell Glenn congratulations and that I'm so happy for you both!"

"Talk later. Bye!"

Casey rushed her goodbye and hung up the phone before succumbing to a full meltdown in the gym parking lot.

---

TWENTY MINUTES LATER, Casey studied her reflection in the visor mirror. Her eyes were pink and puffy, her skin blotchy, and she wore an overall look of defeat. She couldn't arrive home looking like that. She exited her car and ran back into the gym to wash her face again and apply a little lipstick. She thought, *Yeah, all I need is a little lipstick. Now I'm good as new.* She laughed at the ridiculousness of the concept.

On the drive home, she realized she didn't want to be anywhere near Jason. She shuddered at the thought of their big who-gets-what-in-the separation dinner later that night. She was fresh out of optimism and energy to feign a friendly conversation.

She decided to grab a burger for lunch at the closest drive through and then pick up Roxie for a little apartment hunting.

Roxie greeted her at the entry with a wagging tail, big eyes, and a pink tongue panting heavily. Casey picked her up and gave her a squeeze. "Hi, girl. I'm so happy to see you! We're going to go on a field trip!"

Roxie gave her a hug and then tried to wiggle free. Casey placed her on the ground and sat on the living room floor as Roxie rushed to the big rubber frog to play fetch. After Roxie calmed, she picked her back up and yelled up to Jason, "I'm taking Roxie out for a while. We'll be back in a few hours."

He yelled back, "Okay."

She returned her gaze to Roxie, "Girl, are you ready to find our new home?" Casey accepted her lack of objection as a yes.

---

CASEY ENTERED the one-bedroom apartment behind the bubbly, young leasing agent with sleek, shoulder length hair. The agent flashed a bright smile. "Why don't the two of you take some time to look around? We're very pet-friendly here."

Casey thanked her and stepped to the right into the living room big enough for a few sofas and a television stand. It had a fireplace with mantle and a set of sliding glass doors on the left. The agent yelled from behind, "Out there is the enclosed balcony —safe for the dog to run around. It leads to the laundry room."

Casey slid open the door and put Roxie down. She glanced to

the right to the view of Mt. Diablo. She thought, *Not too shabby.* She opened the door to the laundry room that included a full-size washer and dryer with a wooden shelf above them. She swiveled around to find a large space that could be used for storage. Casey moved out of the laundry area urging Roxie to follow suit.

They hopped back through the door to the living room and made their way to the kitchen and dining room that faced each other. Casey stared at the quaint horseshoe-shaped kitchen and paused. She would have her own kitchen. Her own washer and dryer. Her own dining room. Her own fireplace.

She moved on to the bedroom, which was more than big enough for a queen-sized bed and nightstands. She gasped at the size of the walk-in closet. It was huge. She didn't think she had enough clothes to fill it. The attached neutral-colored bathroom had a tub, shower, and sink. She stepped back and covered her mouth with her hand. She would have her own bathroom. She would have her own bedroom.

Never in her life had she had her own room—now she was going to have six. She couldn't believe she would have her very own apartment. No little sisters. No roommates. No uninterested husbands. No fighting. No drama.

"What do you think?"

Casey broke from her trance and pivoted to face the agent. "I love it."

"Great! Let's get you to the leasing office so nobody snatches it up before we get an application in. This is a hot floor plan."

Casey failed to suppress a grin as she signed the rental application. She handed it to the agent across the desk. The agent responded, "Give us about fifteen minutes to process this."

Casey thanked her and peered down at Roxie, content in her lap, and whispered, "Sweetheart, we've got a new home." She scratched behind Roxie's ears and stroked the black and white fur on her back.

While the application was being processed, Casey clipped on Roxie's leash and took her outside for a walk around their soon-to-be new apartment complex. It was massive with twelve cream colored buildings, each three stories high with a backdrop of the mountains. She watched as neighbors strolled with their dogs along the plentiful paved walkways lined with manicured lawn and mature redwood trees.

It hadn't fully sunk in that this was going to be her and Roxie's new home. The excitement of her own place was suddenly clouded with the dread of her impending life event. Was the pit in her stomach her body's way of telling her this wasn't temporary? Or trying to get her to face the reality that her marriage was broken? Was this a step toward reconciliation, or a step toward a new and independent life?

"There you are!"

Casey gave a sheepish grin. "Oh, hey. All done?"

The perky agent nodded. "Congratulations! You're all approved!"

Casey thought, *Congratulations. Your marriage failed, now you get to live here!* She replied. "Great. What's next?"

"We'll set your move in date and get a deposit to hold the apartment. That's it!"

Casey followed her back into the office and discussed details. She wrote a check and handed it to her. The agent stood and extended her hand. "Thank you, Casey. We look forward to having you as part of our community."

Casey wanted to vomit, just a little. She shook her hand. "Thank you." She glanced down at Roxie. "C'mon, girl. Let's go."

They exited the leasing office and made their way to the car. She buckled up and thought, *Is this really happening?*

"HEY. I was wondering when you'd be back." Jason stood in the kitchen wearing blue jeans and a white T-shirt.

Casey replied. "Sorry, took longer than I expected." She glanced at her watch. "Still plenty of time to get ready for dinner. I have good news! Miss Roxie and I found an apartment."

Jason's eye brows arched, and his mouth turned up. "Awesome. Is it the one you told me about?"

"Yep. My application was approved, and I left a deposit. I get the keys on Friday."

Casey heard the words she was saying but was having a difficult time processing that she just told her husband she'd found a new place to live, without him, as if she'd just told him she'd gotten a promotion at work or got a great deal on a new pair of boots. She felt as if she were outside of her body talking about somebody else.

Jason playfully replied, "Good thing we planned our dinner for tonight—you've got to get packin'."

Casey shut her eyes and thought, *Yes, she needed to get packin'. Astutely put, Jason.* "Yeah. Okay. We should get ready for tonight. Should we make a list?"

Jason held up a piece of paper that had been lying on the counter. "Already got it."

Casey's mouth dropped open, and she thought, *Of course you do.* "Good. Cool. I'm gonna take a shower and start getting ready."

She waved and ran up the stairs before she completely lost it. She stripped down, throwing her clothes on the bathroom floor, and stepped into the steaming water.

The rush of hot water effectively washed the tears from her face. She felt like everything she did and said was an act. Her life had turned into a bad television show. Smile and pretend to be happy. Don't let them see you cry. Don't appear weak. Act like everything is fine. All the time. It suffocated her, and she didn't know how long she could hang on. Was she overreacting? Maybe Jason wasn't really trying to push her out as quickly as humanly possible? Could it be that Jason's chipper demeanor was as fake as hers? Maybe he only acted happy because he thought she was?

———

She stood in front of the full-length mirror and stared at her reflection. She contemplated whether or not she'd lost weight. Her therapy of cardio kick-boxing seemed to be paying off in more ways than one. She smoothed the black wrap-around dress and fussed her honey brown hair to give it a fuller look.

She slipped on her black pumps when Jason entered their bedroom wearing a dark suit, white dress shirt, and a funky tie featuring an electric guitar. It had been a birthday gift from his mother.

He said, "You look great."

"Thanks." She couldn't remember the last time he'd complimented her.

"You about ready? My parents are on their way to stay with Roxie."

Casey replied, "Just going to add a little lipstick and I'll be good to go." She thought, *Because today lipstick solves everything!*

The doorbell rang.

Justin quipped, "Just in time!"

They descended the stairs one in front of the other. Jason reached the door and opened it to reveal Betty and Frank. "C'mon in."

Betty knelt down. "Oh, there she is!" She picked up Roxie and looked them up and down. "You guys look great."

Casey forced a closed-mouth grin and thought, *Thanks for watching Roxie so your son and I can go execute our secret plan to separate—and who are we kidding. We'll likely get divorced. Thanks again!*

Jason ushered them into the living room and said, "We should really get going. Traffic over the bridge is gonna be rough."

Frank nodded. "Yes, you better get going."

Betty bellowed. "Have fun!"

Casey thought, *Oh yes. This is going to be super fun.*

They waved as they exited through the kitchen into the garage. Situated in Jason's sleek coupe they drove the forty-five minutes into San Francisco listening to Dave Matthews without uttering a word.

SEATED at their table for two, they surveyed the dark, crowded restaurant lit mostly by tiny tea lights glowing against white tablecloths. They ordered the five-course tasting menu with a wine pairing option for Jason. Upon presentation of the amuse bouche and her single glass of Riesling, Casey gathered the nerve to bring up the purpose of their 'date'. "So, you've got the list?"

Jason reached down to pull it from his trouser pocket. "Right here. Should we just start—get it over with?"

"Sure."

"Okay, from the top. Food processor?"

Casey gave a lopsided grin. "Well, I don't exactly cook. If you want, you can have it."

Jason said, "True. Well if I get that—you want the espresso machine?"

Casey lit up. "Yes please!" She loved that espresso maker.

They went back and forth throughout their meal until they'd crossed all of the items off the list. Jason raised his wine glass. "We're done. Cheers to that!"

Casey raised her water glass, "Cheers!"

She set down her glass and ran her hand down the side of her dress. In an announcer's voice she'd heard on a popular TV ad, she said, "Dress: eighty dollars." She tilted her head to the table. "Wine: forty dollars. Dinner: two hundred dollars." She giggled. "Deciding who gets what in the separation: priceless."

She and Jason broke into laughter.

Casey thought, *At this point it's either laugh or cry.* At the moment, she chose to laugh.

# CHAPTER 10

CASEY PULLED the packing tape across the final box and thought if she had to endure the odor of burnt plastic for another moment she'd hurl. Was it the smell or her nerves? Either way, she was relieved to be done packing up her items and the agreed-upon half of what was formerly her and Jason's belongings.

Jason approached. "All done?"

"Yep. The movers called and should be here in the next five to ten minutes. It's probably better if you keep Roxie upstairs when they're here. You know how she gets."

She glanced down at her feet where Roxie's sweet black-and-white teddy bear face beamed at her. You wouldn't think she'd turn into a vicious ten-pound ball of fluff at the sight of strangers getting too close to her people, but she did.

"Good thinking." Jason scooped her up. "We'll head up now since they'll probably be here any minute."

"Okay." She scratched Roxie's head. "Okay, girl, I'll see you later when we're all done. Be good."

Casey stood and watched as they ascended the stairs. She couldn't will herself to move until she heard the knock on the door. She opened to find a rather burly man with thick arms and dark hair pulled back into a pony tail. She said, "Hi, I'm Casey."

"I'm George. Nice to meet you. The rest of the crew is on the truck. Is it okay for me to come in for a walk-through of what's going?"

She smiled. "Sure."

Casey led him into the living room where she'd grouped her boxes. "Most of the boxes are here, there's a few in the garage, and a dresser and bed upstairs that's going. Everything else stays."

"Cool. Easy."

She thought, *Cool. Easy.* She felt none of those things. She felt flushed and tormented. It was one of the most difficult things she'd ever had to do. The reality of the day became more over-whelming than she'd anticipated. She was glad Jason and Roxie were sequestered in his office. She didn't think she could stand to look at them as she moved out of their home. She certainly couldn't have done it with a smile on her face. She had learned to be quite the actress, but she hadn't yet reached that level of expertise.

With the truck loaded up, Casey climbed into her car to lead the way to her new apartment. Buckled up, her cell phone vibrated. She checked the screen and saw it was Kat calling. She popped in her earpiece and answered. "Hey, Kat. Give me a sec."

She backed out of the driveway and parked until she received the wave from George that the crew was ready to follow.

As she drove down their street, she said to Kat, "Alrighty. Ready now. How are you?"

Kat asked, "I'm good. You? What are you up to today?"

Casey gave an exhausted laugh. "I'm hanging in there. I'm uh. Well…moving."

Kat asked, "Moving? What?"

Casey figured now was as good as time as any to explain what had transpired over the last few weeks. She gave Kat the full story during the drive.

Kat responded, "I'm so sorry. How are you doing with all of this?"

"Some days I'm okay. Some days I'm not okay. One minute I'm okay, the next I'm not. It's unsettling. I don't know what is going to happen with my life in a day or a month or a year. Everything is moving so fast. I feel like I've lost all control." Casey wiped the tear that had escaped.

Kat responded with another, "I'm so sorry."

Casey knew she was sorry, but she also knew Kat had no idea what she was going through. Casey had thought her whole life was set in stone, and now it was all slipping away from her as she dangled on the edge of a cliff. Kat was in the opposite position. Her life was full of happiness, positivity, and plans for the future. They couldn't be in a more different place. She'd thought she'd get comfort from talking about her situation, but it just made her feel more alone.

Casey said, "Hey. I've got to go. I'm at the apartment, and I've got to let the van through the gate and you know, move, and all that jazz."

Kat said, "Okay, call me later if you want to talk."

"Will do. Thanks. Bye."

She tugged at the ear piece and threw it on the passenger side. She pulled some napkins from the glove box and cleaned up her face. She laughed to herself and thought, *If only I'd brought some lipstick.*

---

SHE WAVED in the two massive men carrying her mattress. They crossed the threshold, and she directed them, "Straight back into the bedroom." They nodded and continued forward.

When they finished, the man with tattoos on both forearms approached and said. "Looks like we're about done. George will be up in a minute with paperwork."

Casey said, "Okay."

The tattooed man surveyed the place. "You livin' here alone?"

Casey thought it had been pretty obvious but responded with a nod.

He stared at her. "You got a gun?"

Casey stiffened. "Uh. No."

"Lady livin' alone, you should definitely get a gun."

Casey replied, "Oh. Uh. Thanks. I was considering it." Casey had not been considering the purchase of a firearm. She did, however, catalogue this as her first bit of advice received as a single woman living alone. She shifted toward the kitchen. Thankfully, George returned shortly after.

. "All set here. Everything go okay? Anything else you need help with?"

Casey thought, *Hmm maybe I ought to ask them to get me a gun?* She replied. "No, I'm all set. Thank you."

"Alright. Just go ahead and sign here, and we're good to go."

Casey scribbled on the invoice attached to a metal clipboard.

He ripped off her pink copy and handed it to her. "Casey, thank you, and enjoy your new home!"

She waved as they left. Should she have said she had a gun? Now that he knew she didn't have one, he could return to attack her without fear of being shot. She needed to be more prepared for questions pertaining to her new single-woman-living-alone status.

In the future she could say, "I've got a guard dog!" And "I know martial arts!" And "Oh yeah, I love guns. I've had a collection since I was just a little girl!" It wouldn't be completely false. Who's to say Roxie wasn't a guard dog? She had always alerted Casey when people approached, although she wouldn't be terribly effective at defending Casey against a full-grown human. And, she did partake in cardio kick-boxing, which was sort of martial arts, so not a total fabrication. Sure, the thing about guns was a lie, but sometimes lying is okay to save your life, right?

She studied her mostly empty apartment, which now resembled a small city of buildings made of stacked moving boxes. She went back into her laundry room and returned with a blue folding chair she had frequently used for watching Cara's soccer games, and she set it up in her living room facing the fireplace. She arranged a few boxes on either side and stood back. She thought, *Couch and end tables, check.*

In the dining room, she sat on a box labeled *books* and glanced across at the kitchen. She decided to leave unpacking for another day. She pushed herself up off the box and entered the bedroom. Her bed looked inviting, but, she thought, *Where the heck are my sheets?* She began reading the black marker descriptions on each box until she found the one labeled, *Linens.* Bingo. She made the bed haphazardly and fluffed her pillows. She plopped herself on top and closed her eyes.

Her mind raced. The enormity of the day's events weighed upon her. She was lying on her bed in her new apartment without Jason. This was where she lived now. She didn't live with her husband. She was probably getting divorced.

She opened her eyes, stared at the bright white ceiling, and muttered, "How is this my life now? How did I get here?" And with that, she broke down. Each time she was sure she didn't have any more tears, they'd come back with a vengeance. She told herself she needed to pull it together. She still had to pick up Roxie from Jason, at Jason's house. Not their house. Jason's house. She dragged herself to the bathroom. She turned on the faucet and sank down onto her knees. Head in hands, she cried until there was nothing left.

She stood and stared at her reflection. She thought, *Pitiful.* She splashed cold water on her face and looked back up. She deduced her meltdown would likely go unnoticed if she put on some makeup and of course, some lipstick. She let out a weak chuckle at her ongoing joke. She unpacked her boxes labeled *bathroom* and fixed her face.

SHE KNOCKED on the front door to her previous residence. She heard the click of the lock disengaging and held her breath. Jason stood before her with Roxie in his arms. He smirked. "You could have used your key."

Casey hesitated before replying. "I wasn't sure what the rule was. We didn't talk about that."

"Well, c'mon in."

She sat herself down on the ground to greet Roxie with belly rubs and a game of fetch.

Jason sat on the sofa next to her. "All settled?"

She didn't meet his eyes. "I don't know about settled. I didn't get much unpacked, but I'm all moved in. That's something." She pulled the key to the house from her pocket and handed it to him.

He stared before taking it. He exhaled. "So, this is really real, huh?"

Casey glanced up at him. "Yeah."

Jason cleared his throat. "You'll drop off Roxie on Sunday? And then get her on Friday?"

"Yeah. That's the plan. I do want her to get used to the new apartment so maybe I can keep her longer after that. My company's holiday shutdown starts on Saturday so I'll have a few weeks off."

Jason stared blankly. "Okay. Yeah. She should get used to it. I read sometimes dogs have a hard time adjusting when you move."

"I read that too."

"After the holidays maybe we can come up with a normal schedule."

"Sounds good."

Casey set Roxie on the carpet and braced herself on the couch to stand up. "I should gather her things. I suppose we'll need to get her a second set of stuff for her, like another leash, harness, car carrier, water and food dishes, et cetera."

Jason's leg shook as he looked at her. "I can get her the new stuff. You can keep her old stuff since she's already familiar with it. It's probably better you take it since she's going to an unfamiliar place. It'll make her feel more at home."

"I suppose."

Casey continued to gather things into a brown paper grocery bag. She lifted the sack and said, "I think this is it." She searched for Roxie. "Come here, Roxie."

Roxie pranced over. Casey bent to pick her up with one arm. "We'll see you tomorrow, around eight, okay?"

Jason nodded.

Casey stepped toward the front door and turned around. "Bye."

Jason remained seated and waved his left hand.

AFTER ROXIE HAD SUFFICIENTLY SNIFFED every inch of the new apartment, the two settled down on the gray carpet in their new living room. Casey petted Roxie and said, "Well, girl. This is it. What do you think?"

Roxie kept her gaze on Casey.

"You hungry?"

Roxie stood and wiggled her tail.

Casey climbed up, using the blue folding chair for support. "Alright girl, I'm on it." She searched for a local pizza parlor and phoned in an order.

She continued to unpack Roxie's bag and then mixed together her chicken and rice meal. She decided to hold off on creating the kibble trail until the pizza arrived.

With dinner procured and ready, Casey sat on the floor next to Roxie's food mat and white ceramic water dish. They dined side by side for their first meal in their new home. While they ate,

Casey couldn't help but think how much sadder the current scene would have been if she didn't have Roxie with her.

# CHAPTER 11

CASEY PARKED in the driveway at Jason's with a sinking feeling in her gut. She grabbed Roxie from her carrier and climbed out of her car and made the short trek to the front door of the townhouse. She stared at it for a good thirty seconds before she knocked.

Jason answered wearing a pair of plaid pajamas and blue thermal shirt. She had bought the sleep ensemble for him for Christmas the previous year. He gave a friendly smile. "Hey. C'mon in."

She stepped into the living room and put Roxie down.

"How are things at the new apartment?"

Casey glanced to the right before answering. "Really good. I'm realizing I'll need to shop for a few things, but I'm slowly getting settled." Casey was proud she was able to pull off such a positive view of her new world. Needing a few things was an understatement. She had enough utensils for fifty people, but no dinner plates or bowls. How had she missed those in the split? Not to mention, her near-complete lack of furniture. Should she buy a new couch? Dining table? TV stand? If they got back together and she'd bought an apartment full of furniture, they'd have too much stuff.

"That's good. I was talking to my mom earlier. They're hosting Christmas Eve this year, instead of Christmas because Derrick will be on leave for a few days and he needs to be back on base on the twenty-fifth. Has your family talked about their Christmas plans yet?"

Casey had completely blocked the holidays from her mind. She could barely keep herself together long enough to go to the gym and participate in short social interactions. How in the world would she get through two Christmases pretending she and Jason were still happily married and living together? She had gone through the last year-and-a-half pretending they were happily married, though, so maybe it wouldn't be any different?

She watched Roxie rummaging through her toys when she heard, "Casey?"

She shook her head. "Oh, sorry. I was just thinking. I haven't talked to my mom about it yet, but I'm sure it'll be fine. She usually likes to celebrate Christmas Day. I'll call her later to ask what the plan is."

She realized she still hadn't responded to her friend Maddy's invite for a Christmas party she was hosting at her parents' house the next weekend. Christmas time used to be her favorite time of year, and she always got excited about all of her friends' annual parties. Now she was dreading them.

Casey inhaled and exhaled to prevent the waterworks from turning on again. "I got an invitation from Jerry and Dana for their holiday dinner. I haven't responded yet. Do you want to go? Or should I make up an excuse?"

Jason's face fell. "Oh. I don't know. Maybe we skip. I mean, you can go if you want. They're really your friends anyways."

Sure, Dana was her work friend, but when they'd met Dana and her husband, Jerry, she and Jason were already a couple.

They only did things together as a couple. The dinner was all couples.

Casey shook it off, something, she realized she'd have to learn to do more and more. "Got it. Okay, so I'll pick up Little One on Friday night." She scooped up Roxie from where she was rolling around in a pile of toys and gave her a squeeze and kiss on the top of her head. "You be a good girl. I'll see you in a couple of days, okay?" She put her back down as her heart broke just a little.

Jason stood. "Alright, we'll see you Friday night. Have a good first week in your new place!"

Casey thought, *So positive. I'll have to work on that.* "Thanks. I may text you to see how she's doing. Is that okay?" Casey had no idea what the proper communication etiquette was when you're separated and sharing a puppy.

"Yeah, that's fine."

Casey said, "Okay." And she waved as she let herself out.

On the drive back to her sparse apartment, she only wept during half of the drive. The other half she blared Destiny Child's *Survivor* over and over until she parked in her assigned stall. Empowered, she walked through the front door and began to unpack her clothes and organize the bathroom while blasting that song on repeat. She was a survivor.

Why was she allowing Jason to make her fall apart? She thought, *Uh-uh. I've been through too much to be undone by him.* No way she would let any man bring her down.

By the time she finished unpacking, it was eleven o'clock. She slipped on a pair of flannel pajamas and plopped onto her bed. Her eyes flickered before she fell fast asleep.

---

THE SOUND of her alarm jarred her awake. She slid off the bed and zombie-walked to her shower to turn it on. She glanced at the mirror covering the entire wall above the sink and counter. She thought, *This is the first day going to work and facing people as a secretly separated, living-alone female.* She inched her face closer for a thorough inspection. Eyes not too puffy. Face clear.

She stepped into the shower and let it wash away the days before. She didn't cry. She washed her hair and body like a mentally stable person. It felt good. Drying off, she convinced herself to set a goal of zero tears today. Dressed and primped, she exited her apartment into the morning sunshine and freezing air.

At BayArea BioPharma, she strolled down the hall to her cubicle, where she sat in her chair and powered up her desktop computer. She read emails like it was any other day. The day had gotten off to a better start than the one's before, actually. She had a shorter commute, her own bathroom, and no hostile looks as she exited her home. She thought, *It will be a great day at work.*

From behind she heard, "Hey, girl!"

She thought, *Yes! Javier's finally back from vacation!* She swiveled around in her chair and raised her pinky to the corner of her mouth doing her best Dr. Evil impersonation. "Hellooo."

Javier set himself on the top of her desk. "What's new? What did I miss? Any new office gossip? Tell me!"

Casey giggled. "Careful, you're gonna give yourself a stroke. No new office gossip that I can think of. Oh, you know about Dana, right?"

She'd mostly kept to herself when he was away. She hadn't been feeling especially social these past few days.

"Yes. Heard. Got the going-away lunch invite from Prissy. OMG. What will we do without her?"

Casey suppressed a laugh. "Prissy" was Javier's secret name for their uptight receptionist, Patty. Casey replied. "I don't know. Sucks, right?"

"Totally. Anyhoo. What's new with you? How are..." He sat down in the chair next to her and scooted it closer. "How are things with Jason? Things better? How's counseling?"

Casey chuckled quietly. "Counseling is great. Since we stopped going." She met Javier's light brown eyes. "We are separated. I moved out this weekend. It's a secret." She rolled her eyes and went on to tell him all the sordid details as he sat with his mouth gaped open.

He said, "Girl, I'm so sorry. You're so much better than him anyway. You're like a ten, and he's like—sorry to say, I know you're still married and all—a five. At best." Javier pursed his lips and nodded his head.

Casey had felt the familiar tingling of tears forming, but the action was halted by Javier's special brand of cheer. She grinned. "Thanks, Javi. I needed that."

He gave her a stern look. "No problem. Anything you need— you ask." He shook his head. "So nobody knows? That's crazy. Are you sure you're okay with it?"

Casey threw her hands in the air. "No, not really, but what am I supposed to do? I mean, it would suck to have to tell our families right before Christmas. They'd probably give me a hard time about it anyway. Being super supportive isn't always their strong suit. I mean, I get that we're just delaying the inevitable though. They'll probably be pissed we lied."

She knew it was true, but she also knew from past experience to just let it go when it came to her family's insensitivity and lack of support.

"Oh, who cares about them? I just care that you're okay."

"Hey. I'm a survivor." She sang a line of the song. "Thanks, Javi. Enough about me and my depressing life. How was your and Ben's vacation? I want details!"

Javier went on to describe in hilarious detail the vacation to Maui and all their misadventures on the beach and attempting to hike Mt. Haleakala. Before long, Javier had her doubled over in laughter.

"What's all this commotion?" Dana leaned on the entrance to Casey's cubicle.

Casey regained the ability to speak. "Javi's telling me about his vacation. Apparently Ben is even less athletically inclined than him!"

Dana pushed a strand of dark hair behind her ear. "And here I thought that was impossible."

Javier playfully swatted at her. "Hey. And I'm mad at you. I can't believe you're leaving us!"

Dana crossed her arms. "We can keep in touch! You guys are coming to our annual Christmas Soiree, right?"

Javier beamed. "Ben and I will be there. We'll leave Peanut at home. He's not party-ready."

They'd adopted Peanut the chihuahua shortly after the fateful lunch visit to the humane society where Casey had gotten the idea to get a dog. Now here she was four months later, sharing a Shih Tzu with her estranged husband.

"How about you and Jason?" Dana asked.

Javier exchanged glances with Casey.

Dana's mouth opened. "What? What did I miss?"

Javier lowered his voice. "Just tell her. She's not gonna say anything."

Casey deflated. "Jason and I are separated."

Dana's reaction was Casey's new least favorite: pity. "Oh, I'm so sorry. When did it happen?"

Casey looked at Javier, and he winked. "I got this."

Javier turned to Dana and whispered the story to her while Casey threw in a few nods here and there as Dana's face registered disbelief. By the end Casey said, "So, Jason and I won't be at your dinner, but I'll be there, if that's okay."

Dana said, "Of course. Why wouldn't it be okay?"

"It's all couples. I'd understand if you'd prefer I don't come."

Dana's eyes widened. "We would love to have you. You're always welcome." She wrinkled her nose. "Forget Jason."

Javier giggled. "See. We all know you're too good for him."

Casey gave a sheepish grin. "Thanks, guys."

Dana waved her hand like she was swatting a fly. "Oh, and Jerry wanted me to tell you, you can bring Roxie. He is dog crazy right now!"

"I just might. She's not very used to the new apartment yet, and I don't like leaving her for too long."

"Bring her. Jerry will be thrilled."

Dana and Javier continued on with office gossip while Casey watched her work buddies. She was once again thankful she had such good friends in her life to lift her up as she was falling down.

The week went by with few tears as she busied herself with work and shopping to stock her new apartment. She'd even bought new Christmas stockings to hang on the fireplace mantle for herself and Roxie, and she purchased a six-foot fake tree she decorated with several strands of colorful lights and multi-color ornaments. It brightened her otherwise drab living room. The room was a still a little sad-looking, but it was better with the decoration than without. It prompted her to also began researching sofas and dining tables. She figured if she and Jason worked things out, she could always sell the new furniture on Craigslist. Considering she hadn't heard from him all week, other than replies to her texts concerning Roxie, the need to sell any new furniture seemed less and less likely. She was surprised at herself to realize she was beginning to accept that possibility.

## CHAPTER 12

CASEY SAT on the living room floor with Roxie in her lap. "Hi, girl! I missed you so much! How have you been?" She scratched behind Roxie's ears as the pup chewed on her now brownish-yellow stuffed duck.

"How was your first week in the new apartment?"

She glanced at Jason where he sat on the beige sofa in a pair of light blue jeans and a Golden State Warriors sweatshirt.

She thought, *Right. You're here. This is your house.* Casey said, "It was good—busy. I finished unpacking and shopping for some essentials. I even bought Roxie and me a Christmas tree and stockings. I started looking into a new couch and dining table. It's a little empty without them." She paused to study Jason's face for some kind of reaction to her buying new furniture. His face stayed blank. She said, "I was holding off, since furniture is expensive, but what are you gonna do, right?"

Jason nodded. "Yeah. I get it. I got a new bed on Monday. Luckily, they were able to deliver it fast."

"That is lucky." Her chest ached. She returned her attention to Roxie and gathered the nerve to continue the conversation. "How was the week for you?"

Jason swallowed. "It was quiet. A little weird without you here. Roxie kept sniffing at the front door. I think she was looking for you."

Casey felt like she'd been punched in the gut. She gazed down at Roxie. "Poor girl. You don't know what's going on."

Jason sighed. "Oh, I know. I feel bad for her too. Poor little dog from a broken home."

Casey smirked. "It is a little pathetic isn't it?"

"Yeah. I think so." Jason chuckled. "Oh, I made an appointment with a counselor."

Casey said, "That's great." She paused. "I haven't made an appointment with Malcom—should I, or...?"

"Maybe we hold off until I talk to my new counselor."

She nodded. "Okay. Sounds like a plan." Casey was relieved to not have to go back to the counselor. She and Jason hadn't been on any dates since it was assigned as their homework, and when they'd told Malcom they were separating, he'd explained it was critical for their marriage to keep seeing each other during the separation. Neither of them had initiated any dates.

"Any plans for the weekend?" Jason asked. "I know you usually have a bunch of parties this time of year."

"True! Yes, I have two parties left before the family ones begin. I have a party at Maddy's tomorrow night, shopping with Anna and Cara on Sunday, and then the dinner party Sunday night at Dana and Jerry's. And then Monday is Christmas Eve." She gave a sheepish grin. She relaxed at the change in tone of their conversation. It was like they were old friends catching up for the first time in months. Maybe their separation wouldn't be totally miserable? "How about you?" she asked. "Any holiday stuff with the old gang?" The gang was a group of Jason's college friends that mostly still lived the fraternity brother life.

"Yeah, Matt called. He's doing a thing at his parents' with the whole crew. Apparently, Matt just got engaged, if you can believe that."

Casey's eyes widened. "You're kidding. To whom? Like, how desperate was she?"

They both chuckled.

Jason responded, "Right?"

"I guess tis the season." She paused. "I don't think I told you. Kat's engaged."

"Yeah? That's great. Tell her I said congratulations."

"Will do."

Jason smirked and shook his head. "Man, are we losers or what?"

Casey laughed, "All signs point to yes. At least we can laugh about it, right?" She thought, *Sometimes I laugh. Sometimes I cry. Right now, I laugh.*

"True."

"So what's the plan for Christmas Eve? Should I meet you here and we drive together?"

"That'll work. And for Christmas Day, I can drive out to your place before your family celebration. It's not fair for you to have to always drive out here."

"Thanks. I appreciate it."

Casey thought, *Are we the most amicably separated people, or what?* She realized how nice it was not to fight with him anymore. Each time they'd fought, it was as if she turned into a different person. A person who screamed and threw things. It wasn't a person she liked or a person she wanted to be. When they'd fought, she'd felt like part of her soul was being ripped out.

"Well, Roxie and I should probably head out." She stared at Roxie, still content in her lap, "You ready to go, girl?" Roxie jumped up and stood at attention.

Jason laughed. "I think that's a yes!"

"I think so."

Casey picked up Roxie and headed for the door. She extended her hand to the knob, hesitated, and turned around. "Bye, Jason. See you Monday."

CASEY APPLIED SPARKLY gold eye shadow to her lid. She blinked and opened her eyes. *Definitely festive.* She finished the look with a bright red lipstick. Her goal had been to look as cheerful as possible considering tonight was her first social gathering as a secretly separated woman. She hadn't even told Maddy about it. Not that Maddy would've been able to comprehend what Casey was going through. Maddy was two years younger, a recent college graduate living at home with her parents. She didn't think Maddy had ever even had a serious boyfriend. Casey avoided telling her mostly to avoid that look of pity she received far too frequently now. Despite their difference in age and places in life, Casey adored Maddy and her never-ending optimism and chipper personality. Casey was ready for a fun, think-about-nothing-serious kind of night. She knew one of Maddy's parties would certainly deliver.

She gave Roxie a quick rub behind the ears and told her, "Roxie, stay. You be a good girl. I'll be home in a little bit."

Roxie attempted an escape by running full speed toward the door. Casey picked her up and said, "Roxie, I'll be home soon. You stay here." She put her down in the living room near a pile of her toys. Casey backed out of the room and opened the front door just a crack and slowly slid out as Roxie stared at her with a look that could've only meant, I can't believe you are abandoning me. Casey stood in front of her door and breathed in and out the frigid air. She told herself, "You can do this. She'll be fine. It'll be just a few hours." Convinced, she stepped away from her apartment and made her way to the car.

CASEY HURRIED down the path to the two-story ranch-style home booming with the sounds of the "Jingle Bell Rock." She entered through the open front door and was greeted by Maddy, who wore a shimmering kelly green A-line dress, standing at the end of the staircase, directly ahead, with two women Casey didn't know. "Hey! Welcome to the party. I hope you are ready for a rockin' good time!"

Casey gave a nervous grin. "Hi!"

Maddy wrapped her five-foot-two frame around her for a generous hug. "I'm so glad you made it!"

She pivoted toward the two women, who also seemed a bit apprehensive at the level of cheer that was being thrown around. Maddy said, "Let me introduce you all." She pointed at the woman with long dark brown hair who wore a red wrap-around dress and four-inch heels. "Casey this is Gina. Gina this is Casey." And she waved at the woman with wispy blonde hair and sharp features who clung to the banister. "Casey this is Natalie. Natalie this is Casey." Maddy paused. "A few fun facts. One, you're all the first to arrive! And I know Casey through Kat, whom I met at St. Mary's, and now we're buds, and I'm so glad. Casey's super fun." Maddy's eyes sparkled as she grinned.

Casey suspected Maddy had started partying before her arrival.

She continued. "Fun facts about Gina. She works with my dad, and now we're buds. 'Nuff said. And Natalie I know from soccer. She's an amazing player. Fierce." Maddy winked a twinkling green eye at Natalie.

The three newly introduced women exchanged glances that said they needed to catch up with their mutual friend's sobriety level.

Maddy continued. "Deets for the night. We've got a make-your-own-taco bar. Copious amounts of fun drinks. And for dessert, assorted yummies and an ice cream sundae bar!" She displayed jazz hands before exclaiming, "And I just made punch! You guys want a drink?"

Gina said, "If that's what *you* had, that's what I'll have."

Maddy giggled and slapped a hand on Gina's arm. "Oh, you're hilarious. Follow me. It's all in the kitchen."

The three women trailed Maddy down the hall in single-file fashion and into the large kitchen, which smelled like a mix of taco meat and freshly baked sugar cookies. Red and green Christmas lights lit the tops of the cabinets. Sugar cookies and peanut butter balls on the countertops were displayed on ornament-shaped platters. A large punch bowl full of green foamy liquid with tree-shaped ice cubes sat to the right of the sweets. Maddy grabbed a plastic cup with a candy cane on the side and scooped a ladle of green liquid into it. "Here you go, Casey!" She repeated the action for her other two guests.

The sound of the doorbell chimed. "Be right back!" Maddy said, running out of the kitchen.

Casey heard Maddy squealing hello to newcomers. Casey eyed Gina and Natalie. "How long have you known Maddy?"

Gina sipped her drink apprehensively. "Sorry, I don't normally drink frothy green things." She scrunched up her button-nose and chuckled. "I met Maddy a few months ago. She's really fun. You?"

"It's been a few years now. We used to hang out with Kat together, but then Kat went off to grad school, and the two of us have hung out ever since. And of course I try not to miss any of her parties. They usually have high entertainment value."

Gina laughed. "I can see that. How about you, Natalie?"

Natalie chugged about half of the green punch. "Samesies. Just met her a few months ago. We play on a recreational soccer team together. How big are her parties usually?" Natalie glanced over at the stove covered in trays of taco fixings. "There is a ton of food."

Casey grinned. "Maddy knows a lot of people. Usually thirty to forty."

Natalie's pale blue eyes bugged out. "Holy moly. I don't know anyone."

Gina gritted her teeth. "Me either."

Casey said, "No worries. I can usually recognize some of the regulars, but I don't really know anyone other than Maddy."

Gina raised her cup. "Well, now we know each other. Cheers!"

Natalie and Casey joined cups and exclaimed, "Cheers!"

Within a half-hour, more than thirty people filled the house. Some brought cases of beer, and some brought their dogs. It was an anything-goes kind of party, and the only rule was that you had to have a good time. To Casey's surprise she stuck pretty close to Gina and Natalie, with whom she quickly picked up a good rapport. She learned more about each of them. As she listened to their stories she thought, *Fast friends. That was the term.* Gina had a not-so-serious guy she was dating, but she wasn't looking to settle down anytime soon and worked in internet sales. Natalie had a long-term boyfriend, Peter, and was a graduate student working part time at a school. Both of them were warm and funny and liked to have a good time. No surprise, considering they all were friends with Maddy.

At one point in the evening, Maddy made a reappearance at the dining table where the three women had sequestered themselves. "Hey, ladies. You having a good time?"

Casey smiled. "Yes M'am."

Gina and Natalie nodded enthusiastically.

Maddy took a seat next to Casey. "So what's new? Natalie, how's Peter?"

Natalie finished chewing her taco. "He's good. His parents are in town, so he's entertaining his brother and sister."

Maddy turned to Casey. "How's Jason?"

Casey's face fell. She stared down at the brilliantly cut diamond solitaire and slim platinum band on her ring finger. She glanced up at Maddy. "Not great. Well, I mean he's fine. We're not great. We're separated." She surprised herself with the disclosure.

Maddy gasped. "What? What happened?"

Casey shook her head. "It's a long story. I'd rather not talk about it." Casey held up her cup of green juice and gave a fake grin. "I'd rather drink!"

Natalie and Gina exchanged glances. Casey had purposefully not brought up her marital situation during their get-to-know-you conversation.

Maddy gave her a hug. "I'm so sorry. We'll do lunch next week and catch up, okay?"

Casey nodded. The table fell silent.

Casey shook her head. "New topic. I'm dying for that sundae bar!" Casey was proud of herself for how quickly she was able to change the subject of their conversation.

Natalie cheered, and Gina said, "Yes please!"

Maddy slid out of her seat and stood. Her eyes widened. "I almost forgot! You wanna help me set it up?"

They all agreed and followed Maddy back to the kitchen.

Gina scooped vanilla ice cream as Natalie poured sprinkles and candies into little dishes. Casey grabbed the bag of plastic spoons and arranged them in a cup. "I think I'll put hot fudge and caramel on mine!" she declared.

Natalie nodded. "Oh yeah, and peanuts and sprinkles too."

Maddy said, "All the good stuff!"

Gina nudged Casey and whispered, "Speaking of good stuff. That guy has been eyeing you."

Casey turned and looked to her left. She watched as the guy quickly averted his attention to Maddy's parent's chihuahua, Tonka. The man was medium height, with a slight build, a round face, and bright blue eyes. She supposed he was attractive enough, but she was still married. She and Jason weren't supposed to be seeing other people. Although, she had to admit it felt good to have someone admire her. She brushed off the thought and faced Gina. She gave a light-hearted chuckle. "Now he's eyeing Tonka. I suppose he's not terribly selective."

Gina hesitated before she giggled. "I suppose not."

Casey guessed Gina got the hint. "So, what do you guys like to do for fun?"

"I love to dance!" Gina exclaimed.

Natalie stopped pouring almond slices and started swaying her slender hips. "Me too. Salsa's my favorite."

Maddy approached with a pile of snowman napkins. "Hey, ladies. Are we starting the dance party in here?"

Natalie stopped dancing. "Not yet. That was a preview. First, we eat sundaes, and then we dance."

Gina and Casey cheered.

Casey grabbed a bowl of ice cream and added hot fudge, caramel sauce, mini chocolate chips, and rainbow sprinkles before heading back to the dining table to devour the sweets before initiating the dance party.

---

CASEY STROLLED BACK to her apartment feeling good about the night out. She'd made some new friends, had a great time, and only had to endure the briefest of pity parties.

She arrived at her door and slid her key into the lock. She paused at the sound of scraping from the other side of the door. She continued unlocking the door and pushed it open to find Roxie jumping with a crazed look in her eyes as if she were an animatronic ball of fluff designed to bounce from wall to wall. Casey picked Roxie up to stop her from hurting herself, gave her a quick hug, and set her back down on the ground to get a toy. Roxie ran over to her pile and grabbed the big green frog. They played fetch on the living room floor for nearly ten minutes while little Roxie's nerves settled. Then she was ready for bedtime.

Casey didn't notice the scratches and chunks missing from the wooden molding outlining the front door until the next morning.

DRESSED FOR THE EVENING, Casey glanced down at Roxie, who'd managed to follow her every step since she'd gotten home the night before. She thought, *Thank goodness I can bring her tonight.* After she discovered Roxie's destruction of the door and a wet spot in the dining room, Casey realized she needed to give Roxie a bit more time to acclimate to her new home before leaving her alone again. "Don't worry, Roxie," she told her as she approached the door, "You're not getting left!"

She buckled on Roxie's new rhinestone-studded collar, clipped on her leash, and headed out for their first couples' dinner together.

On the drive, Casey blasted more of Destiny's Child to pump herself up for another evening of facing those who may give her that dreaded pity face. By the time she arrived at Jerry and Dana's townhouse, she was ready. Casey inhaled the frigid air as she and Roxie strutted down the concrete path, lined with manicured lawn, to the front door.

Jerry opened up the large wooden door wearing a pair of dark jeans and a blue button-down dress shirt. "Roxie!" He exclaimed. "So glad you could make it! Welcome!"

Dana stood next to him and playfully punched him in the arm.

Jerry chuckled. "Oh, hi Casey, didn't see you there. Welcome to you too!" He squatted down to pet Roxie before he stood back up to hug Casey. She caught a whiff of his sandalwood cologne as he patted her back. He laughed playfully. "I kid. I kid. C'mon in."

Dana gave Casey a quick one-armed hug before ushering her into the couple's tri-level townhouse. Casey inhaled the scent of freshly cut pine tree as they strolled past the living room and into the dining room outfitted with a table set for ten. In the center of the oval table, a poinsettia sat atop a bright red cloth. Wine glasses, dinner plates, and utensils adorned the matching place-mats. Two couples Casey had met the previous year, waved as she approached. She was about to take a seat when Jerry called out. "Casey, I have something for you. Come here a sec."

Casey shrugged playfully to the couples and carried Roxie over to the living room. Jerry was standing next to the small tree that he towered over. "What's up?" she asked.

Jerry scratched Roxie's head. In response, she angled her furry head back in an attempt to bite him.

From under the tree, he pulled out a soft purple baby blanket and a yellow miniature tennis ball. He gazed at Roxie. "It's your own blanket and toy to play with for when you come over to visit!" Jerry laid the blanket on the rug and tried to get Roxie to play fetch.

Casey put Roxie down to investigate. While Roxie was off retrieving the ball, Jerry spoke in a hushed tone. "Just so you know, I told the other people here about Jason. I told them not to bring it up. Tonight we just celebrate! How are you doing?"

Casey said, "I'm doing alright. Adjusting. It's only been a week and a half, but for some reason it seems longer."

Jerry grabbed the ball from Roxie and threw it across their cream-colored carpet once more. "Well, if you need anything, you let us know. Anything. Oh, and I almost forgot. We want to formally invite you and Roxie over for New Year's Eve. We'll have dinner and drinks. It'll be fun! We'd love to have you."

Casey nodded. "Thank you."

She redirected her focus to Roxie chewing on the ball, refusing to give it back to Jerry. She was touched by Dana and Jerry's thoughtfulness. She hadn't been particularly close to them and, besides seeing Dana at work, she only hung out with them every few months when they would go out to dinner with Javier and Ben.

When Casey and Jason decided to separate, she didn't know how people would treat her. She'd anticipated having the stigma of being separated or divorced attached to her and figured she would stop being invited to couples' events. She was even prepared for people to think she was a quitter or toxic, fearing that divorce may be contagious. She hadn't anticipated the flood of encouragement and support from everyone she told.

"Hey, girl! Ahhh, and this is Roxie!" Javier, wearing a purple velvet blazer and matching fedora, hurried toward Casey and Roxie in the living room. He bent down and gave her a kiss on the cheek. "Good to see you. We are partying tonight!" He glanced down at Roxie who was actively sniffing his feet. He put his palm to his chest. "She is the cutest." He lowered his hand for her to sniff and then picked her up and clutched her to his chest. He studied her furry face. "Hi there."

Roxie stared at him with wide eyes as if to say, "Who are you and why are you holding me?"

He scratched her head. "Oh my god. She's too precious. I can't even… Oh my god, Casey, I'm stealing her from you!"

Casey gave a hearty laugh. "Over my dead body!"

"That can be arranged." He winked and looked over his shoulder toward the dining room. "Ben! Come here. You have to meet Roxie. She is the cutest!"

Ben, a dark-skinned Adonis, approached and waved with a wide grin. "Hi, Casey." He stood next to Javier and let Roxie sniff his hand before petting her back. "She is adorable."

Javier pretended to whisper. "We're stealing her."

Jerry called out from across the room. "Drinks anyone?"

Multiple cries of, "Yes, please!," were returned.

Jerry exclaimed, "Alright, c'mon into the dining room, and we'll get you hooked up. Dinner will be ready in about thirty minutes."

The group made their way to the dining room where the newcomers said hello to the other guests, and they kicked off their evening of great food, cocktails, and company.

# CHAPTER 13

ON CHRISTMAS EVE, Casey watched Jason from the passenger side of his car. He had dark circles under his eyes and his skin looked pale. She asked, "Rough night?"

Jason groaned. "Party at Matt's last night. I drank way too much. I'm so hungover."

Casey felt like she'd received a punch to the gut. Her thoughts raced to the last time he'd declared he'd drank too much. Was there another confession coming? After a long pause, she assumed there wasn't. Or if there was something to confess, he was keeping it to himself.

"That sucks. I cut myself off at two last night."

"You were drinking?"

Casey had been drinking far more over the last few months than she had in the last few years. "A few cocktails at Jerry and Dana's."

"Oh, that was last night. How was it?"

She wondered if he was hoping she had felt lonely or uncomfortable being the only non-coupled guest. Although, she'd had Roxie with her, so she was technically part of a couple.

"It was really fun. Jerry got Roxie toys for when she visits. She even had her own seat at the dining table. It was a little ridiculous, but we had a great time." Casey meant it.

Nobody had given her the pity face or even mentioned Jason or her life changes. It was awesome to be surrounded by people who loved to laugh and enjoy each other's company.

"Cool. Did they ask where I was?"

Was this the time to fess up that she'd told everyone about their separation? What was he going to do, leave her? She explained, "Well, I'd already told Javier and Dana about us. Jerry filled in everyone at the party before I arrived and told them not to say anything."

Jason darted his eyes at her. "You told Dana too? Who else did you tell?"

Casey thought, *Here we go.* "I told Maddy. I think that's it."

"I thought we agreed not to tell anyone, except Kat and Javier?"

*We also agreed until death do us part and this is what you're upset about?* "Yeah, it just came up. I didn't want to lie to my friends."

He sighed. "How did they react?"

She kept her cool. "Surprised. Supportive."

He smirked. "You think our families will react similarly?"

Casey laughed. "Surprised—maybe. Supportive—not so sure. I think they'll try to talk us into moving back in together no matter how..." She paused to refrain from using the word miserable. "How it may not be the right thing for us."

He shook his head. "That's what I'm afraid of too." He parked in front of the two-story yellow house with white trim, perfect lawn, and a short white picket fence. It was the epitome of the American dream, and it was a far cry from the dumpy houses and cramped apartments she'd grown up in.

He faced her. "Here goes."

She forced a tight-lipped grin before exiting the car.

They strolled up the walkway. Before they could knock on the door, Betty stood in the entry wearing a red sweater with a colorful Christmas tree embroidered on the front. She chirped, "Merry Christmas!"

She and Jason mumbled, "Merry Christmas."

They walked into the smell of fresh gingerbread. It was heavenly. Before they were even two steps in, Frank and Derrick stood into the entry eagerly awaiting for their greeting. Frank's brown eyes lit up at the sight of Roxie. He gave a quick, "Merry Christmas" before extending his hands, cooing, "Come to Grandpa!" Casey smiled and handed her over. Frank hurried off to bring Roxie into the living room a few yards away.

Casey gave Derrick a brief hug and a "Merry Christmas."

Derrick, who looked a lot like Jason except for the buzz cut and muscular physique, turned to his brother. "Hey little bro! How the heck are you?" He followed the greeting with a bear hug.

After being released Jason responded. "Good. Really good. Welcome home!"

Casey was impressed at Jason's ability to sell their lie. Or maybe for Jason it wasn't a lie? Maybe he was doing really well?

Derrick nodded his head. "It's good to be home and to be back in sunny California. It's so cold in Germany! It sucks I have to go back tomorrow, but I should be home for a bit longer in the spring. Anyway, let's get you two in here."

He ushered them into the living room where two sofas sat in an $L$ shape and an arm chair waited on the end. In the corner by the window stood an eight-foot Christmas tree covered in lights and ornaments and topped by an angel with a gold halo and a gown of white silk. The coffee table was covered in platters of cheese and crackers as well as a tower of assorted chocolates with foil-covered Santa candies on top.

One of the sofas held Betty's mother, known as "Grannie," her sister Ellie, and her sister's husband, Ron. Jason insisted they didn't get up. He and Casey approached, giving half-seated hugs and hellos before finding a spot on the couch to the right of them. Derrick sat in the armchair while Frank stayed on the floor playing with Roxie.

Grannie said, "Frank, should you be down on that floor?"

"Don't you worry about me. I'm fine here playing with my grandpuppy."

Derrick laughed and faced Jason and Casey. "Imagine what it will be like when you two have kids!"

They exchanged glances.

Derrick boomed. "What was that? Are you guys pregnant?"

Casey thought, *Oh jeez. He couldn't have misunderstood that look more*. She shook her head violently and waved her hands. "No. No. No. Not pregnant."

Jason's eyes bugged as he shook his head back and forth.

Derrick teased, "Are you sure?"

She responded with a definitive, "So sure."

*So very, very sure.*

Betty entered a moment later with eyes wide. "Did I hear someone is pregnant?"

The room broke into laughter as Jason explained the mix-up. Betty deflated and gazed at Casey. "Oh. Well, when you do get pregnant, I want to be the first to know, okay?"

Casey was stunned at the command. "Oh. I don't know. I think I'd tell Jason first." She chuckled to cover the pit deepening in her stomach.

As conversation resumed and all eyes were no longer on her, she swallowed hard, realizing how devastated Jason's parents would be when they found out about the separation. They'd treated her like family from the first time she'd met them. They were her family. She wasn't sure how it hadn't crossed her mind before. If she lost Jason, she'd lose them too.

Seated for dinner at the dining table, Casey listened intently to Derrick describing his time in Germany. She turned to her right. "Jason, doesn't Germany sound amazing? We ought to take a vacation there!"

He nodded enthusiastically. "Definitely."

She smiled and thought, *He seems sincere*. She placed her hand on his thigh, but he quickly brushed it away. She felt physically ill and excused herself to the restroom to conceal the tears she felt forming in the corner of her eyes.

She reemerged and spent the rest of the evening engaged in polite conversation and opening gifts. Roxie was the winner of most gifts, with eight new toys and an assortment of treats, mostly from "Grandma and Grandpa."

At nearly ten o'clock Jason and Casey feigned exhaustion, saying it was getting late. They said their goodbyes with hugs all around and smiles on their faces.

As Casey buckled her seat belt, she contemplated how they'd convincingly pulled off pretending they weren't separated. On the other hand, they had been pretending to be happily married for a year and a half. How much more difficult would it be to not disclose her change of address? Before they drove off, she glanced out the window to her in-laws' home, and a sadness washed over her. Would it be their last Christmas together?

They drove in silence.

Jason stopped in the driveway instead of going into the garage. "I should probably let you out here."

Right. She said, "Yeah, more room." She unbuckled, secured Roxie, and climbed out. "See you tomorrow." She hurried over to her car and entered, setting Roxie down in her carrier. She gave her a quick scratch behind the ears and backed out of the drive-way. By the time she hit the freeway, tears flowed in a steady stream. She cursed herself for getting upset. She was a survivor. She was strong. Isn't that what she'd convinced herself?

## CHAPTER 14

ON CHRISTMAS DAY, Casey was sitting on the living room floor playing fetch with Roxie when she heard a knock on the door. She rubbed Roxie's fur and said, "We've got a visitor." She opened the door and said, "Hey."

Jason replied, "Hey. Merry Christmas—again."

Casey nodded. "Yes, Merry Christmas—again." Last night's cry-fest had zapped her energy, and she didn't have enough left to be friendly.

Jason stared at her. "So, this is your new place?" He knelt down to greet Roxie.

Casey threw her hands in the air. "Oh, right. You haven't been here. Come on, I'll give you the grand tour." She thought, *Everything is great, everything is fine.* Just breathe.

"It's nice. Roomy." Jason added.

"Yeah, I like it." She reminded herself that she did like it. She just didn't like that it came at the expense of her marriage as the life she knew was being stripped away. "We should probably head out to my mom's." She grabbed two shopping bags full of wrapped gifts from next to the tree.

Jason asked, "Can I help with one of those?"

"Sure. Thanks."

She picked up Roxie and led Jason out.

She concentrated on the road without speaking.

Jason asked, "Is everything okay? You seem quiet."

Casey thought, *Is everything okay? Yes, just super duper. I'm celebrating Christmas for the second time with my estranged husband. Everything is fucking great.* She answered, "I'm fine. Just tired."

"Didn't sleep well?"

"Not really."

She'd barely slept. Her mind was running wild with worst-case scenarios. Divorce. Losing Jason and his family. She realized she'd been going on auto pilot, and Christmas Eve had been like a slap in the face bringing her back to the reality of all she had to lose.

Sure, she'd been relieved by the separation. The home she and had Jason built had suffocated her. His indifference was killing her. She needed a break. It hadn't meant she wanted to break up. After being with his family, she knew she didn't want a divorce. She wanted her husband and her life, but she didn't want a husband who didn't love her or want to be with her. She felt defeated. Her marriage was broken, and she didn't know how to fix it.

"That sucks. Is the party at your mom's new place?" he asked.

Casey nodded. "Yep. She's so excited to have people over. It's a two-bedroom, one-bath condo. It's a decent size for her and the girls, but I'm not quite sure how it'll fit everyone."

"Who all is going?"

"Kelly and the kids—maybe Paul, my grandma, not sure about Sam. That's all I know. It changes each time I ask." The truth was Casey didn't really care. She just wanted to get the day over with.

"With all those kids, how do you think Roxie will do?"

Casey hadn't thought about it. "I don't know. Maybe we'll try to hold her. We shouldn't just let her loose. It could scare her."

"True. I'll keep an eye on her so you can catch up with the kids and not have to worry about Roxie."

She glanced at him. "Thanks." It was thoughtful. He wasn't usually thoughtful. Casey told herself to be more optimistic. Nothing was final. They hadn't even talked about divorce. She needed to get out of her head and be more patient.

She parked in front of the condominium complex. "Here goes."

Jason gave a friendly smile. "Here goes."

Casey unloaded the gifts and gave herself a pep talk. *Smile. Laugh. Focus on the kids. You love the kids. Kids are endlessly optimistic and spirited—try to be like them.*

She led Jason and Roxie toward the first-floor condominium, where a wreath made of holly decorated the front door. She knocked and stepped back. Footsteps pounded closer from the other side before the door swung open. In the entry, Cara stood grinning, wearing black leggings with rhinestone pattern down each leg and a fuzzy red sweater with a penguin on the front. "Merry Christmas!"

Casey entered and gave Cara a hug. To the right, Agatha was inspecting the contents of the oven in the small kitchen that emitted the smell of bacon. She shut the oven door before greeting them with hugs and Merry Christmases. She offered Casey and Jason apple cider and seats in the living room.

Two sofas lined the walls and a five-foot tree stood in the corner between them. A few dining chairs had been scattered about. The tree was filled with colorful ornaments and lights, topped with a ceramic angel with a light-up halo. In the sofa to the left was Casey's youthful grandmother, and Anna sat on a chair next to the couch.

"Hi, Grandma. Hi, Anna."

Anna got up to hug both Jason and Casey. Grandma remained seated but said, "Oh, hi there. Merry Christmas." She paused. "Is that a dog?"

Jason replied, "Yes, this is Roxie. She's just a puppy."

Grandma had strong resemblance to Agatha with dark curly hair, although hers was much shorter. She had the same intense blue eyes. "She's so cute."

Jason smiled. "Thanks."

Jason and Casey sat on the sofa across from Grandma, and Cara strutted over and parked herself on the other side of Casey.

Casey asked Cara, "What did you guys get from Santa?"

Cara's eyes lit up. "I got the new Sims game. It's so cool. And I got some new clothes and lip gloss. I'll show you." Cara hopped off the couch and ran back to her and Anna's room.

"Wow. Lots of stuff. Anna, how about you?"

"Mostly clothes, makeup, and a new purse. Mom took us shopping to pick out most of our stuff."

Jason faked surprise. "What? They weren't really from Santa?"

Anna smirked. "Apparently not. Mom blew it on that one."

Casey laughed. "I think so. How do you like the new condo?"

"It's cool I guess. I still have to share a room with Cara. Ugh. She's the worst. She gets into all my stuff."

From their bedroom came a faint, "Do not."

Anna shook her head and lowered her voice. "She totally does. And she's a total slob. Clothes and her school stuff are scattered everyone. She leaves her soccer cleats and her stuff on my side all the time. She's so annoying. I can't wait to move out."

Casey chuckled. Yes, she remembered her own childhood. The only thing that kept her going was knowing that one day she'd move out and be on her own.

Cara reentered wearing a pair of denim jeans with glitter on the pockets and a black lace top. "What do you think?"

Casey grinned. "Very cute! Stylish. You may beat out Anna for family fashionista if you keep it up."

Cara smirked at Anna. Anna rolled her eyes and shook her head. They were rivals and adversaries most of the time. Agatha often complained about their constant bickering. When they visited, Casey had strict rules: they fight, they go home. They behaved most of the time.

Cara left the living room to continue the fashion show.

Casey studied the room. "When's Kelly supposed to get here?"

Anna shrugged. "Who knows. I hear she's bringing Paul. Kelly's super excited because his divorce is final."

"Oh, wow." The word *divorce* made Casey shrink.

Anna added, "But don't tell anybody I told you. It's supposed to be a secret."

Cara returned for her second showing. They all admired her outfit and said they loved it. Cara, satisfied, retreated to put her Christmas outfit back on.

Agatha entered the living room in a fitted black dress with a Santa pin on her left shoulder, looking stunning as usual. "Anyone need anything? Brunch is almost ready."

Grandma said, "I'll take some more cider."

Agatha shuffled across the room to grab Grandma's glass to refill. "Anyone else?" They shook their heads.

The doorbell sounded. Agatha glanced over at the front of the home. "Must be Kelly and the gang! Perfect timing."

From the living room, Casey could hear the opening of the door and multiple voices exclaiming Merry Christmases and good to see yous. Olivia entered the living room running at full speed. At three years old, she seemed to only have one speed. Casey pushed off the couch and grabbed her for a hug. "Hi, Olivia!"

Olivia was cherubic with auburn hair and wide hazel eyes. "Hi, Auntie."

"Merry Christmas, Olivia!"

Olivia responded with something that sounded a bit like "mewwie kismas". She stared at Roxie. "Puppy!"

Casey knelt next to Olivia. "This is Roxie. Do you want to pet her?"

Olivia nodded her head enthusiastically.

"Okay, but you have to be very gentle." Casey demonstrated. "You ready?"

Olivia nodded again. She extended her tiny hand onto Roxie's back. Roxie responded by trying to bite at Olivia. Olivia giggled. "She funny."

Jason responded. "Maybe that's it for now."

Casey turned to Olivia. "Roxie has to rest cause she's just a baby. She needs lots of sleep."

Olivia looked at her. "Like baby Brie?"

"Exactly."

"Ohhh."

Casey was amazed by Olivia's ability to comprehend logical explanations.

Olivia ran over to Angelina. "Sissie. Auntie has puppy. Roxie."

Angelina's dark brown eyes shined down at her sister. "Oh really, Olivia? You want to show me?"

Olivia nodded.

Casey grinned. "Hi ,Angelina. Merry Christmas!"

Angelina flipped her long, mahogany colored hair before extending her arms for a hug and a Merry Christmas.

"This is Roxie."

Angelina said, "She's so cute. Can I pet her?"

Olivia patted Angelina on the arm. "Have to be gentle." She demonstrated in the air. "Like this."

Angelina cracked a grin, "Okay. I'll be gentle."

"And. And. She needs rest like baby Brie."

Angelina chuckled. "Okay, I'll just say hi for a little bit."

Olivia nodded, seemingly satisfied by her big sister's plans.

Casey was pained by the sight of how much Angelina, at only eleven years old, had been thrown into a role similar to the one Casey had played growing up, especially since the arrival of Brie six months earlier. Angelina was expected to cook, clean, babysit, and change diapers on a regular basis. Casey feared Angelina's childhood was being stolen from her.

By the time Kelly, Paul, and Brie entered the scene, the living room was full of people, and the temperature had risen twenty degrees. Agatha quickly pulled additional chairs from the dining room to accommodate Paul and Kelly.

Kelly sat Brie's carrier down and exclaimed, "Merry Christmas everyone!" She proceeded to walk around to everyone, giving hugs and reintroducing Paul, a tan-skinned man of medium height and build. They reached Casey and Jason on the sofa.

Paul bobbed his head at Jason, "Hey. Looks like we're the only guys here!"

Jason chuckled. "Yeah. Thank goodness you're here. I'm usually the only one!"

They laughed over that for a bit before Paul pulled his chair over to sit near Jason. Casey found the sight of the two men sequestering themselves away from the nine women amusing.

Agatha returned. "Brunch is ready! It's buffet style, so help yourselves."

Casey reflected on their Christmas Eve dinner at Jason's parents', where dinner had been served at a formal dining table and there were zero children laughing and running about. She wasn't sure which she preferred. Christmas with her family was certainly livelier, but the calm and quiet on Christmas Eve was nice too.

When everyone was seated in the living room with their colorful paper plates nearly empty, Kelly stood up and placed her plate on her chair. She waved Paul over, and he begrudgingly stood next to her. Kelly beamed. "Everyone, I have something to say. First of all, I'm so glad we are all here together. It makes my heart full. Merry Christmas!"

The rest of the group exchanged glances.

Kelly continued. "Paul and I have an announcement to make." She paused and wiped a tear from her eye. "Paul and I are getting married!"

Casey froze. Was she freaking kidding? The room was silent for a bit too long before Agatha said, "Congratulations to you both!" She approached to hug them. "I'm so happy for you."

The rest of the room took the cue and began with various forms of congratulations and "that's so exciting."

Kelly hugged Casey. "I'm so happy. We're going to be married sisters. And I want you to be my matron-of-honor! Okay?"

Casey wanted to run away. Hide. Put the covers over her head and scream. She replied. "Of course. Yeah, I'd be honored. This is so great."

She glanced over her shoulder at Jason. He sat emotionless, not making eye contact with anyone.

Casey couldn't figure out why Kelly would want her to be the matron-of-honor. They were sisters, but they weren't close. Why not one of Kelly's girlfriends? Why her? Why was all of this happening to her?

Kelly grinned. "Great! There is a ton of stuff to do. We should get started right away. First—dress shopping!"

Casey no longer wanted to hide under her covers. She wanted to hide in another country. What were the odds she'd be separated from her husband at the same time she was the matron-of-honor in two weddings? What had she done to deserve this? Was this karma? She thought she was a good person. Maybe she had been an evil warlord in a previous life?

She breathed in and out and then replied, "Great!"

The words "time for presents" emanating from her mother were music to Casey's ears. She'd passed the limit of her ability to smile and nod. She wanted to go home.

Agatha appointed Cara and Angelina as elves, and they dug under the tree for presents and then handed them out to all in attendance. Paper flew through the air as squeals of delight, thank yous, and "oh this is cool" rang out from various points in the cramped room.

Afterward, when the mess was cleaned up, Kelly and gang

made their exit, saying they had to go to Paul's parents' next. Casey stood. "Yeah, we've got to go too. Roxie hasn't eaten." She thought, *Thank goodness for Roxie.* They spent the next ten minutes saying goodbye before they were able to make their escape.

On the drive back to Casey's, Jason stated flatly, "Well, we survived Christmas."

Casey glanced at him and refocused on the road. "Yeah. Done. Thank God."

She made no attempt to further their conversation. She didn't want to chit-chat. She didn't want to put on a happy face. She wanted to break down with a pint of Ben and Jerry's, watch bad TV, and cuddle with Roxie.

# A NEW YEAR

# CHAPTER 15

ROXIE RAN TO THE DOOR. Casey followed and asked, "Who's here girl?" She opened the door. Jason stood with a faint smile. "Hi."

"Hey, come on in."

Casey surveyed the living room. "I'd offer you a seat, but I don't really have any furniture yet. I did order a new couch. I'm super excited, but it won't be here for another week or two."

Jason gave a friendly laugh. "It's cool. I can stand." He leaned against the living room wall. "So how are you? Have a good New Years?"

Casey propped herself up next to the fireplace. "It was good—quiet. Roxie and I went over to Jerry and Dana's. It was just Dana, Jerry, Roxie, and me. It was fun though. You?"

"Went over to Matt's. He resurrected beer pong and we played all night—well, until we passed out."

"Sounds fun." Casey wondered how she hadn't realized she'd married a frat boy. All his friends were in fraternities. Why had she thought he was different?

"How's Roxie been? Getting used to the new place?"

"I think so. I've been leaving her at regular intervals to let her know I'm coming back. No accidents, but I'm sure I'll be losing a part of my security deposit on the door molding." Casey nodded her head toward Roxie's destruction.

Jason's eyes widened. "Oh my gosh. I didn't think she had it in her. How is she doing it?"

Casey shook her head. "With her teeth. I came home the other day and she had slivers of wood in her whiskers."

He picked up Roxie. "Did you do that, Roxie?" She responded by licking his nose. They shared a short laugh.

Casey got back to business. "So, does the Sunday pick-up work for you?"

Jason nodded. "Yeah this works fine. And you'll pick her up from my place on Thursday nights?"

"I plan to pick her up after work so that it won't be too late when I drive out to your place." Saying 'your place' felt like a little dagger to her midsection. But it meant something that they were still sharing Roxie, right? It meant there was hope, right?

"It's settled then." He glanced at Roxie in his arms. "You hear that Roxie, custody is all worked out." He looked at Casey. "I feel bad she's being split."

She shrugged. "Well, I can just keep her. I think she'll adjust. Plenty of dogs stay home by themselves."

He gazed at Roxie. "No, I couldn't give her up. I love her too much."

Another dagger. *At least he loved someone who he couldn't give up —unfortunately for her it wasn't his wife.*

Casey responded. "Well, it sounds like we have a schedule." She paused. "How is counseling going?"

He set Roxie back on the floor. "It's going well. I've been twice now. I'm already beginning to feel better."

She was shocked.

He continued. "My therapist diagnosed me with clinical depression. Explained that a lot of my feelings and lack of motivation are related. I've started some medication. It's too soon to see if it's working. It's kind of a trial-and-error approach."

She thought, *What did that mean? What did it mean for them?* She said, "That's great. Did your therapist say anything about our marriage counseling?"

Jason stared at Roxie on the living room floor chewing on her duck. "He thinks I should stop. Until I'm in a place to do that."

She thought, *In a place to do that? What the heck did that mean?* She crossed her arms across her chest. "So, we'll stop. Okay. Any idea for how long?" Not that they'd attempted to spend time together or mend their relationship in any way. Maybe it was good they were officially taking a break from counseling too?

He didn't look at her. "I don't know."

Casey's body temperature rose, and her hands shook. He didn't know? She was going to be in marriage limbo indefinitely? Indefinitely? She wasn't sure she could handle it.

She said, "Oh."

Jason finally looked at her. "I'm really sorry. I did want to tell you thank you. If it wasn't for you suggesting marriage counseling and us separating I would've never gotten help—and this didn't start with us. I've felt like this for a long time. It feels so good to have someone to talk to about all of it. I feel hopeful for the first time in I don't even know how long—probably forever."

Forever? Casey felt a knot form in her throat. "Oh. Good." She paused. "Sounds like progress." She forced a laugh. "Now to tell our families. When are you going to tell your parents?"

"I already told them—everything. About the depression about the separation. My therapist told me it was important I am honest with them so they can support me."

They? Not her? Casey nodded. "That makes sense."

"He also said it wasn't right to keep it a secret. Especially for me to ask you to keep it a secret. He says you likely need a lot of support right now too. So, I'm sorry about that, too."

Casey stared at Roxie playing contently. He was sorry? What could she possibly say to that?

He continued. "It seems like you're doing alright with all of this."

Alright with all of this? Ha! That was because she'd hid it from him. She'd hidden all of her tears from him. All of her melt-downs. All he'd ever seen was the anger masking the pain.

She replied. "Yeah. I'm okay. It's weird, but I'm hanging in there."

"Have you told your family yet?"

*That was going to be a blast.* She hadn't even thought about telling them. She said, "No. I think I'll just tell them as I see them. I just have to tell one for them all to know." She forced a laugh. *Yes, it's hilarious that my separation would reach the top of the family gossip charts.*

"True," he mused. "Well, Roxie and I should get going." He knelt to pick her up. "We'll see you Thursday."

"See you Thursday."

She shut the door and slid down to the carpet and broke down. What just happened? Apologies? Clinical depression? What did that mean? What did it mean for them?

She had the nagging feeling something major had just happened, but she didn't know what it was. She forced herself up, with help of the door handle, and marched into the dining room to pull her laptop out of her tote. She sat on the floor, resting her back on the wall. She powered up the laptop and researched clinical depression.

She clicked on the first website offering answers. She hunched over as she skimmed the text and gasped. She'd just thought he was bummed out by Ian's death. Major depressive disorder had nothing to do with life events. It was a medical condition.

She read on. Sadness. Hopelessness. Loss of interest or pleasure in most or all normal activities. Sleeping too much. Lack of energy. Weight gain. Feelings of worthlessness. She began to sob.

Why hadn't she seen it? She supposedly loved him and didn't see it. She should have seen it. What if he'd killed himself?

She wiped her face on her sleeve before getting up to blow her nose and wash her face. In the bathroom, she stared at her reflection and thought, *What a freaking mess. My face. My life.*

After she cleaned herself up, she continued her internet search for how to be in a relationship with a person suffering from depression. Everything she read said that first step was getting help. He was doing that. He was on medication. The article had said that relationships can last as long as the patient is getting help and progressing. Maybe this wasn't the end of them? Maybe the sense of dread was just her own fear manifesting?

Her fear of their marriage ending wasn't based on anything concrete, not really. He never said he didn't want to be with her, and he'd never mentioned divorce. Maybe her fear was based on the things he didn't say? Like, "I love you" and "I can't lose you." He apparently felt that way about Roxie, but what about her?

She sunk into herself. She forced herself up and into the kitchen. She opened the freezer. "Hello, Mr. Mint Cookie." She pulled the tub of ice cream out and scampered over to the living room where she plopped into her camp chair and clicked on the TV.

# CHAPTER 16

THURSDAY MORNING, she dragged herself out of bed and into the bathroom to get ready for work. She stuck her face up to the mirror. *Crap. Puffy eyes again.* She opened her medicine cabinet and snatched her new eye cream that took care of the puffy eyes in under an hour. She unscrewed the lid on the tiny jar and dabbed her finger in the cool gel and dotted it beneath her eyes.

She stood back. "Now I'll be as good as new! Or at least hide the fact I cried myself to sleep last night. Thanks, Clinique!" She gave a phony grin at her reflection.

She slithered over to the kitchen to make a pot of coffee. Casey knew she'd be a little late to work, but it didn't really matter. If she got there at nine or nine fifteen nobody cared. Heck, she could probably stroll in at ten and nobody would question it. Except Javier who would be all up in her grill, asking, "Where you been, girl?" She'd have to explain, "Hello! My new eye cream is super, but it doesn't work instantly. So chill." She wouldn't really. She'd blame it on traffic or something believable. The only saving grace for the day was that she'd get to pick up Roxie. What would she do without that dog? She couldn't be sad with that fluffy ball of sunshine hopping around demanding treats or chewing on toys while lounging in her lap.

She poured herself a cup of coffee and hoped the work day would fly by fast. Maybe she'd set up some new experiments to keep her busy so she wouldn't have time to think about anything else. It could work. She realized that despite her love-life falling apart, at least she had a job and career she liked. And, she had good friends too. Maybe you can't have it all?

Fully caffeinated, she strolled back to the bathroom and inspected her eyes. She sighed, "Good enough for now." She stripped down and stepped into the shower.

---

CASEY SAT in her cubicle and texted Jason. "Leaving work soon. I'll be there to pick up Roxie around six."

Jason responded, "I'll be at my parents'. Can you pick her up there?"

"Sure."

Casey placed her phone on her desk and thought, *Super.* It was going to be the first time seeing them since they found out about the separation. She wondered if it would be awkward or if they'd try to talk to her about it? Or would they act like everything was fine?

She pulled up to the two-story American dream and parked her car. Her nerves rattled as she approached the front door. She knocked. Betty answered wearing a purple velour tracksuit. "Oh, hi, Casey. Come on in."

"Thanks."

Roxie ran toward her. Casey picked her up and beamed. "Hi, girl! I missed you!" She put her down and played fetch as Betty asked, "How was work?"

"It was good. Busy." Casey looked around. Roxie had a bed set up in the corner of the living room with an overflowing basket of toys next to it. "Is Jason here?"

"No, he had to run an errand."

"Oh." She couldn't help but think maybe he was avoiding her.

"Are you settled in okay?" She paused. "At your new place."

Dagger to the heart. "Yeah. I'm sure Jason told you—I've been there a month and a half or so. Furniture is being delivered soon, which will be nice. Close to work. So..."

"That's good. And Roxie is adjusting okay?"

That's good? Did she know something Casey didn't? Casey turned to Roxie and grabbed the stuffed bunny from her and threw it. "Yes, I think so."

Betty's eyes widened, accusingly. "Oh? Jason says she's chewing up the door."

Casey thought, *Oh boy—now she had to answer to Betty too?* "She did at first. She doesn't really do it anymore. She hasn't had any accidents when she's been alone, for a few weeks now, either."

"That's good."

Casey stood up and grabbed Roxie. "Okay, well we better get going. Tell Jason I said hi."

Betty replied. "Will do."

"Bye."

"Bye."

Casey forced herself to walk, not run, back to her car. She drove off and succumbed to the tears. This time they weren't sad tears. They were angry tears. She cursed Jason for making her face his parents for the first time since their separation, alone. Why would he do that to her? That's right, because Jason only thought about one person—himself.

---

SUNDAY NIGHT, Jason stood with Roxie in his arms, rolling his eyes as Casey explained, "I just would have liked to have had a heads-up that you wouldn't be there. I didn't know what you told them or how they were reacting. I went in blind."

"Look, I said I'm sorry. I had to run an errand."

"Can you at least let me know next time?"

He closed his eyes and reopened them. "Yeah. I will."

Casey nodded. "Thank you."

"I've got to get going. I'm supposed to be at my parents' for dinner."

Casey shook her head. "Alright." She scratched behind Roxie's ears. "Bye, girl. See you Thursday."

She shut the door and waited a full sixty seconds before she screamed at her apartment. "Yeah, just go, asshole! Can't even be bothered to let me know you aren't going to be where you said you are? Not to mention—what ever happened to through sickness and health? Oh yeah—that. Did you forget we're married? Jerk."

Casey's patience was wearing thin. She knew he had a medical issue, but did that mean she didn't deserve common courtesy? Or updates on the outlook on their marriage? It all seemed so unfair. She just had to sit around and wait like a dutiful wife to figure out what he wanted. Everything she'd read said that those seeking treatment for depression could continue their relationships and even start new ones. Why not him? They were married. Didn't that mean anything?

As the tears fell, she shook her head. "No. I'm not crying tonight. I won't. Not tonight. Forget him."

She stomped over to the kitchen, grabbed a pint of Chubby Hubby, and ate angrily while leaning on the counter. She wiped her eyes. "He's such a jerk anyway. What did I ever see in him? He's not considerate. He never cared about what I wanted. No, everything is all about Jason all the time." She stabbed the ice cream and yelled, "Fuck you Jason! My life no longer revolves around you!" She strutted into the living room and sank into her new purple microfiber sofa.

She clicked on the TV and finished off the pint. She placed the ice cream container with the spoon inside, down on the floor, thinking, *It's not exactly the dinner of champions.* She made a mental note to hit the gym the next day. After all the new things in her life, she didn't need a new, bigger wardrobe too.

# CHAPTER 17

A FEW WEEKS LATER, Casey added a short vase with a small bouquet of wildflowers to the center of her new four-top dining table and stepped back. She grinned at the pleasantness of the dining room now that it had a table set with lime green place-mats, wine glasses, and dinner plates. It was no longer the cry-on-the-floor-with-your-laptop room. It was a real grown-up dining room.

Satisfied, she pivoted back into the kitchen to check on the boiling water that was making a rumble. Sure enough, it was time to add the tortellini. Casey opened the refrigerator, which finally held food items other than take-out, and pulled out the pasta. She was about to drop it into the water when she heard a knock at the door. She set it down and headed toward the door.

Casey grinned. "Hi there! C'mon in."

Maddy chirped, "Hi!" and entered with her arm extended, clutching onto a bottle of white wine. "For you! A housewarming gift."

Casey said, "Thanks—it's my first housewarming gift actually, but then again you are my first real guest!"

. "I feel so special." Maddy surveyed the living room, dining room, and kitchen. "It's nice—so roomy." She paused and glanced down at Roxie. "Oh, hi puppy! You want to play?" Maddy knelt down to throw the famous once-bright-yellow duck for Roxie. Roxie sprinted across the living room after it. She glanced back up at Casey. "She's too cute."

Casey looked at the molding on the door and said, "Yes, she's a cutie. A bit of a rascal too. I was just making the pasta. Are you hungry yet?"

"Sure, and I could definitely go for some wine!"

Casey grimaced. "You wouldn't have happened to have brought a wine opener?" Casey hadn't even thought to get a wine opener. She'd have to add it to her to-buy list.

Maddy chuckled. "You don't have a wine opener?"

"No, I don't usually have wine."

"Girl, we've got to get you set up, but for now, you're in luck." She pulled out a multi-purpose knife from her purse. She flicked open the wine screw and said, "Viola! No problem."

Casey exclaimed, "I wouldn't even know how to use that!"

"No prob. I'll teach you." Maddy sprang over to the kitchen and did a demo.

"You're very handy!"

Maddy winked. "I try."

They moved across the kitchen and made the five-foot trek to the dining room, where they poured wine into the carefully placed wine glasses.

They sat and sipped chardonnay as dinner cooked. Maddy asked, "How is it being on your own?"

"It's okay. Quiet mostly. Actually, it's nice to be able to be as messy as I want! Some days I get home from work and just kick off my shoes and throw my coat on the floor—just because I can."

Casey had enjoyed that aspect of living alone. Actually, she enjoyed most aspects of living alone. The only thing that continued to keep her up at night was the uncertainty around her and Jason.

Maddy nodded. "How are things with you and Jason?"

Casey sipped her wine. "I see him when I drop off Roxie or he picks her up. That's it. We don't talk other than that. It's mostly chit-chat. Nothing real. Nothing about us."

Maddy tilted her head. "You guys are sharing Roxie?"

Casey sighed. "Yes. We have an agreement. He picks her up here on Sundays and I pick her up on Thursdays at his place, or his parents'. It's like joint custody of a kid." She paused and looked at Maddy. "I know, it's a little crazy, but it kind of works out too. Roxie hates being left by herself. She shakes and runs after me when I try to leave. It's heartbreaking."

Maddy's eyes widened. "Wow. Okay. That's different." She paused. "How is it seeing him and not being together? That's gotta be hard."

"It's not great. Some days I'm sad. Sometimes I'm angry. Sometimes I just feel defeated. It's been two months since I moved out and no sign of us getting back together. We just act like two buddies who happen to share a dog. It's a routine."

"Have you told him how you feel?" Maddy asked. "Have you thought about maybe asking him out on a date?"

Casey shook her head. "No. I kinda feel like he needs to initiate it. I have been the initiator for so long I think if he wanted to spend time with me, he would ask. Or at least hint at it. I've gotten no hints. Plus with his depression—I would think his therapist would be advising him when and if he should be trying to mend things with me." She poured herself another glass of chardonnay.

Maddy tilted her head. "I'm so sorry. I wish I could help."

Casey gave a half grin. "You are helping. You're here, and you brought wine." She raised her glass. "To good friends!" They clinked glasses and cheered.

They chatted and laughed until nearly midnight.

After Maddy went home, Casey was once again reminded of how lucky she was to have supportive friends whom she could always count on to cheer her up—and to bring wine. She was starting to feel good for the first time in a long while.

Casey decided to leave the mess for in the morning and proceeded to get ready for bed. She thought, *Another perk of living alone, or at least for not living with a neat freak like Jason. I can leave the dishes overnight and clean them up whenever I feel like it.* Content and a bit tipsy, she snuggled under the covers with Roxie and watched old episodes of the Golden Girls until she fell asleep.

# CHAPTER 18

LATER THAT WEEK, Casey took a deep breath, put on her best smile, and opened the door. She said in the most chipper tone she could muster, "Hi."

"Hey. Can I come in?"

Casey hesitated. He wanted to come in? "Yes, of course."

He knelt to greet Roxie. He stood and leaned on the living room wall. Casey thought, *Huh.* It was the farthest he'd come inside since Casey had given him a tour shortly after she'd moved in. "You want to sit? I have a place to sit now." She joked, trying to break whatever weird vibe she was getting from him.

"No, I'm okay with standing. There is something I want to talk to you about."

Casey shrugged. "Okay."

He stared right at her. "I think we should get a divorce."

She didn't hear him correctly. She couldn't have. They hadn't even gone back to counseling or talked about other scenarios like dating or how long the separation would be. The only thing they'd ever discussed was Roxie.

"What? Why? I don't understand."

He remained straight-faced. "I've been talking to my therapist, and we agree I'm not in a place where I can be in a relationship."

She shook her head. "But that's temporary. I can wait for you to get better. We agreed through sickness and health. This is just a setback. I can wait. As long as it takes. I'll wait." She heard herself. Was she begging him not to divorce her?

"I don't think that's fair to you."

"It's not, but it's our marriage. Life isn't always fair. Believe me, that I know." She'd learned that long ago. She continued, "It's okay. It's just a setback. We were happy once, weren't we? I think if you continue therapy and we go back to counseling we can be happy again."

He smiled gently. "No. That's the thing. We weren't. You always talked about how we used to be happy—about how things were in the beginning. I never understood why you'd say that... because I was never happy."

She froze. "Never?"

He glanced at the floor. "I'm sorry. I just don't have those feelings for you."

Casey felt like she was outside of her body listening to a different couple. It couldn't be her and Jason.

She mumbled. "What does that mean?"

"I don't love you that way. I don't love you the way married people are supposed to love each other."

Casey stepped back as fire rushed through her. She would make him say it. She was done with ambiguity. "So, what you're saying is that you're not in love with me and you never were and you were never happy with me. Did I get that right?"

Jason picked up Roxie. "Yes. I'm sorry."

She laughed bitterly. "Okay. Well, I guess there is no amount of counseling or compromise to get over that." She wondered if she was in shock or simply stunned.

Jason scratched Roxie's neck. "We can talk about the details later."

Casey stared at the floor as her whole body shook. "Yeah, okay."

"Casey, I am sorry." He paused.

She had no more words for him. She just wanted him to leave. He said, "See you Thursday."

Casey remained frozen in place until she heard the door shut.

She stared at the back of the door and whispered. "What just happened?" Divorce. They were getting divorced. He was never happy. He had never loved her.

She backed into her dining room and sat down. Maybe she'd always known. She did. So why did it feel like she'd just taken a meat cleaver to the chest? Who knew it would be so much worse hearing it than thinking it? Maybe because she could tell herself she was being silly and insecure? Five years. For five years, their entire relationship had been a lie. Their marriage. Their love. None of it was real. How had she gotten it so wrong? The most wrong of any way of being wrong. She couldn't have been more wrong. If it were a contest of who was the most wrong, she would have won. She'd been that wrong.

Her hands vibrated as she wiped her eyes. Was this her fault? She had married him knowing in her gut he didn't feel the same way she did. Why did he stand up in church before God and all their friends and family promising to love and cherish her the rest of their lives? Why would he do that? It didn't make sense.

She laughed out loud with a puffy face and streams falling from her eyes. She said aloud, "Congratulations, Casey! Not only are you getting a divorce, but while you are in the middle of said divorce you will also be the matron-of-honor in two different weddings!" She thought, *Ha! Scratch that. Now I'll be the maid-of-honor, not a matron.* Casey stared up at the ceiling and shook her head. "Un-fucking-believable." How had things gone so wrong?

# CHAPTER 19

CASEY GROANED and clutched the side of her head. She shut off the blaring alarm with a heavy fist before crawling out of bed. She shuffled into the bathroom and stood in front of the mirror staring at the person before her, but her eyes were so puffy she could barely see. She grumbled, "F— you, Jason," and exited the bathroom.

She pulled the laptop from her bag and powered it up while seated at her dining table. She ignored all of her work emails and created a new message.

*Hi Eddie.*
*Out sick. Migraine.*
*Casey*

She closed the lid of her laptop and forced herself into the kitchen. She shook a few ibuprofen into her palm and swallowed the pills for the pounding in her head that refused to let up. She climbed back into bed, rolled over, and buried her face in her pillow.

The buzz on her nightstand startled her awake. She picked up her cellphone and saw it was Javier calling. She didn't want to talk to anyone. She didn't want to see anyone. She wanted to hide in her dark apartment until ... she didn't know for how long. She placed the phone back on her nightstand and rolled over.

Another buzz. Casey sat up and cursed at her phone. It was Kat. She hesitated before answering. She didn't feel like having a conversation, but she figured she might as well get her I'm-getting-divorced announcement out of the way.

Casey answered and mumbled, "Hello."

There was a pause.

"Casey. Hi this is Kat. I got your message from last night. I was going to leave a voicemail. I didn't think I'd get you. Are you at work?"

Casey didn't remember calling her. Shoot. It came flooding back. Midway through the previous night's meltdown she'd called Kat to tell her the news, but instead left a message telling her to call her back because she had *news*. Casey lay back down and turned on her side with the phone clutched to her exposed ear. "No. I'm at home."

"Is everything okay?"

Casey said, "No."

"What's wrong?"

She muttered, "Jason told me he wants a divorce. He said he never loved me and was never happy."

"Oh, Casey. I'm so sorry." She paused. "He actually said that?"

"Yep."

Silence.

"Casey, he's an asshole. You know that, right? Total asshole."

"I guess."

"No guessing. He's an asshole. You are one of the most beautiful, intelligent, fun, and loving people I know. Only an asshole would say that. Screw him. You can do so much better. You know that, right?"

Casey didn't answer. It was the same speech she'd given Casey when she had told Kat he'd cheated on her right before the wedding—when he'd broken her heart. She didn't think it could be broken any further. Now it felt like it was shattered into a million pieces with no possibility of being put back together. Her eyes opened wide.

Why had she not realized it before? He probably only cheated so she'd break up with him and call off the wedding. It wasn't a moment of weakness or as he claimed, drunkenness. She'd been so stupid, it made her stomach hurt. Why hadn't she broken up with him? Because she had loved him. Because she had been weak. Because she had been too worried about what everyone would think if they'd called off the wedding. Gifts to return. Notifications to be made.

"Is there anything I can do?"

Casey pulled up her blanket. "No. I'm heading back to sleep. Can we talk later?"

"Of course. Casey, you'll get through this. You are the strongest person I know. Call me anytime, okay?"

Casey fought the tears welling up. She didn't feel strong. She felt broken. She said, "Thanks. Bye." And she hung up. She threw the phone to the other side of her queen-sized bed.

Casey wiped the corner of her eyes with her comforter. She thought, *He is an asshole.* Then why was she so upset? It had been years since things had been good—or if you were Jason—it had never been good. She laughed bitterly. She knew their relationship had been on life support for longer than it should have, but to have never been happy?

She'd at least taken comfort in the idea they'd been in love and happy, at one time. He didn't have to take that from her. He took her only good memories and shit all over them. He could've let it go. He could've said his feelings changed instead of saying he never had any at all. Why take away the memory that she had been loved, even if it wasn't real? Couldn't he give her that? That *was* an asshole thing to do.

She knew he'd exceeded the allowable number of tears, yet there they were. Why? Did she even miss him? They'd lived apart without seeing each other, with the exception of Roxie pick-ups and drop-offs, for more than two months. Never once had she thought, *oh I wish Jason were here*. Or *I miss Jason*. It hadn't occurred to her until that moment. She didn't miss him. Then why was she such a mess?

Was she mourning the death of her marriage? Good or bad, she thought the rest of her life was mapped out. She knew what was coming. She'd have a few kids, stay home to raise them, and live a perfectly vanilla life. She would have a family of her own. Two parents. Two kids. A house. No drama.

Is that why she was so upset—was it the fear of what was next? The fear that she'd never find real love. The fear that she'd never have a family. The realization that she had no idea what she would do with her life now.

She pulled the covers over her head in an attempt to hide from her feelings.

The vibration woke her. She reached across the bed and pulled the phone up to her face. It was Kat. She answered. "Hey."

"Hi. How are you?"

Casey yawned. "Super."

"Are you still in bed?"

"Yeah, why?"

"It's almost six o'clock! Have you been out of bed at all?"

Casey had gotten up to use the bathroom a few times. Did that count? Probably not. "Not really."

She felt a grumble in her stomach. She wondered if this latest development would drive her into a deep depression where she wouldn't eat for days at time, like right before the wedding. She had gotten so skinny. Silver lining? She didn't recall being hungry in the slightest. The days leading up to the wedding, even the thought of food made her want to revolt. Another growl from her belly. Looks like she wouldn't be so lucky this time. She was ravenous.

"Are you feeling any better? Plan to go to work tomorrow?"

Casey hadn't thought that far ahead. "Not sure. Maybe." She began to wonder what to have for dinner. She didn't have much. Maybe order a pizza?

"Do you want to talk about it?"

Casey didn't really, but she knew soon she'd have to tell everyone. It wasn't a bad idea to start with Kat, someone she knew wouldn't judge her or make her feel like crap.

"I don't think I miss him. Is that bad? Should I miss him? I didn't want a divorce. Yet, I don't miss him. What does that mean?" She knew she was rambling.

Kat said, "Despite loving him, he's been a crappy husband and partner since I've known you. Why would you miss him? I don't think it's weird at all that you don't. I shouldn't say this, but I think you are so much better off without him. You have your whole life ahead of you. I think he's been holding you back from all you're capable of. What has he ever done for you? He had you pegged to be the mother to his children. That's it. He never cared about how you were doing at work or activities you were interested in. He was only interested in what he wanted—a Stepford Wife. Casey—you are no June Cleaver, and I mean that as a compliment."

Casey sat up, and her head spun. She needed to eat. Kat was right. She'd spent so much energy trying to be what she thought he wanted her to be. Even then she'd always fallen short despite the part of her soul she sacrificed.

She rubbed her eyes. "You're totally right." Casey was glad she'd answered the phone. "I still feel like I failed. I was so sure about getting married. Not even two years later and I'm getting a divorce."

Kat retorted. "Casey, you didn't fail. Your marriage was doomed from the start—you know that. Your marriage failed—

you didn't. You never gave up. I honestly believe you did all you could. The good news is that you're only twenty-five. This is just a blip. You've got the world at your feet."

In her gut, Casey had known the marriage was doomed. She knew he didn't want to be with her. She knew he didn't love her. She'd second-guessed herself and stayed with him. She'd told herself she was being crazy or insecure. Come to find out, she'd been right. She usually liked being right, but not this time.

Casey said, "Thanks, Kat. I needed to hear that."

"It's true, Casey. I wouldn't make that up. If you were some loser who was now destined to walk the earth alone with the exception of a shifty one-eyed cat, I would've said something more like … There, there. It's okay. There's more fish in the sea."

Casey laughed heartily. "What do you have against one-eyed cats?"

Kat chuckled. "They're shifty!"

They both laughed until Casey was able to collect herself enough to speak. "Oh man, too funny. I am starving. I think I'm going to order a pizza."

"Okay, I'll let you go. Call me—seriously—any time if you need to talk. And don't forget—you're awesome."

"Thanks. You're pretty awesome too."

Kat laughed. "True."

Through her giggles, Casey said, "Talk to you later. Bye."

"Bye."

Casey put her phone down on the nightstand and wandered into the kitchen. She pulled a glass from the cupboard and filled it with water from the tap. She braced herself on the counter and gulped until the cup was empty.

She rummaged through her junk drawer to find the phone number for the local pizza parlor that offered delivery. She ran back to her room for her phone and dialed. As she waited for her dinner, she washed her face and brushed her teeth. She glanced at her reflection, "Better late than never, right?"

While chowing down on her cheese pizza and binge watching the Golden Girls, Casey decided she'd go into work the next day to face the rest of the world. By the fourth episode, she wondered if she'd end up like those Golden ladies. Single and surrounded by her best girlfriends eating cheesecake. She chuckled. After living with Jason for the last four years, it sounded like a fantastic plan.

# SPRING

# CHAPTER 20

A FEW WEEKS LATER, Casey trudged up to the front door and knocked. It opened, and Jason smiled. "Hey."

Casey chirped, "Hi," before bending down to pick up Roxie. She snuggled the fidgeting fur ball before letting her down to get a toy.

Jason stared at Casey with what looked like concern in his eyes. "C'mon in. It's cold out there."

Casey entered into Jason's living room and stood near the hall.

Jason asked, "How are you doing with everything?"

Casey glanced up. "I'm good." There was no way she was allowing him to see one moment of sadness, fear, or remorse from her. He didn't deserve it. He deserved a punch in the nose.

Jason's face fell. "Oh. Good. I wanted to talk to you about the, um, divorce."

Casey asked, "What about it?"

Jason averted her gaze. "Well, I was thinking maybe we should use a filing service instead of using lawyers. We don't have any shared assets. It should be simple."

She thought, *Yes, so simple. You married me under false pretenses, and now you're divorcing me. Simple.*

Casey shrugged. "Yeah. Sounds good. Have you done any research on it?" She had a feeling he had.

Jason remained standing as Casey played with Roxie. "Yeah, there's a few not too far from here. It's about five hundred dollars, but they handle all the filing. All we have to do is fill out a questionnaire."

"Sounds good."

Their wedding had cost twenty thousand dollars, but their divorce would only cost five hundred. What a waste. Waste of money. Waste of time. Waste of energy.

Jason seemed caught off guard by her nonchalant attitude. What did he think, she'd be a mess? Her whole world would fall apart without him? She had let it for a little while, but those days were over. Casey was ready to move on.

Jason nodded. "Okay, I can go down there and get the paperwork."

Casey thought, *Aww how thoughtful.* She said, "Sounds great. Thanks."

Jason sat on the couch next to Casey and Roxie. "What about Roxie?"

Casey squinted at him. "What about her?"

"I don't want to give her up. Can we agree to keep sharing her?"

Casey remained calm despite the flames rushing through her veins. "Is that really necessary? I can keep her. I'm the one who wanted her in the first place."

"C'mon. You know I love her. My parents love her. I don't want to give her up, and you work full-time. And you know she hates being left by herself. I think it's best for her. We can have the same arrangement we have now?"

She thought, *I know you love her? I don't know who and what you love! I thought you loved me, asshole!* Casey wanted to run out and never return. She could flee the state with Roxie and never speak to him again. She brushed off the idea, which wasn't terribly practical. Maybe it wouldn't be so bad? Roxie did hate being alone. Maybe it was what was best for Roxie?

Casey exhaled. "Fine. Same arrangement."

Jason leaned back into the sofa. "Great."

She was and wasn't surprised at how expeditious he was on filing for divorce. It hadn't even been two weeks since he professed his lack of love for her. He didn't skip a beat, exactly like their separation discussion and agreements. Quick and transactional.

"Oh, one other thing. I'd prefer you don't use my last name anymore."

Casey stared at him. Maybe she hadn't heard him right. He was telling her she couldn't use his last name anymore? After all she had to do to change her last name after they got married? It wasn't even two years ago. Like Pepper was such a great freaking name? Kat was spot-on with this one. He was an asshole. How had she not seen this before? She ought to keep his last name out of spite. He can't tell her to change her name! She told herself to calm down. She would be sharing custody. They'd have to get along. For Roxie's sake.

She responded with a polite. "Sure. Well, Roxie and I should get going." She gazed down at her. "You ready, girl?" Roxie leaped out of Casey's lap.

Casey waved and let herself out. Roxie in tow.

On the drive home, she yelled at an invisible Jason. He had some nerve. What a jerk! She couldn't believe she had ever wanted to be with him. Why did she marry him? There was no way he was all of a sudden a jerk. Why hadn't she seen it?

———

AT HOME, she snuggled on the sofa with Roxie as they watched

TV. The question of why she married Jason plagued her. She was twenty-four when they'd gotten married. None of their friends were getting married or even in serious relationships. They were all recent college grads partying and having fun. It was her who had pushed for it. Why had she pushed so hard?

Sure, they'd been dating for three years and lived together, but living together was really a logistics thing, not a romantic gesture. It was their junior year of college, and they both wanted to live off campus. It made sense, at the time, to live together.

Oh, how she'd loved the response from her family at them for moving in together. What was the phrase Agatha had used? Yes. It was, "Why buy the cow if you can get the milk for free?" Is that why she wanted to get married—so her family wouldn't judge her? Or was she so in love that marriage and babies were all she could think about? It wasn't. She was in school. She dreamed of winning a Nobel Prize for chemistry—not changing dirty diapers. She'd done enough of that growing up and taking care of her sisters. How did she go from wanting to win a Nobel Prize to wanting to be Jason's stay-at-home wife who minded the children and the house? Why *did* she want to marry him?

She sank into the cushions and sighed. Because she loved him. It was true. It was real, even if he didn't love her. She would've done anything for him—for their relationship. She had put up with his mother calling five times a day and visiting several times a week. She'd put up with Jason's snarky attitude toward her family. She'd put up with him doing whatever his parents asked him to do despite how it affected her. He was a momma's boy, through and through. She never stood a chance at being the most important person in his life. Not even second or third. She was probably somewhere between a cousin and a professor at school. It all made perfect sense now. What is it they say about hindsight being twenty-twenty?

She glanced down at Roxie, curled up next to her, and scratched behind her ears. "At least I've got you girl."

A FEW DAYS LATER, Casey parked in the driveway of Jason's town-house. It seemed like a million years ago that she had lived there. She hurried up the path to the front door. She was ready for this to be over with. She knocked and heard rustling around inside before Jason opened the door.

Jason stood with papers in his hands. "Hey, thanks for stopping by."

She cocked her head. "No problem." Casey looked at the room behind him. There had to be fifteen people milling about. Her mouth dropped open. "Are you having a party?"

Jason remained in the door frame, blocking most of her view. "Just a few people over from my new golf team."

Casey was shocked. New golf team? He was having a party? That in itself was alarming, but why would he have her stop by to pick up the questionnaire for their divorce papers while he was having a party? That was un-freaking-believable.

She snatched the papers from his hands. He didn't move aside to let her in. He stood firm blocking the entry. It was clear that he didn't want her to come inside. She studied each page slowly and thoroughly, flipping the papers over one-by-one. In her peripheral, she saw his arms drop to his sides as she read slower. His hands fidgeted. She enjoyed making him squirm.

She glanced up. "Looks complete. It just needs my signature. I'll sign it and drop them off at the office, so we can get this thing going." Now that the initial sting had worn off, she couldn't wait to be divorced from him.

"Thanks. I appreciate it."

She thought, *Sure you do*. She did all she could to keep her cool despite the heat searing through her. She told herself she must stay calm, for Roxie. She said, "No problem." As he began to shut the door, he paused and opened it back up and said, "Bye," before quickly closing it.

She stood frozen. "Bye."

She walked back to her car shaking her head. What the heck was that? If he just had golf buddies inside why would he be in such a hurry to get rid of her? Was it possible he was already seeing someone? Him? Is that why he'd been progressing at lightning speed to square away their divorce?

As she drove, she couldn't shake the feeling he was definitely trying to hide something. She shrugged. She didn't even care anymore. If there was another woman, he was her problem now. Good riddance.

CHAPTER 21

CASEY STUDIED the monitor and thought, *That doesn't look right.* She rechecked her lab notebook to ensure her calculations for the experiment had been correct. Had she run the wrong protein standard?

From behind, she heard footsteps approaching. She glanced over her shoulder and watched as Javier and a man in a dark suit and a cheerful smile chatted while Javier pointed at doors and benches. Casey thought, *Ahhh. Is he the Analytical Chemist candidate, the replacement for Dana, who Javier had been talking about?* She vaguely remembered Javier telling her that he had worked with the candidate at a previous company and had referred him for the position. Javier hadn't mentioned how good-looking he was, but then again, she wasn't exactly on the market. Was she? Huh, maybe she was. Yes, she was kind of. She shook off the thought. He was probably married anyway, and besides, she had zero desire to be starting up any new relationships anytime soon. That was the last thing she needed.

She busied herself with the notebook as she saw them approaching.

Javier grinned. "Hi, Casey. This is Seth Donavan. He's interviewing for the Analytical Chemist position." He looked at Seth. "Seth, this is Casey Pepper, she's on the analytical team."

Seth's ocean blue eyes twinkled as he extended his hand. "Nice to meet you."

She shook his hand. It was warm and dry. "Nice to meet you too. Good luck today."

He chuckled nervously. "Thanks!"

Javier winked at her as he led Seth away. She thought, *What was that? I filed for divorce only two weeks ago. He better not be trying to set me up already.*

She refocused her attention to her lab experiment and realized the issue. Simple entry error into the chromatography program. She updated the information on the computer and was about to head back to her cubicle when Javier approached her again.

Javier's eyes widened. "Soooo...what did you think of Seth?"

Casey glanced up at him. "He seems nice."

He pursed his lips. "Word on the street is, he's single now."

Casey sighed. "And?"

"You're single. He's single. I sense romance…"

Casey exhaled. "Oh. My. God. I just filed for divorce. I won't even be legally single for like, six months."

"Honey, you're single now, maybe not on paper, but you're single. And Seth is super nice and easy on the eyes." He looked her up and down. "You're looking fierce by the way."

Casey had been hitting the gym five days a week and giving her appearance more attention than normal. It made her feel better to take control of her life. However, it was in no way related to trying to catch the eye of the opposite sex. She had decided she wasn't going to be a sad sack who ate pints of ice cream for dinner and turned into a couch potato. Not anymore. She still ate ice cream, but she'd kick-boxed it off at the gym instead of letting herself balloon into the spokeswoman for Ben and Jerry's.

"Thanks, Javi. I'm just not ready to date. Or even think about dating."

Javier gave an exaggerated. "Okaaay." He glanced over at the clock. "Gots to run. Lunch later?"

"Sure."

Casey shut her notebook and headed back to her desk. She grabbed her cellphone and texted Jason. "Hi. I'm going over to my mom's after work, I'll pick up Roxie after. Is 8:30 p.m., okay?"

Jason replied. "Sure no problem. I might be at my parents.'"

"Ok, I'll text you before I leave my mom's."

Jason replied, "OK.".

"Thanks."

She slid the phone back onto her desk. She slouched into her chair. This was her life now.

---

"Hi, Casey! C'mon in." Agatha beamed as she hurried to the back of the condo outfitted in a bubblegum pink tracksuit.

Casey entered the condo. "You about ready for our power walk?"

"Yep, I'm in need! It's been weeks since I've gotten any exercise. I just need to put my shoes on and I'll be ready."

"Where are the girls?"

Agatha shouted, "Cara is at soccer practice and Anna's at the library." Agatha returned. "Ready!"

They exited and Agatha locked the front door, stashing the key into her jacket pocket. "We can get to the trail from over here." Agatha led the way down the busy street.

On the trail, Casey inhaled the scent of eucalyptus. She took a moment to appreciate the weather, chilly but sunny too. Casey asked, "So what's new? How are the girls?"

Agatha swung her arms from side to side like a soldier.

"They're good. Both doing well in school. Cara is really into soccer this year. How are things with you and Jason?"

Casey squinted her eyes. "Still getting divorced. We actually filed a few weeks ago."

Agatha pursed her lips. "I still can't believe you want a divorce. I'm so disappointed."

Casey shook her head in disbelief. Who says that? She'd never said anything to make her think she actually wanted a divorce, but then again, she hadn't told her the whole story either. Her mother didn't even know about Jason's indiscretion before the wedding. Casey had done a stellar job at keeping the truth about her and Jason's relationship from her family.

She sighed. "It's not that I want a divorce. It's that I'm getting a divorce."

She was tired of her family's lack of support on the issue. Everyone else in her life had been nothing but supportive.

Agatha continued. "Well, maybe you should have kept at counseling longer?"

Casey's blood boiled. "More counseling would not have helped."

"I'm just trying to be helpful. Marriage is about compromise. I think maybe you didn't try for long enough."

Casey's eyes bugged as she breathed in and out of her nose. "There is no compromise for Jason not loving me."

"Oh, Casey don't be so dramatic. I don't think that's true. I know he loves you."

Casey was about to explode. Did she really have to spell it out? She took a few more breaths and said, "He told me he didn't love me and didn't want to be married to me anymore."

Agatha shook her head. "Oh, I don't believe that."

Casey stopped walking and stared at Agatha in disbelief. Agatha turned, eyes wide. "What?"

Casey threw her hands in the air. "What? You don't believe me. He said it. Yes, my husband, Jason, told me he didn't love me and wanted a divorce. He told me he never loved me and was never happy. Now we're getting a divorce. There is no compromising. That's it. It's over. I'd appreciate a little support, not accusations. Or any marriage advice. I'm not married anymore!"

Agatha approached and put her hand on Casey's shoulder. "I'm sorry Casey, you're right. I believe you. And that Jason is an idiot."

Casey shouted. "Yes, he is!" She lowered her voice. "Next topic please."

Agatha gritted her teeth. "Okay, okay. Next topic. We are thinking about planning a trip to Spain..."

Casey half-listened for the remainder of their power walk. She just hoped her mother finally understood what was going on. She was tired of defending her divorce. Despite her progress in moving on from Jason, having to explain to people her husband didn't love her wasn't exactly pleasant.

Agatha finished her long-winded explanation of the Sagrada Familia's history and asked if Casey was staying for dinner.

She shook her head. "No, I still have to swing by the craft store to buy supplies for Kat's bridal shower invitations and pick up Roxie."

Agatha furrowed her brow. "You're really going to keep sharing Roxie?"

Casey glared at her. "Really."

Agatha fanned out her hands. "Okay. Okay. No need to be dramatic. Although, I bet he's just doing that to stay in contact with you."

Casey rolled her eyes. "I seriously doubt it." Casey couldn't wait to get back to the condo so she could stop talking about her estranged husband and pending divorce. It was killing the endorphin rush she normally enjoyed during exercise.

CASEY SAT on her living room floor bent over her coffee table studying the packets of diamond ring and three-tiered wedding cake stickers. Next to the stickers was a stack of ivory- and sage-colored card stock. It was bridal shower invitation craft time.

She grabbed the three-dimensional diamond ring stickers and paused. She set them back down and lifted up her left hand. Was it silly she still wore her wedding rings? It hadn't been a conscious decision to keep them on, but seeing them now, it seemed wrong. Out of place. A lie.

She began to tug off the platinum diamond solitaire and stopped. A fever seared through her and a single tear escaped. She quickly brushed it off her cheek. She didn't even know why she felt anything. It was just a ring. Was removing her rings the final nail in the coffin of their marriage? That seemed silly. Her marriage was dead. Cremated. No coffin needed.

Or was it the memory of how happy she'd been when they'd picked out the ring together, blissfully unaware it was all a lie? She convinced herself that it didn't matter why she was upset. She wasn't married anymore. She reinitiated the removal of her rings and carefully placed them on her apothecary-style coffee table.

She stared down at her naked finger that displayed a wedding ring sized groove in her skin like a cruel tattoo. It was the marking of a previously married person. A sign to others to stay away—divorce lives here.

She took a deep breath, gave Roxie a scratch, forced herself off the ground, and walked into her bathroom. She opened the top drawer and removed a small red and gold Asian style pouch with a drawstring. She slid the rings inside and put the pouch back into the drawer.

She and her pint-sized shadow, Roxie, returned to the living room and began to design the invitation using the supplies she had purchased. She decided on the ivory cardstock with the sage cardstock layered on top. The text of the invitation would be printed on a third loose layer of off-white vellum. The wedding cakes with a sage-colored ribbon would adorn the top of the invitation. Casey studied her prototype and was quite pleased with the design and realized how much she'd enjoyed the crafting. Which was a good thing, considering she had a long list of maid-of-honor projects, like wedding favors, games for the shower, and bachelorette weekend planning. She hadn't even started on the work for Kelly's wedding yet. Between socializing, work, and wedding duties, she had barely a spare moment.

She chuckled to herself. When she'd found out she would be in two weddings the year of her divorce, she'd thought she'd been cursed. A fate worse than death. Now, she understood how much time and effort it required to be a maid-of-honor; it had been a great distraction from the fact she had no idea what she'd do with the rest of her life. For now, her life was filled with crafting and wedding party planning. Easy.

For some inexplicable reason, she didn't equate Kat and Kelly's weddings with her own or the failure of her marriage. She thought she'd be feeling sorry for herself or constantly bummed out by the constant, "Congratulations" and "beautiful couple" in reference to the engaged couples. The same phrases that had been bestowed upon her and Jason when they'd announced their plans to wed. It was the opposite. Instead of being miserable, she basked in the surrounding positivity. Sure, she'd thought some of their ideas were a bit naive, like her favorite saying, "we don't believe in divorce," but she kept it to herself. Her previously non-divorcee self had said the same thing. She hadn't believed in divorce until she'd gotten married. That was the truth. She thought, *Hmm. Maybe I'm becoming a little jaded, but how could I not be?*

# CHAPTER 22

TWO WEEKS LATER, Casey set the red and white cartons onto the small round dining table. She glanced over at Cara sitting on the floor playing with Roxie, still wearing her soccer clothes. "Are you going to change before dinner?"

Cara twirled her strawberry-blonde ponytail. "Do I have to?"

"I guess it's fine." Casey found it increasingly difficult to not spoil her baby sister.

Cara threw her arms up in a victory pose. "Yes!" Giggling, she took Roxie's plush alligator from her and threw it across Agatha's living room. She looked over at Casey. "What did you get? You bought potstickers, right?"

Casey smirked, playfully. "As if I would forget them? Who do you take me for?" She chuckled. "I got the usual. Do me a favor and tell Mom and Anna dinner is ready."

Cara leapt up and ran toward the bedrooms. Roxie followed.

Anna strolled through the kitchen into the dining room wearing jeans and a burgundy sweatshirt with her high school mascot on the front. She said, "Hey, Casey—I didn't know you were here." She gave her a hug. "Ooh, and you brought Chinese food. Awesome."

"What have you been up to? Homework?"

Anna stuck out her tongue. "Blah. Yes. Never-ending homework. I have decided I hate Algebra."

Casey's mouth opened, and her eyes widened. "What? Hate Algebra? You're breaking my heart. Algebra is the best. I loved it."

Anna laughed. "Well then you can have it, cause Algebra and me, we don't get along."

Anna sat on one side of Casey and Cara was on the other side. Agatha still hadn't finished cleaning the bathroom. Anna yelled out, "Mom! Dinner!"

"I already told her. She's like all crazy obsessed with cleaning."

Anna nodded. "For real. Casey, she's crazy."

Casey giggled as the girls continued their rant. There wasn't any other company she preferred to her two little sisters. They'd grown up to be two of the funniest, sweetest, and smartest young women she'd ever met. Not to mention they kept her endlessly entertained. It was one of the reasons Casey and Roxie updated their weekly routine to include dinners at the condo after Casey picked Roxie up from Jason's or his parents.

"There she is!" Casey cried.

Agatha waved sheepishly. "Hi, Casey. Sorry, I just can't stand a messy bathroom."

Anna and Cara exchanged glances.

"Well now that you're here, let's dig in. What do ya say?"

Agatha exclaimed. "I say, yes!"

Deep into their moo shoo, Cara's amber eyes widened. "Did Mom tell you about our trip to Spain? It's gonna be so cool!"

Casey had to scan her memory. She'd mostly tuned her mother out when she had talked about it during their walk. She said. "I think so. Is that for sure now?"

Agatha nodded. "Yep! We're going for a week to Barcelona. You should come with us!"

Cara tugged on Casey's arm. "Yes! Please come with us! You have to come! Please, please, please!"

Casey raised an eyebrow. "Cara, do you want me to go too?"

Cara's ponytail bobbed as she nodded.

Anna cheered. "Yes, Casey! You have to come with us. That would be so fun if we all went together."

"I'll have to find out if I can take time off work, and if Jason will be able to keep Roxie. When are you going? I have Kat's bridal shower and wedding in a few months."

Casey hadn't thought of going on a trip before, but it was intriguing. The idea of leaving town sounded awesome. She knew she could take the time off work since she hadn't taken a vacation in almost a year. She'd do some research when she got home and check with Jason about Roxie. It did seem fun. She'd never been to Europe. None of them had.

Agatha gritted her teeth. "Speaking of weddings. Kelly's upset nobody is doing anything for her engagement."

Casey rolled her eyes. "She hasn't even set a date. What does she want us to do?"

"I think she wants to go dress shopping with everyone and wants to start planning her bridal shower and bachelorette party. She already has a place picked out for her bridal shower."

Casey sighed. "I'm fine with going dress shopping, but she's not supposed to plan her own parties." A sinking feeling settled over Casey. What if her maid-of-honor duties amounted to her being Kelly's assistant whom Kelly would expect to be at her beck and call?

Agatha shrugged. "It's just what she said. Maybe you can call her?"

Casey thought, *Great.* She was actually surprised it had taken Kelly this long to complain that her impending nuptials weren't center stage. She'd call her. Who didn't love dress shopping? Someone going through a divorce? Nah, it would be fun. She lied to herself.

Casey said. "I'll call her and see about organizing a dress-shopping outing. Now tell me more about this trip to Barcelona."

Agatha rattled off the details. This time Casey listened.

After dinner, they said their goodbyes, and Cara made one last plug for Casey to join them in Barcelona. Casey explained she'd look into it and hugged her and promised to see her the next weekend at her soccer tournament.

Later that night, snuggled in bed with Roxie, propped up by her pillows, Casey hunched over her laptop researching European vacations. She'd never been out of the country other than on an ill-fated cruise to Mexico during her childhood. She hadn't the first clue on what there was to do and see in Barcelona, let alone the rest of Europe.

Her research pulled up photos of grand cathedrals, palaces, and museums with world-famous art. She wasn't much of a fine art aficionado, but even she'd heard of the Mona Lisa. It seemed like something she needed to see.

She quickly realized she didn't want to go for just a week, and she didn't want to just go to Barcelona.

Into the wee hours of the night, she plotted out a two-week vacation starting in London where she'd see the Crown Jewels and stroll along the Thames. From London she'd take the Eurostar to Paris, where she'd eat baguettes, drink espresso, and see the Eiffel Tower. She noted she may need to buy a beret. And by "may" she meant she "must" buy a beret. From Paris she'd take an overnight train to Barcelona and meet up with Agatha and the girls where they'd strut down La Rambla and soak in the whimsical sites created by Gaudi. From Barcelona she'd take a flight to Rome where she'd eat her body weight in gelato and explore ancient ruins. It would be amazing.

She realized it was a bit last minute to try to partner up with Rachel or another one of her girlfriends on the trip. Should she go by herself? Why not? She'd traveled for work by herself—why not Europe? It was settled. She would take herself on a grand European adventure as a young, single woman with her whole life ahead of her. Girl power.

Casey was too amped to sleep, but she nearly had a fit when she saw it was two in the morning. She had work tomorrow. She shut the lid of her laptop, adjusted her pillows, and laid her head down. A moment later, a grin spread across her face.

―――――

SUNDAY NIGHT, Jason shook his head. "Seriously no problem. Between my parents and me, we'll watch Roxie. The trip sounds awesome. Where all are you going?"

Casey told him all about her trip and where she planned to visit.

He smiled. "That's so cool. And you're going by yourself. That's so brave! I'm not sure I'd go by myself."

Casey thought, *Yeah. I am brave.* She grinned. "It'll be an adventure, for sure. It's safe. I'm not worried. I think I'm too excited to be worried." She laughed.

He nodded. "I can't wait to hear what your favorite places are. I was thinking of going with some of my buddies in the fall. Rome is on the list."

Casey listened to him, and to her it was strangely normal how friendly they'd become, or remained. Which was it? Become or remained? She raged from time to time when her anger bubbled up, but she'd decided there wasn't a reason to have an adversarial relationship with him, and they shared Roxie. They had to, at the very least, be cordial. Was it his fault he didn't love her? No, you can't choose who you love. Boy, isn't that the truth. However, it was his fault he married her and led her on all these years, but she decided to bury that little tidbit at the moment. She couldn't change the past. It wasn't as if she were still in love with him. No, she'd come to that conclusion when she realized she didn't miss him. She didn't even want to dig into the question of when she'd stopped loving him. No reason to open that can of emotional worms. Or was her lack of love a defense mechanism? She shook it off. It didn't matter. Now when she looked at him, all she saw was an acquaintance. Like a coworker she may have a conversation with around the water cooler. A coworker with whom she just happened to share a dog.

Casey said, "I'll give you the full report. Thanks again for agreeing to watch Roxie."

"No problem."

"We better get going. Bye."

"Bye."

She waved as she and Roxie walked to her car. She settled inside with a huge grin on her face. She was headed to Europe!

## CHAPTER 23

A FEW WEEKS LATER, Casey drove into the parking lot of Julia's Bridal in downtown Walnut Creek. She parked in the stall farthest from the entrance and slipped one leg out of the car and hesitated. Why had Kelly decided on this bridal shop of the gazillion bridal salons in the Bay Area? Was it to rub it in that Casey was getting divorced? Was she still mad she wasn't the first to get married? Was this payback?

She thought, *Chill out, Casey. Not everything is about you and your stupid divorce. Get a grip.* Casey continued out of the car. She tried and failed to shake the familiar pang in her chest as she remembered her own fun-filled day of wedding dress shopping. She'd sipped champagne and shared all the details of her upcoming wedding and honeymoon. She had been on cloud nine.

The last stop on Casey's wedding dress shopping tour had been Julia's. It was there Casey slipped on her gown and she saw her future. In the strapless beaded bodice and layered tulle skirt, she saw herself standing next to Jason in the church, smiling for pictures, and thanking guests as they complimented her on how stunning she looked. She had to have *that dress*. When she'd gotten home she'd run up to Jason and wrapped her arms around him. She'd said, "I found it! I found the dress!"

He'd smiled. "That's great!" He stopped smiling when she told him the cost. It had been well above their budget, and he was adamant it was crazy to spend that much money on a dress. He wouldn't allow it. After days of pouting, he'd finally given in and allowed the extravagant purchase. She had beamed and thought, *He does love me.*

Now the ball gown and her optimism for a happily-ever-after were stuffed away in a box in the back of her closet.

Refocusing on the present and Kelly's special day, Casey pushed the glass door open. The scent of lavender wafted up her nostrils. She approached the two women standing behind the counter covered with bridal magazines and a vase of calla lilies.

"May I help you?"

Casey forced a grin. "Yes, I'm here to meet my sister and family."

She was cut off by the woman who had doted over her just a few years before. Before, when she was the blushing bride-to-be. "Oh, you must be with Kelly." She giggled. "There's quite a few of you."

Casey said, "Yes, we're like a built-in entourage."

The woman looked her up and down. "Well, let me bring you back to her fitting room."

Casey begged the universe for it not to be the same room she'd had. She was relieved when they stopped at the first private suite on the right.

The keys on the woman's rubber bracelet jingled when she knocked on the door. A faint, "come in" was heard.

The woman said, "We've got one more!"

Casey entered the parlor-style suite donned with full-length mirrors with a pedestal for the bride, and an assortment of arm chairs and a sofa for the admirers.

She faced Kelly, who was wearing a poufy princess style ball gown and said, "Hey, I made it. Sorry I'm late." While she thought, *Sorry, I didn't crash on the way over, so I wouldn't have to be here at all.* She gave her a brief hug and proceeded to give the rest of the gang one too.

Kelly returned her focus to the mirror and brushed her hands down the heavily beaded skirt. "What do you think? Is it me?"

Casey thought it was a bit much for a mother of three. She said, "It's beautiful. Really dazzling." Casey wanted to crawl into the corner and cry. She thought she was okay with all the wedding stuff. It had been a great, positive distraction, hadn't it? Why was this killing her?

Casey squeezed into a spot on the couch that Cara and Angelina offered. From across the room, Anna gave a shudder at the dress choice. Casey had to contain herself from giggling.

Agatha gave an over-the-top smile. "It's just lovely. You are going to be such a beautiful bride."

Kelly wiped a tear. "Thank you. I'm just so happy."

Agatha left her chair to embrace an emotional Kelly while Anna rolled her eyes and suppressed a giggle at the sight of the two most dramatic members of their family. Casey was thankful she at least had her little sisters for amusement. If she hadn't, she might've been faking an illness right about now and speeding home to cry alone in her spinster apartment.

Another knock on the door. A woman in navy slacks, a pinstriped shirt, and a gold scarf entered. "How is that one? Do you love it?"

Kelly said. "I do, but do you have something a little less beaded, maybe not strapless? Just for comparison?"

The woman nodded, and her earrings jingled. "I have a few that I think would be lovely on you. Give me a few minutes, and I'll bring them right out."

Kelly tilted her head. "Thank you." She returned her attention to the mirror.

Casey wondered if she'd been that self-absorbed when she'd

had her day of fittings. Probably. Weren't all brides? She was suddenly thankful that Kat's mother was making her dress and Casey hadn't been forced to go along for dress shopping. Kat would've picked up on her fake enthusiasm in a heartbeat. Casey didn't even have to go bridesmaid dress shopping with Kat. Kat had told her and the other bridesmaids she didn't care what they wore as long as it was a black dress. Casey had a sneaking suspicion that wouldn't be the case with Kelly.

Anna scooted her chair next to the sofa and spoke softly. "Hey, Casey, are you super excited for our trip or what?"

Casey said, "Totally. I can't wait! Just a few more weeks!"

Anna grinned showing her perfectly straight teeth. "I've already started packing. Is that weird?"

Casey said. "No, not at all, but I haven't even started. We're supposed to have awesome weather. How many suitcases are you bringing?"

"Mom says we can only have one." Anna grimaced.

Cara flung herself toward Casey and Anna's huddle. "Are you talking about the trip?"

They nodded.

Cara replied. "So excited!" She giggled.

Someone yelled Casey's name.

Casey glanced over at Agatha and Kelly who stood near the pedestal. "Yeah?"

"We were thinking of going to Beautiful Gowns in Concord to look for bridesmaids' dresses. I've heard they have really good prices. What do you think?"

Casey lifted her wrist and studied her watch. "Today? I thought we were just looking at dresses for you. Don't we still have two other places left?"

Kelly said, "Yeah, after all of my appointments we'd go. A girlfriend of mine told me they have knock-offs of the dresses most of these fancy places have, for a fraction of the price. That's why I want to go there last. Once I find the dress I like, Mom's going to take a picture and then she'll match it to a discounted one."

Agatha slipped the top of the camera out of her purse as if it were top secret documents and winked.

Kelly continued, "Cool?"

Dread fell over Casey. It would take hours and hours before this shopping event would be over. She wasn't sure she was up for it. Casey widened her eyes. "Cool."

The woman came back in the suite with an armful of gowns. Agatha retreated to her seat and tucked her satchel-style purse under her chair. Casey sank back into the sofa, preparing herself for the rest of the show. She was glad she'd made plans with Maddy to go dancing in San Francisco later that night. She would need a few cocktails and an opportunity to let loose.

Kelly climbed out of the last high-priced gown while the group began to pack up their belongings to head to their next appointment. Casey couldn't wait to leave Julia's Bridal Salon. As she strolled out of the salon she vowed to herself to never return.

She was knocked out of her thoughts when she heard a voice behind. "Can we ride with you Casey?"

She turned to see Anna and Cara. "Sure, if it's okay with Mom."

Anna waved back at Agatha. Agatha nodded.

Anna said, "It's cool."

Casey was usually happy to spend more time with her sisters, but she'd hoped for a little rage-alone time to get all her frustration and anger out before the next stop on Kelly's wedding-dress-shopping trip.

On the way to the next location, Anna and Cara spoke nonstop of details of the trip to Barcelona. Casey was pleased with the distraction from her own dark thoughts.

Kelly's next two appointments were similar to Julia's, except this time Casey wasn't late and didn't miss the champagne offering. She gladly accepted the champagne offered at both high-end salons located in nearby Orinda. After Kelly's appointments, they enjoyed a pizza lunch before heading to the discount warehouse in gritty downtown Concord.

Casey drove into the parking lot of what looked like a big box store, except they had tuxedos, wedding gowns, and tacky brides-maid dresses in large display windows. The store was huge compared to the quaint alcohol-slinging bridal boutiques they'd spent most of the day at.

They strolled to the entrance where Agatha stood with Kelly and Angelina in a semi-circle studying the digital camera in Agatha's hand.

Kelly looked up at them. "We're on a mission, ladies. Do you choose to accept?"

Casey smiled and nodded while thinking, *do I really have a choice?*

Agatha handed the camera to Casey. "The mission is this. We find Kelly's dress. This is what we're trying to match. Got it?"

Casey studied it and passed the camera to Anna. "Got it."

Kelly continued. "Once the first mission is complete, we move on to our second mission. The second mission is to find all of your bridesmaid dresses and a flower girl dress for Olivia. Do you accept said mission?"

Casey gave a serious expression. "I accept this mission."

Anna bowed. "I accept, and I will bring much honor."

Angelina and Cara giggled and assured Kelly they had accepted the mission.

The gang entered the massive warehouse. The center of the store contained a dozen racks of long white gowns in plastic followed by dozens of rows of bridesmaid dresses in all colors of the rainbow. The walls were adorned with mirrors, racks of men's tuxedos, shoes for men and women, and every accessory anyone in a wedding party may need from veils to flower girl baskets.

Casey turned to the group. "Okay, I think we should split up.

We've all seen the photo. There are six of us and twelve racks, we each take two racks. Deal?"

Kelly said, "Perfect. We'll be done lickety-split."

Casey thought, *That's the point*. She said, "I'll take the first two. We alternate racks. First one to find it is the winner!"

Kelly laughed. "You heard the MOH. Let's get to it!"

Casey rushed over to the first rack and flipped through the heavy plastic dress filled bags. First row, no luck.

Halfway through the second row she heard, "I've got it! I think I've got it!" from a few rows back.

Casey took a mental picture of her place on the rack and ran over to where Agatha stood with Agatha's eyes wide holding a dress half out of the plastic bag. She said, "Kelly, is this it?"

Kelly pulled the rest of the dress out of the bag and studied the lace bodice with a sweetheart neckline, the beaded belt, and the single layer of tulle that made up the full skirt. She stood back. "I think so." She studied the price tag and chuckled. "It's only two hundred bucks! I'm gonna try it on." She glanced up at all of them. "Ladies, follow me."

Casey glanced at her watch. It had only taken ten minutes to find Kelly's dress. Thank you, Universe.

They gathered outside the single-stall dressing room and waited for Kelly to put the dress on. A moment later, she pushed back the curtain and exited wearing the gown. She smoothed out the skirt and stood tall. "What do you think?"

Agatha shook her head. "I think it is *the dress*! How lucky is that?"

Casey smirked. "So lucky." She meant it. Now all they had to do was find their dresses, and they'd be done. Forever. Casey grinned. "On to the second mission! Kelly, what color should we be looking for?"

Kelly twirled around, watching her reflection in the mirror. She stopped. "I was thinking maybe tangerine or kiwi? Those colors are so in right now." She tapped her finger to her chin.

"How about each of you bring me two dresses to evaluate, one in tangerine and one in kiwi. Sound good?"

Casey's face fell. Kelly had fancied up the wording, but she was pretty sure Kelly told them they would either be wearing an orange or lime green dress. Yikes. She put another happy face on. "Sounds super fun! Let's do it!"

Kelly laughed. "You heard her. Let's go. I'll be here waiting for the presentations." Casey followed the order with a curtsy.

They giggled as they ran toward the racks.

---

KELLY SAT on the cheap plastic chair outside the fitting rooms taking notes on all the dresses each girl presented. She said, "I'm still not seeing the one. Angelina, you're up next. Show me what you've got."

Angelina chirped, "Okay. I hope you like it." She walked into the dressing stall and closed the curtain.

Kelly turned to Casey. "What do you think of the one Anna brought out—the kiwi halter?"

The words kiwi and halter together made Casey want to revolt. She said, "Oh, I don't know about the color. It's a bit bright."

Kelly's face fell. "You don't like the color? I like it."

Casey shook her head. "It's your wedding. Whatever you want, we'll wear it."

Kelly frowned. "But I want you guys to like it, that way you'll wear it again."

Casey thought, *Nobody is going to willingly wear these awful things ever again.* Casey tried to backtrack. "It's not that bad. I could see wearing it during the summer. It's perfect for summer."

"You think so?"

Casey nodded. "Totally." She was getting good at this lying thing.

Kelly put her hand on Casey's arm. "Oh my gosh, I love it!"

Casey looked up to see Angelina wearing a tangerine, also known as bright orange, dress with one off-the-center strap. Lace overlaid the bodice, and it had a straight, flowing skirt. It was a bit like Kelly's dress, but with the awful shoulder strap and bright color.

Kelly said, "Oh, it's perfect. It matches me. What do you guys think?"

Casey said, "I think it's great. I love that it matches your dress." She thought maybe if she acted like she liked it, this day would finally be over. Her enthusiasm for all things married and wedding had worn thin. She couldn't wait to go home and cry into her pillow before going out with Maddy. She thought she was over her and Jason. Why was she feeling this way? It was like a sneak attack, and she hadn't been prepared. What other surprises would be in store for her?

The women gave convincing adoration for the dress and praised Angelina for finding the perfect dress for all of them to wear. They sorted out sizes and found a white flower girl dress with tangerine sash for Olivia. Kelly beamed that it had been a productive day and tried to convince them all to go to dinner to celebrate. Casey thanked the universe once again that she had plans with Maddy.

Casey hugged and goodbyed her way to her car. She reached for the handle and heard, "Wait, sis!" She turned around and saw Kelly jogging toward her with her wedding dress bag in hand. "Can you store this at your place? I don't want Paul to see it. It's bad luck!"

Casey's mouth dropped open. "Oh. Of course."

Kelly said. "Thank you. It can't get wrinkled though. Is there somewhere you can hang it, out of the bag?"

Casey toured her apartment in her mind. Not really. She said, "It might get a little crinkled in the closet, but you could steam it out right before."

Kelly cocked her head to the side. "That could work. Okay. Sounds good. Thank you again for today. It was everything I've ever dreamed."

Casey gave her last performance of the day. "I'm so glad. It was really fun. I can't wait for the wedding!" It wasn't a complete act. She was happy for Kelly and that she'd had the day she'd always dreamed of. Casey just wished the day had been three years ago when she hadn't been jaded or had her heart stomped on.

They hugged one last time. She set the dress in the back seat and hopped into the driver's side. As soon as she was out of sight from her cheerful family, she broke down and sobbed until she reached her apartment.

She sat in her parking stall and cleaned up her face with the bottom of her T-shirt. She took a few deep breaths and climbed out of the car. She told herself, *Everything will be fine. It's not a setback. It's just a few tears.* She hoped.

She lugged the dresses to her apartment and situated them in her closet. Outside of the bag, Kelly's wedding dress took up a lot more room than she had considered. It took up a third of the closet, and it hung there like the ghost of weddings past haunting her. She sighed and strolled over to the bathroom to get ready for a night out—with a cocktail or maybe two.

---

SHE GRIMACED at the familiar sliming of her face. She turned over and hid under the covers. Roxie hopped over her and began to dig at the comforter. Casey groaned. "What, Roxie? Normally you let me sleep."

She peeked from under the blanket to see the clock. Casey thought, *Crap. No wonder Roxie was anxious this morning. It was almost noon.* She pushed back the covers and greeted a hyper-active Roxie. "Okay, girl. We'll go on a walk. Give me a second."

She slid out of bed and threw on some clothes, knowing Roxie could only wait for so long before Casey would find herself cleaning up a mess instead of taking her on a walk. Casey's head pounded. How many drinks did she have last night? What time did she get home? There was no way she drove. Where was her car? She rubbed her eyes and grabbed Roxie to put her harness on.

Casey chased after Roxie as she made her way down the path in-between the buildings. It was bright out. Why hadn't she grabbed her sunglasses? Roxie made a pit-stop and relieved herself on the grass. From behind, she heard, "Hi." She glanced to her right. It was one of her neighbors with a fluffy white Maltese that Roxie liked to clown around with. She forced a smile. "Good morning." She stuck her hand out for the Maltese to sniff. "Morning, Teddy."

Teddy's owner, a bookish thirty-something man, chuckled. "Is it still morning? Late night?"

What gave it away? Was it her slow movements, the shielding of her eyes with her hand, or the fact she thought it was morning?

Casey smirked. "A little bit."

"All right, well have a good walk. C'mon, Teddy."

Casey waved as they strolled past. She gazed down at Roxie. "You done yet?" Roxie responded by panting and hopping back on the concrete path to continue her morning exercise.

As Roxie did her thing, Casey replayed what she remembered of the night before. She vaguely remembered tequila shots and a taxi. Her car must be at Maddy's. She'd call when they were back in the apartment.

Why did she get so wasted? Right. Wedding dresses. Why had she let shopping get to her? She was over Jason, right? Wrong? She knew she was still angry with him for tricking her into believing they were in love. How could she have been so wrong about their relationship? She'd spent five years thinking he was the one and thinking she was the one for him. He'd fooled her. More than that, he'd made a fool of her. How could she ever trust herself again? How could she ever trust another man who claimed to love her?

She watched Roxie rolling around in the grass. "Are you done yet, silly girl?" Roxie ran toward her. She bent down and scratched Roxie being the ears. "You're a good girl. Let's go home and get some treats."

She pushed her thoughts of love aside and told herself to focus on her upcoming trip. Her trip she needed to get ready for like, yesterday.

# CHAPTER 24

## LONDON

BACKPACK on and roller suitcases in hand, Casey rushed through the airport to get to her gate. As sweat dripped down the sides of her face and down her back, she scurried up to the boarding attendant and handed the woman her ticket. The heavily made-up blonde gave a genuine smile. "Hello!" She took the boarding pass and chirped. "Have a great trip!"

Casey spat out a breathless, "Thanks," and strutted down the jetway.

The male flight attendant checked her boarding pass and escorted her to her seat. He grinned. "Here you are. Now, let's see if we can find some room overhead." The attendant began opening and closing bins until he found one that would accommodate her bag. He gallantly picked up her suitcase and stowed it away.

She gave a relieved grin. "Thank you."

"You are very welcome."

Casey plopped into her seat with her backpack and complementary blanket in her lap. She pulled out a Laurell K. Hamilton novel and stuffed her backpack under the seat in front of her.

With her breathing back to normal, she clicked on her seatbelt and surveyed her fellow passengers. Half were engrossed in a book while the other half were covered by their navy blue blanket with neck pillows in position, ready for the overnight flight.

Casey leaned back and turned on the overhead light. There was no way she would be able to get any shut-eye. In ten hours she would be in London!

---

EXCITED AND EXHAUSTED, Casey found her way through the crowds to the passport control at London Heathrow Airport. Giddy, she pulled out her camera to commemorate the first time getting a stamp on her passport. She froze when she heard a stern, British accent yell, "Ma'am there are no photographs allowed."

She shoved the camera into her backpack and shuffled to the passport officer. The officer took her passport without expression. Casey studied the airport and grimaced at the numerous *no camera* signs. *Oops.* She'd blame it on the jet lag. Finally freed from the less-than-friendly Brit, she headed off toward the exit to catch the London Underground to her hotel.

She stepped through the archway with the universal sign for exit and was startled by the noise. There was a loud sea of excited people on either side of the walkway with *Welcome Home* signs and flowers anxiously awaiting loved ones. She strolled past, and a sadness washed over her as she was painfully aware of how alone she was. She knew it was silly to feel that way. Of course no one would be waiting for her. Why would there be? It was her solo part of the trip, and she was a young, independent woman on the adventure of a lifetime. It wasn't a pity party. She shrugged off the empty feeling inside and studied the airport map to find the entrance to the Tube. She needed to figure out how to get to her hotel. By herself. She didn't need anyone—certainly not Jason.

With a newfound sense of confidence, she purchased her ticket and followed the signs to the train. She hadn't realized how far underground the underground was until she lugged her suitcase down too many flights of stairs to count before she made it to the platform. Drenched in sweat she sat on her suitcase as she waited for her train. She watched the crowds of English people and wondered if they knew she was an American.

A train whooshed by before it made a full stop and an electronic voice announced, "Mind the gap," repeatedly until she entered the train and the doors shut. She clung to the overhead bar to steady herself, in an effort to prevent herself from crashing into the other passengers, on the way to Victoria Station.

As she exited the station, it dawned on her that what goes down must go up. She was happy to discover the escalator up instead of a staircase. She was tired and sweaty and just wanted a shower. Not to mention, she wasn't convinced she had the strength to carry her suitcase up umpteen flights of stairs.

She reached the open air and stepped out onto the sidewalk. She grinned as the wind struck her face and the scent of wet pavement filled her nostrils.

She pulled out the printout of the details for her hotel and reread the instructions from Victoria Station to her hotel. She glanced up and across the street and let out a faint laugh. In front of her stood a tall gray building with a red awning displaying the name of her hotel.

The online reviewers hadn't exaggerated—it was a great location. She marched across the crosswalk painted with white lines, zebra crossings as the locals called them, to the entrance to her home for the next two nights. A gentleman in a smart suit held the heavy glass door open for her. She thanked him and approached the check-in desk.

A blonde woman with wide eyes said, "Checking in?"

Casey nodded. "Yes, the reservation is under Casey Pepper."

The woman clicked at the keyboard. "Okay, I have it here. Says you'll be in a single for two nights."

The word *single* stung. "Yes, that's correct."

"Okay. The room isn't quite ready yet. It'll be a few hours. You're welcome to leave your luggage until it's available."

Casey knew check-in wasn't for several more hours but had hoped for a small miracle. She replied, "That would be great."

She checked her suitcase with the bellhop and found a bench in the lobby to plan out her day. She studied her guidebook, which didn't seem to have a section on sites to visit while exhausted and in desperate need of a shower.

The map showed several major sights within walking distance. Buckingham Palace, Westminster Abbey, and a dozen others a bit further or a short Tube ride. She decided to head out on foot to see the Palace and hopefully find a coffee shop along the way.

She made her way back out to the street and began walking toward the Palace when she happened upon a Starbucks. She was hoping for something a bit more British, but she would happily accept a little comfort from back home. She strolled in. The coffee shop was just as they were back home, with the exception of a few food items she'd never seen before. She ordered a double espresso and a pastry. She needed all the energy she could get.

She took a seat near the widow and chugged her espresso and nibbled on her croissant. She took out her travel journal and made a quick entry.

*Arrived in London. Tired. Dirty. Stopped at Starbucks for coffee and food. Love the crisp, cool weather.*

She people-watched until her energy waned and took it as a clue to keep moving so she didn't pass out on a bench somewhere. That was all she needed, to lose all her money and passport on her first day of the trip. Wouldn't that be a kick in the teeth?

She reinitiated her journey to the Palace. She knew she was near as the crowds thickened. She strolled with her gaze upward to see the concrete and gold statue and the massive gray building with an imposing black and gold fence surrounding it and two massive golden emblems on the gate guarded by two British soldiers.

She planted herself across the street from the main gate in front of the Victoria Memorial and soaked it in. She couldn't believe she was actually standing in front of Buckingham Palace. She'd seen it in movies and on the news, but there it was. Awestruck, she fought the tingling sensation in her sinuses she knew all too well usually led to tears. She didn't know what she was feeling, but it wasn't sadness. Was it pride that she had become successful enough to take herself on a European vacation? Or was it happiness to be somewhere new and exciting? Or was she just plain old exhausted? She sniffled and refocused. She raised her camera and snapped pictures from every angle before moving on to her next destination.

Exhilarated by the magnificence of the Palace, she decided to do a big sights day and see all the major monuments. She opted for the nearest Tube station instead of walking the wet streets in fear of passing out due to lack of sleep.

She took the train to Westminster Station and exited up the stairs, which were considerably easier to deal with when one didn't have to carry a packed suitcase. She stepped out of the stairwell and was struck by the most famous clock she'd ever seen. Big Ben. It was right there. She pulled out her camera and took a few photos of the tall, golden clock before finding a way to cross the busy street. As she searched she spotted the infamous red double-decker buses and black cabs she hadn't been sure still existed circling the roundabout. She spent the next hour walking outside the Parliament buildings and ended with a tour of Westminster Abbey before searching for something to eat along the River Thames.

Over a kebab and fries, she examined her photos on the tiny screen of her digital camera. She still couldn't believe she was actually in London. A world away from everything she knew.

She checked her watch, and under her breath said, "Thank you, universe." It was late enough to check into her room. She'd shower, take a nap, and then head out again for dinner and sightseeing at Piccadilly Circus. She hadn't realized one could be exhausted and excited at the same time.

AFTER TOWELING off in her tiny bathroom, smaller than her bedroom closet at home, she flung herself onto her twin-size bed and grinned. She thought, *What an awesome start to the trip, and it was only day one!* It was better than she'd imagined.

In fresh clothes, she organized her backpack for her evening out. She felt so alive. More alive than she'd felt in the last two years. She couldn't wait to see London at night.

She took the Tube to Piccadilly and was mesmerized by the lights. It was like a British Time's Square, not that she'd been to Time's Square in New York, but she'd seen it on television each New Year's Eve since she could remember. She continued to wander the streets taking pictures and people-watching. The hordes of people, big and small, young and old, all were having a merry time.

She didn't want to miss a thing, so for dinner, she ate a giant slice of cheese pizza while standing and soaking in the sights. She absorbed the energy of the city, and in that moment, she knew she was where she should be—seeing the world and experiencing different cultures. It just felt right. It felt like her life was heading in the exact right direction. She didn't know where she would end up, but in her gut, she knew she wouldn't be disappointed. She tossed her greasy napkin in the trash and continued her journey. By the end of the night she'd seen Trafalgar Square, played the slots at what seemed like an all-male casino, saw Harrods lit up, and took goofy photos with wax figures at Madame Tussauds.

Jet lagged, she tried to will herself to sleep in order to be well rested for the next day's tour of the Tower of London, Tower Bridge, and all the museums along the way.

Around two in the morning, she finally won the battle, and the next day was filled with more wonder and amazement. She found herself hating the fact she'd be leaving London the next morning. Well, as much as one could hate being less than twenty-four hours from seeing Paris for the first time.

# CHAPTER 25

## PARIS

Aboard the Eurostar, Casey sank into her seat and began reading up on all the things to see and do while in Paris. It had been a quick decision to do the whirlwind trip, and she hadn't spent a lot of time researching the ins and outs of the cities she planned to visit. She let go of the idea of a planned itinerary and went for impulsive instead. It worked well for her in London, although it had been a bit rushed. She decided it didn't matter, because she knew this would be the first of many trips. As she opened her guidebook to Paris, she vowed to the city of London to one day return and spend more time.

She thumbed through the pages of the book and realized she'd need to prioritize what she would see and when. There wouldn't be enough time to see all of Paris in the two and half days she'd planned. It would be a highlights tour. What were the main things she couldn't leave Paris without doing? Obviously she'd need to see the Eiffel Tower and the Mona Lisa at the Louvre. She'd need to taste all of the French pastries and baguette sand-wiches. What else must she do?

By the time she arrived, she had crafted a rough itinerary for her time in Paris. Off the Eurostar, she once again had to navigate her way to her hotel by way of public transportation. According to the hotel notes, she should take the Metro to the Chatelet stop on Rue de Rivoli. Focused, Casey trekked through the crowded station with an air of confidence and determination.

She climbed the stairs out of the Metro station and onto one of the most famous shopping streets in Paris, Rue de Rivoli. She consulted her map and notes and dragged her suitcase over the cobblestones down a narrow street, announcing her arrival to all those within earshot. She got sharp looks from locals offended by her noisy suitcase that kept catching on the uneven path. She passed a pastry shop with macarons and eclairs in the window. She took a mental note to return once situated in her hotel.

Fifteen minutes later, drenched with sweat and not feeling closer to her destination, she attempted to get directions from a woman wearing four-inch pumps. Casey had no idea how she didn't twist an ankle on the never-ending cobble stone. The woman nodded and pointed the opposite direction Casey had been heading. Casey eeked out, "Merci," and turned around to where she'd come from.

At last, she found the hidden alley to her hotel and opened the tiny glass door that seemed more appropriate for a small flower shop than a hotel. She was greeted with, "Bonjour. Checking in?"

Casey wondered how the woman immediately knew she was an American. She said, "Oui." In an attempt to use as much of that one year of high school French as possible.

She gave the woman her paperwork and was given a key with a huge fob that looked like a rubber mallet attached.

The woman explained, "Use the key to open, pack up, and then return to office. Front desk is closed at eleven. Must be back by then or you take key. To get to your room, you take the lift around corner to third floor. Yes."

Casey smiled. "Okay, great. Thank you—er—merci." Casey

accepted the key and found the elevator that was roughly the size of a telephone booth. She shimmied her and her suitcase into the musty smelling elevator and pressed three. The elevator jerked up and slowly ascended to the third floor.

Relieved to be out of the death box, she found her room straight ahead and unlocked the door. She was pleasantly surprised as she studied the spacious room with a desk, dresser, and full-size bed. Compared to her tiny London hotel room, it was a palace. She unpacked her suitcase, situated her backpack with essentials and set out to see the sights of Paris before dark.

Back on the streets of cobblestone, she was happy to find the pastry shop still open. She squeezed in through the door and said, "Bonjour," to the gray-haired woman behind the glass display of macaroons, cookies, eclairs, and chocolates.

Casey's eyes widened. "English?"

The woman shook her head. "Non."

Casey thought *no problem* as she studied the goodies in the display case. She pointed at the chocolate macaroons and said, "Deux, sil vous plais" and the next treat, "deux et...trois."

The woman gathered the sweets into a white paper bag and told Casey the amount owed. Casey was relieved she understood. She handed her a five-Euro bill, received her change, and said, "Merci" as she waved and left the narrow shop.

Nibbling on macaroons, she window-shopped and people-watched. There were high-end boutiques and galleries, tourist clusters staring at maps, and locals dressed as if going to a dinner party. She enjoyed her stroll but realized her itinerary was wrong. It was her first night in Paris, and she needed to see the Eiffel Tower. She turned back toward the Metro and its sign with black dripping letters with a yellow backdrop. It looked like it belonged outside a haunted house rather than a subway station. She accepted the deviation to her itinerary and boarded a train headed toward her next destination.

She stepped out of the station and was once again awestruck by a larger-than-life vision. There it was across the Seine River, the famed Eiffel Tower. She knelt down and angled her camera up and began snapping pictures. She stood up and marched across the Pont de Bir-Hakeim and strolled along the pea-soup colored river, taking closer shots of the imposing gray monument every few yards.

Dusk approached, and she picked up her pace to get a few final photos before she would start taking photos of the Tower all lit up. She reached the sprawling green in front of the tower. She watched as families began to pack up their picnics and the younger generations settled in.

She pulled an extra sweatshirt out of her backpack and smoothed it flat onto the ground. She sat with her neck arched up, staring. It was industrial yet beautiful. She regretted not packing a baguette—that would have been so French to sit outside the Eiffel Tower eating a baguette. She heard the pop of a champagne bottle and glanced to her left. A group of twenty somethings were celebrating who knows what. She surveyed the rest of the people in her vicinity, mostly coupled or grouped. A pang of loneliness shot through her. Why had she chosen to go to the romance capital of the world mid-divorce?

Night fell, and she took a few more photos of the Eiffel Tower emitting red, blue, and white lights. She exhaled and packed up her make-shift blanket and headed toward the shops for a baguette sandwich dinner on the go. She walked the streets for what seemed like hours before she gave up on her evening exploration and settled on the nearest Metro stop to take her back to her hotel.

Her alarm sounded at eight in the morning, Paris time. She shut it off with a push of her thumb. She sat up and studied her quaint Parisian room decorated with reds and golds. She jotted down a few notes in her travel journal and dressed for the day.

She strolled down Rue de Rivoli and stopped at a cafe with tables out front for espresso and chocolate croissants. She sat in the sun and people-watched while she sipped and ate. Finished, she nodded at the waiter and muttered, "Merci," and continued her journey down the street until she reached the Louvre.

She walked around the square admiring the dark gray baroque style building from the 12th century surrounding the modern glass pyramid entrance. She thought, *Interesting choice of entrances.* However, there was something about the old and new that she found striking. The building itself was a must-see attraction.

She stepped into the pyramid and took the escalator down to the museum that housed some of the world's most renowned art. She stood in line for twenty minutes and bought her ticket. The museum was larger than any other museum she'd ever visited. There were four floors and multiple exhibits. She now under-stood why her guidebook said you could easily spend a week in Paris, visiting the Louvre each day, and each day see something new. Casey had only planned an afternoon. She giggled to herself and thought, *This is the highlights-only tour.* She studied her map for top attractions and set out to see each one.

The first stop appeared to be major, based on the size of the crowd. At the top of the stairs, The Winged Victory of Samoth-race stood. Casey leaned against the staircase and studied the statue. Something inside her was pulled toward this headless woman at the top of the stairs, wings outstretched. It was beau-tiful and strong at the same time. She admired the goddess's ability to fly off to wherever she liked. The goddess was free and in charge of her own life. Nobody messed with her. The symbolism resonated deeply with Casey. She wanted to be like the goddess. Free and in charge of her life. She grinned and continued up the stairs to the next must-see.

There were mummies. Ancient Egyptian statues. The Mona

Lisa. Greek figures from tens of thousands of years ago. It was mind-bending.

Exhausted, she sat at the Louvre's cafe drinking espresso and eating eclairs, reviewing her pictures on her camera. She realized there was so much in this world she hadn't seen. So much she didn't even know existed. What other amazing things was she missing out on that she didn't know she was missing out on? She reflected on her feelings at the Eiffel Tower the night before. Had she and Jason stayed together, she would've never gone to Paris or London or anywhere. She would have lived in a bubble made of white picket fences filled with diapers and homemade baby food. Would she have been happy? She smirked and muttered under her breath, "Guess we'll never know."

Sugared up, she exited the museum and initiated her journey to the Arc de Triomphe. Along the way she saw fountains, gardens, and statues. All just out in the open. Hordes of people were out, also enjoying the sunshine and beautiful scenery. The crowd was so thick that when she got to the Champs Elysses she could barely get by on the sidewalk. Too often stuck behind a group of slow-walkers, she slowed her own pace down to a crawl.

When she reached the Arc de Triomphe, she took pictures from across the street. Content with her photos, she strolled along the other side of the street and was startled when she heard a, "Bonjour," directed at her.

She glanced to her right. Next to her was a man, probably thirty, wearing a backpack and casual attire. She said, "Bonjour." She wondered if he was a pick pocket. She thought, *Well, he's outta luck. Money belt, baby.*

He said, "American?" with a French accent.

"Yes."

"Oh, very nice. Are you enjoying Paris?"

Casey assumed he was a con artist of some sort. "Yes, it's lovely."

He said, casually. "You are visiting for pleasure—how you say, fun?"

She shifted her eyes around. There were plenty of witnesses if he tried to murder her. She said, "Yes. Fun."

He nodded. "Ah. Yes. I try to go to America for the job."

Casey thought maybe she was being a little paranoid. Maybe he was simply friendly or trying to date her. "Oh, what do you do for work?"

"I make the houses nice. How do you say? Decorate. No. The word? Ah?" He mimed frustration.

Casey arched her brows. "An interior decorator?"

"Ah yes. That's it. Interior decorator."

He didn't look like an interior decorator. He looked like a guy who lived on someone's couch. She picked up her pace.

She said, "That's cool." She opted to not initiate any further conversation for a few yards.

He said, "Okay. Enjoy Paris. Nice meeting you."

She said, "Bye." And he scurried off. She shook her head. He had to be pulling some kind of con, gave up, and went off to seek his next mark. She was sure of it, in her gut. The gut she needed to start listening to more often.

She stopped at a restaurant menu and studied it. She was soon greeted by a waiter with sharp features and a maroon apron around his waist. "Dinner?"

Casey still couldn't figure out how all of Paris knew she was a tourist from the United States. She responded. "Oui."

"Just one?"

She nodded. "Oui."

She was led into the large, dark dining room containing at least fifty tables with seating in deep burgundy. White candles flowed at each table. She was seated at a two-top and given a menu. Casey studied the menu and decided on the chicken and fries with red wine. She grinned as she realized she was taking herself out for a fancy dinner. She didn't need someone to take her out—she was an independent woman on an adventure.

She watched the dining room patrons all paired up or in groups. Some seemed to stare at her a bit longer than what was considered polite. Was it because she was alone or clearly an American? She shrugged it off and enjoyed her dinner. French fries in France. It was perfect.

The waiter cleared her plate and asked, "Dessert menu?"

She thought, *Heck yeah!* She responded, "Oui. Sil vous plait."

His face twisted. "I'll be back. You can just speak English."

It was a command. She had stumbled a bit when she'd tried ordering her meal en francais, but her guidebook said locals appreciated tourists trying to speak the language. At this point, she was pretty sure that wasn't true. He gave her a menu and stood as she read it. She grinned. "I'll have the dessert platter."

He cocked his head. "The platter?"

She continued the grin longer than natural. "Yes, the platter."

She leaned back in her chair and sipped her wine. She thought, *This is the life.*

The waiter returned with her dessert. She had to suppress a giggle. She now understood his questioning of her choice. It was clearly intended for at least two people. She didn't care. She ate every pastry, cake, chocolate, macaroon, and cookie.

---

THE NEXT MORNING she woke up extra early and packed up her suitcase and gave it to the front desk to hold for the day. She adjusted the straps on her backpack and set out for the walk to Notre Dame.

For the first time since she'd arrived in Paris, the streets were quiet and devoid of massive crowds. There were a few odd folks here and there, but the booksellers and artists hadn't set up their stalls, and she didn't see anyone begging for spare change. The path along the Seine River was empty.

She strolled along enjoying the wind in her face and the brisk air she could feel through her scarf and jacket. The gray of the city was breathtaking. It was as if everything was frozen and Casey was the only person on Earth. She realized she'd never felt or seen anything like it. There was no chatter or horns or yelling or fighting or doors slamming. She stopped and stared across the dark green river with all its concrete bridges like laces on a beautiful shoe. She steadied herself on the railing as it hit her. She finally understood what she was feeling. It was peace.

She spent the rest of the day wandering the interior of Notre Dame, marveling at art at the D'Orsay Museum, and frequenting cafes until it was time to go to the train station.

---

SHE SAT on a bench waiting to board her overnight train to Barcelona when a tall, lanky man wearing a baseball cap sat next to her. "Bonjour," he said.

She replied, "Bonjour," and clutched her backpack tighter.

In a thick French accent, he said, "Where to next?"

She thought, *Again with the English?*

She said, "Meeting family in Barcelona." Yes, someone would notice if she went missing.

"Very nice. You're from America?"

Obviously. "Yes."

"I wanted to go to America and work. I decorate houses."

She thought, *You've got to be kidding.* She smirked. "Oh, are you an interior decorator?"

He fidgeted. "Yes."

She was now fully convinced her gut was right once again. How could it be possible the only two men she'd talked to in Paris were both interior decorators? Not very likely.

She stared directly into his eyes. "Really? You're the second one I've met on this trip. Must be a popular profession here in Paris."

He ejected himself from the bench. "Oh yes, popular. Must go. Have nice time in Barcelona."

She grinned and waved. "Au revoir!"

She chuckled and said under her breath. "Note to self, listen to your gut from now on—no more second-guessing."

# CHAPTER 26

## BARCELONA

CASEY CLUNG to the door handle in the back seat as the cab driver navigated the streets of Barcelona as if they were an obstacle course. As they whipped past the Placa de Catalunya, Casey swiveled in her seat to catch a glimpse of the fountains before they sped off. She braced herself on the front seat as she was flung forward at the driver's sudden stop. The portly cabbie glanced over his shoulder. "We here."

Casey climbed out and stood on the curb as the driver pulled her suitcase from the trunk and set it next to her. She gave him his fare and said, "Gracias."

He nodded and hurdled himself back into the yellow and black cab.

She studied the printout for the hotel to verify it was the right hotel and marched through the glass entry into the modern lobby with beige sofas and silver fixtures. She approached a woman behind the desk and suddenly regretted the decision of never learning how to speak Spanish.

She grinned. "Hola. I'm checking in."

The petite woman with Disney princess features responded. "Hola. Name please."

Casey explained the reservation was actually under her mother's name, but she was the first to arrive. The trusting woman gave her a hotel key and instructions up to their room. Casey thanked her and took the elevator up to the eleventh floor. She found the room and slid in the electronic key that resembled a blank credit card.

She opened the door, and her mouth dropped open. Straight ahead was an executive style dining table, and across from it was a lounge area. She continued to the bedroom with a king-size bed and fluffy white linens. She turned around and went back through the living area to the biggest bathroom she'd ever seen. It had marble floors, a toilet, a bidet, a vanity with double sinks, a full-size shower, and a jetted tub atop a set of steps. She shook her head. There had to be a mistake. There was no way Agatha booked this room.

She placed her things down near the dining table and started leafing through the hotel guides and amenities list. She glanced to her left and realized there was a balcony too! She ran over to the sliding glass doors and pushed back the curtains. A view of the city. Now she really knew there was no way Agatha had booked the suite. It must cost a fortune.

She sat back down. There was no way she would unpack. She was sure that as soon as Agatha and the girls arrived they would straighten out the mix-up and they'd be moving rooms. She checked her watch. They weren't due to arrive for another forty-five minutes. She peered into the bathroom. A sly smile formed on her face.

She unzipped her suitcase, pulled out fresh clothes and her toiletry bag, and headed for the giant bath. With a tub full of steaming water, Casey dipped her big toe in. She grinned. "Ahh. Yeah." She fully immersed herself into the tub and turned on the jets. She inhaled the scent of the lemon-verbena-scented hotel soap and shut her eyes. She opened them and looked around. She thought, *Oh, I could definitely get used to this. Note to self, become successful enough to afford to go to fancy hotels all the time.* Her body relaxed, and she soaked until the water became lukewarm.

Fresh and clean from her tub time, Casey plopped down on the sofa and began to read the Barcelona guidebook she'd brought. Not long after, the entry door opened, and in came Agatha, Anna, and Cara with wrinkled clothes and messy hair. Agatha exclaimed, "Hola!"

Casey got up and hugged the family with a mix of "Holas" and "check out this room". The girls ran throughout the suite screeching each time they found something new and more luxurious than anything they'd ever seen before.

Casey asked Agatha. "Are you sure this is the right room?"

Agatha's eyes were still wide. "This is the room number they gave." She shrugged. "I would assume so."

From the balcony, Anna yelled, "Hey check this out—come out here!"

They all stepped out onto the balcony that was covered in terra-cotta tiles with a backdrop of the entire city. It was large enough for the four of them, with two lounge chairs and an end table. They posed for photos as they giggled over their good fortune.

Agatha pushed a loose curl behind her ear. "I'm going to take a shower to wash the airplane and cab off of me." She chuckled. "I'd rather take a nap. I'm so tired I could pass out!"

She faced the girls and pointed her finger at them. "But we can't go to sleep! We have to stay up to avoid jet lag. Okay?"

Anna and Cara nodded.

Cara said, "I'm too excited to sleep!"

Anna seconded the emotion.

Casey yelled out, "The tub is nice too—you should check it out!"

Agatha glanced over her shoulder. "I might just do that! I can't think of the last time I took a bath."

While Agatha enjoyed her bath, the girls and Casey started

laying their claims to beds and drawer space and figuring out the first stop on their tour of Barcelona. After Agatha's soak, Cara and Anna had insisted on taking baths too. It was almost like old times with the four of them and only one bathroom. Except for the fact their old bathroom was about a tenth of the size of their new luxury accommodation.

Several hours later, they were ready to hit the town.

THE FOUR STRUTTED down Las Ramblas refreshed and ready to bask in the Spanish culture. Cara's eyes widened. "Ooh look, Casey, it's a little dog dressed as a clown!"

She giggled as she veered off to get a closer look at the street performer and their black-and-white Jack Russel terrier. The group followed through the thick crowd but soon moved on to admire the outdoor flower shops and a living statue painted head to toe in gold paint. Trying not to get lost in the sea of people, Agatha warned them to all stay together.

Anna stopped. "Ooh, can we go in that shop? Look at all the cool stuff. Can we?"

Casey shrugged. She hadn't done much shopping in London and Paris, so she didn't mind perusing with her family. "Fine with me. Mom?"

Agatha pursed her lips. "Maybe for a little bit. There is so much to see other than shopping, though. Cathedrals and monuments." She stared out into the open as if imagining the sights.

Anna pleaded. "Please, for a little bit?"

Agatha agreed.

Anna nudged closer to Casey and said under her breath. "She's been talking non-stop about all the cathedrals like she wants to go to all of them. All."

Casey suppressed a laugh. "Oh, I'm sure she does."

Agatha was famous for trying to drag her children to church

not only on Sundays but other days of the week too. It was no surprise she'd want to visit some of the oldest and most famous cathedrals on their trip. Casey was relieved she'd only be there for three days. She'd already visited several churches on the trip and was nearing ancient-church overload. She was in highlights-only mode, not see-everything mode.

They traveled the length of the vibrant and overcrowded street until they hit the water where they took obligatory photos of the monument to Christopher Columbus. After a few wacky poses and a hearty dose of laughter, they slowed their pace to revel in the glorious sunshine and views of the glittering Mediterranean Sea.

Cara rubbed her stomach. "When are we going to eat? Isn't it almost dinner time?"

Agatha turned to Casey. "That girl is always hungry."

Cara smirked. "I'm a growing girl. I need fuel to be big and strong. Isn't that what you always said to us?"

"A smart aleck too!" Agatha retorted.

Anna said, "I'm getting hungry too."

Casey threw her hands in the air and in the worst Spanish accent said, "Tapas! Sangria! Want now!"

Cara grabbed Casey's arm and mimicked her. "Tapas! Want now!"

Agatha chuckled at her daughters' silliness. "Tapas it is! My guidebook recommends a place down Las Ramblas closer to our hotel. It's supposed to be muy bueno! What do you say?"

The three girls danced and cheered, "Tapas! Tapas! Tapas!" They linked arms and giggled as they strutted back down Las Ramblas.

They eventually found the upstairs restaurant through the use of Anna's limited high-school Spanish. They dined on tapas, and the older three imbibed fresh sangria while laughing and talking about the old days of living three to a room or lack of a home telephone forcing the girls to use a dirty old pay phone they'd claimed as their own. Cleaning and taking care of as if it were a sacred shrine. To two teenage girls and a toddler, it kind of was. Now here they were wining and dining in Barcelona. Who would've thought?

THE NEXT DAY they sought out the architecture of Antoni Gaudi. Agatha had convinced them the walk to Parc Guell wouldn't be too bad, no need for some overpriced taxi. After ninety minutes of getting lost and hiking the hilly streets with the sun beating down on them, they were thrilled to finally reach their destination.

Soaked with sweat, they approached the Casa del Guarda, which bore a strong resemblance to a whimsical gingerbread house, and entered the queue to purchase their tickets. Giddy to have arrived, they discussed their plan of attack for exploring the park.

Twenty minutes later, with tickets in hand, they ran for the center of the staircase to meet the famed dragon that was situated like it were climbing down the center of the stairs. His body was made of blue- and green-hued mosaic tiles with its mouth open in what looked like a permanent smile to greet visitors.

After group photos with the friendly dragon and a game of hide and seek in the dark and cool area below the esplanade with its tiled ceiling ornaments and columns, perfect for hiding, they made the final ascent to the top.

Casey looked out over the city to the Mediterranean and inhaled the fresh air. The girls buzzed around taking pictures and climbing on the benches to get better views. Casey opted to take a seat and relax for a bit. The breeze felt heavenly, and she preferred watching the excitement in Anna and Cara's eyes almost as much as the views of Barcelona.

Soon they joined her on each side, attempting self-portraits with both serious and funny poses. Agatha stood next to them with guidebook open and read, "In 1885, Gaudi's patron, the industrialist Eusebi Guell, acquired the terrain on a mountain ridge with a fantastic view of Barcelona. In 1890, Guell instructed Antoni Gaudi, the architect, to build a garden city, in which nature and equal housing should form a symbiosis. In addition to the Sagrada Familia, this was the largest project of Gaudi." Agatha lowered the book. "We're visiting Sagrada Familia too! Shall I read about that too?"

The girls exchanged glances and let out a soft giggle. Anna said, "Yes, definitely."

Agatha was completely unaware of her daughters' teasing and lack of interest in the history of the colorful and playful park. It was like they were sitting inside a Dr. Suess book with a history professor who thought she was in a classroom.

Ready to move on to the next adventure, Anna pleaded with Agatha to take a cab back to the hotel. "It's so far. My feet hurt."

Agatha shook her head. "It's not so bad. We'll take breaks. There's a perfect path past the Gaudi apartments and a few cathedrals I want to check out. It's all downhill, can you hang on a little longer?"

Anna rolled her blue eyes. "Downhill? I guess, if we take breaks."

They trudged to their next destination with Agatha as their unofficial walking tour guide. At the second church they stopped at, Cara complained. "Another church? Aren't we seeing the Sagrada whatever tomorrow?"

Agatha sighed. "La Sagrada Familia is completely different. It's a huge basilica they've been building for over a hundred years. One more church won't kill you."

Anna batted her eyelashes. "Maybe we can we go in that shop over there while you're in the church?"

"Fine. I'll meet you at the shops when I'm done. Casey, are you coming with me?"

Casey gritted her teeth. "I think I'll shop with the girls."

"Okay. See you later," Agatha huffed.

Casey understood her mother was annoyed, but really how many churches were they going to see? They were beginning to all look the same to her. Not to mention, she would be visiting The Vatican in just a few days. There was no way some little church on the way to the Gaudi apartments would compare.

The girls entered the souvenir shop and surveyed the soccer gear, T-shirts, jewelry, and all the other things nobody really needed. By the time Agatha joined them, they'd decided on a few trinkets and were ready to get back on the road.

By the time they'd seen the Gaudi apartments from across the street, eaten dinner, and made it back to their hotel room, they were bushed. Within minutes of hitting the pillows, they crashed.

FROM THE LIVING ROOM SOFA, Casey heard, "Come on girls! We didn't fly halfway across the world for you to sleep all day!"

Cara protested, "Just a few more minutes!"

Agatha yelled, "No! Up now or I'm never taking you on another trip ever again!"

Anna sassed back, "Fine. I'm getting up. Jeez. Don't have to get all crazy."

Agatha strutted into the living room. She shook her head at Casey. "Can you believe those two? We come all the way to Barcelona, and they want to sleep all day."

Casey shrugged. "Jet lag sucks." She was glad she was over her initial jet lag, otherwise she'd probably be yelled at too.

Anna dragged herself into the bathroom. Agatha called out, "No baths, we don't have time. You can take a shower."

Anna grimaced at her. "Seriously?"

"Seriously."

Anna declared, "Fine," and shut the bathroom door.

Agatha turned to Casey. "These kids! I need to make sure Cara is up. That girl will sleep all day if you let her."

A few minutes later, Cara walked into the living room and said, "Why is the bathroom door closed? How am I going to get ready?"

Agatha explained, "Anna is in there. You have to wait a minute."

Cara threw her arms in the air. "Then why did I have to get up! I can't even take a bath yet."

Agatha warned, "Don't take a tone with me!"

Cara grunted, "Whatever," and went back into the bedroom.

Agatha yelled back, "You better not go back to sleep!"

The bickering caused Casey to go to her happy place along the Seine River and the memory of peace washing over her. At that moment, she longed for Rome where she'd once again be by herself with no arguing and no drama and no being forced to go places she didn't want to go. Total freedom. Who knew solitary travel would be so freaking awesome?

An hour later, still at the hotel with Cara and Anna still primping, Agatha threw her hands into the air and said in a bad British accent, "I give up! We do not travel well together!"

Agatha's dramatic declaration caused the girls to break into laughter.

Cara imitated Agatha with arms up in a *V*. "I do declare, Anna, we do not travel well together!"

This was followed by hysterical laughter from both Cara and Anna.

Calmed down, Anna said. "Cara! We do not travel well together!"

Casey tried to stay out of the mother-daughter struggle by suppressing her grin as Agatha slammed the door to the bedroom.

She turned to her little sisters, attempting not to laugh. "You guys. She's gonna get really mad. You have to get ready, and fast. Okay?"

Cara gave an exaggerated, "Fine."

Anna responded, "Yes, sister darling." Followed by a giggle.

Casey adored her sisters, but she didn't adore their fighting among themselves and their mother. It caused her anxiety she didn't need or want. She told herself, *it's okay, just one more day and I'm off to Rome—alone.*

# CHAPTER 27

## ROME

FROM THE BACK seat of the stuffy Italian cab, Casey stared out the window, sunglasses protecting her from the bright sunlight, less-than-impressed by the scenery before her: brown flatland on one side and warehouses and old junkyards on the other. After the grandness of London, the beauty of Paris, and the whimsy of Barcelona, she hoped Rome wouldn't be a letdown. She thought, *The airport must be further from the heart of Rome than I had assumed.* Entering the town wasn't much better with its tall, gray wall and grimy streets. The cab stopped abruptly, and the driver said something in broken English about her hotel down a narrow street, straight ahead. She paid the man in Euros and shimmied herself and her luggage from the compact car.

She studied the cobblestone path and row of doors in front of her. She got a whiff of cigarette smoke before embarking on the journey to her hotel. The familiar loud clattering of her suitcase wheels over the uneven walkway rattled in her ears as the few passersby looked her way. She thought, *Yes, a young American woman traveling on her own—so interesting.* She stopped at the red door with the number *57* and three gold stars. She had arrived.

She completed a quick check-in before hurrying up to her room in the tiny elevator, which she now realized was the standard in Europe. She surveyed the room and nodded in approval at the twin-size bed on one side with a writing desk and wardrobe lined up on the adjacent wall. She could easily pirouette in the center of the room, unlike her room in London where she had to side-step to get from one end of the room to another, and according to the hotel's website, she was walking distance to all the major sites of Rome and Vatican City.

Anxious to get outside and explore, she lightened up her backpack, threw in a bottle of water, and headed out on foot to see the sights and get her hands on some of that world-famous gelato. Map in hand, she made a left onto the street with the ugly cement wall. She chuckled as she read the map. It was the wall that surrounded Vatican City, and here she'd thought it was bad city planning. She was wall thickness away from Vatican City. It was surreal.

She continued on to explore St. Peter's Square. As she approached, her mouth dropped open. St. Peter's Basilica loomed as a majestic baroque backdrop with an obelisk in the center. She stepped closer to take pictures. She glanced up and studied the statues atop the semi-circles of columns with wonder. She was standing where people stood to listen to the Pope. She wasn't terribly religious, but a spirit of unknown origin seemed to wash over her. It was as reassuring as it was alarming. She brushed it off and finished taking photos.

Satisfied she'd seen enough of the outside, she strolled off the square in search of gelato. A few shops down, she found a small store with a large case of gelato in a rainbow of colors and flavors. She grinned at the young, tan woman. She prayed she understood English and asked, "Can I try?"

She nodded and answered with a thick Italian accent. "Yes. Which one?"

Casey bent over and studied her choices. She loved mint chip, but Nutella was appealing too. She saw one labeled, *Bueno*, and she lit up. She had made herself quite familiar with the Bueno candy bars since arriving in Europe. She said, "Bueno, please."

The woman grabbed a small metal spoon from near the register and scooped the beige gelato with bits of candy bar on top. Casey took the spoon and slipped it in her mouth. Spoon in mouth, she moaned, "Mmm. I'll have a double of that."

She took the cup of deliciousness and exited the shop. She followed her map to the Tiber river and walked along the muddy, green river eating her gelato. The crowds were out, but she enjoyed watching the calm waters and the old buildings. There was something about a stroll along the water, crowds or not, that brought her peace.

She reflected on the past ten days of traveling. She loved the big-city feel of London. The energy made her feel renewed and like there was a whole world out there she was meant to discover. In Paris she felt at peace and comfortable in her not-so-new single status as well as the desire to be free and in charge of her life. Barcelona reminded her of how much she treasured being around her mom and sisters, but also how much she loved the freedom to do whatever she wanted without having to compromise on what to see, what to do, and what to eat. Now here in one of the most ancient cities in Europe, she felt childlike in her interest in doing nothing but see giant monuments, the freedom to skip museums if she wanted to, and her desire to eat gelato and candy all day. There was nobody to judge her. Total freedom.

She rechecked her map after she threw away her gelato cup and spoon. The Coliseum was a bit further than she'd calculated, but she continued on. By the time she arrived, she was once again covered in sweat, but she didn't even notice when the huge amphitheater came into sight.

She froze and stared at it like it were an alien from outer

space. She'd seen it a million times on TV and in movies, but to stand in front of the two-thousand-year-old structure that hosted kings and gladiators was unreal. She felt like she was standing in a history book. She stared at the looming, round, grayish-brown structure. One half was four stories tall with window-like archways all the way around, while the other half was only two stories with the same window-like archways. It was like a round birthday cake that had the top right quarter of it cut away. She walked around with her head up, trying to take it all in.

She began to think about all the places she'd never seen. In comparison to the last ten days, she'd lived her life in a tiny speck of the world. She was born, raised, and currently lived in the San Francisco Bay Area. She'd only been to a handful or two places outside of California. She stopped walking and shook her head. She thought, *I need to get out more. A lot more.*

With dark approaching, she found herself a small restaurant with outdoor seating for a ravioli and chianti dinner with views of the hustle and bustle of tourists and the ruins. She assumed she was paying a hefty tourist fee for her meal, but she didn't care. She could stay there all night absorbing the ancient vibes of the nearby Flavian Amphitheater and Roman Forum.

After ravioli, wine, and a gelato trio, a wave of sleepiness overcame Casey. She contemplated why she was beat at nine o'clock at night. Was it the miles and miles she walked today? Or was it having to navigate the chaotic airports and taxis of Barcelona and Rome? Either way, she opted to call it a night and take the Metro back to the comfort of her hotel room.

A zippy ten minutes later, Casey collapsed on her bed.

---

THE NEXT MORNING, she woke refreshed and ready to explore the interiors of all the great sights she'd surveyed the night before. She stopped at a nearby cafe for a chocolate croissant and double espresso before retracing the prior days steps. She reached St. Peter's Square and thought, *Yes, today is the day I shall stand in line.* She was glad she'd done the exterior walking tour the night before so that she could enjoy the views without using up her energy and patience standing in line.

She shuffled into the basilica and looked up and around. It was the most ornately decorated building she'd ever been in. The marble statues. The gold. The art. The colorful imagery—and that was just the ceilings! She was sure she'd have a crick in her neck by the end of her visit.

She continued along slowly with the ebbs and flows of the crowds. It was too much to take in. It was to churches what the Louvre was to museums. Overwhelming. She approached the chair of St. Peter. She thought, *A chair? Try more like the fanciest throne ever.* Above it was a beautiful round window with slats of yellow and amber with a dove in the middle, which the light from outside shone through. There was something about it that called to her. Sure, the rest of the church was amazing with works of the world's most famous artists, but for her, there was something about that window. Peace? Freedom? Hope? She stood and stared for some time before she consulted her guidebook on what it was. It was the dove of the Holy Spirit. She said, "hmm," and pulled out her camera and proceeded to take a dozen photos before moving on.

Back outside, she opted to Metro back to the Coliseum to spare her feet. At the Coliseum, she stood in line for her ticket with the rest of the crowd and then began exploring the massive amphitheater that once sat up to eighty thousand spectators.

With the countless stairs and climbing endeavors required to explore the dusty and cold structure, she was glad she'd decided on the Metro versus another four-mile walk along the river. She leaned on a railing on the lowest level and peered into the arena where the people would watch gladiator fights, executions, and dramatizations dating back to AD 80. It was so odd to think that nearly two thousand years ago, there was a person standing where she was watching a man fight a tiger. Crazy!

From the Coliseum she explored the ancient ruins at the Roman Forum and enjoyed a bit of espresso and gelato before further exploring the city on foot. It reminded her a bit of Paris with the baroque architecture, but with more castles, piazzas, and ancient ruins in every direction. It was nothing like her boring cab ride from the airport.

By nightfall, she had climbed the Spanish steps and studied the Pantheon while lounging at a cafe sipping espresso and eating cake. The finale of the evening would be gelato at Trevi fountain after a pizza dinner. She couldn't leave Italy without having pizza, right?

She approached the fountain surrounded by more crowds. She squeezed her way through to get a better look. She made her way to the front and realized how much easier it was to get through a crowd as a party of one. She glanced up at the massive monument with the sea god Oceanas center-stage and thought, *Now that's a fountain*. She snapped a few pictures and pushed her way back to the surrounding shops for her final gelato before flying home the next day.

---

CASEY SHOT up out of bed at the sound of her travel alarm clock. She thought, *Why oh why did I choose a seven a.m. flight? Oh right, it was cheaper than a later one.* She hopped out of bed and took a quick shower before packing up her suitcase for the last time. She entered the tiny, coffin-like elevator for her final ride. She checked out of the hotel and stepped out into the brisk air, instantly spotting the black cab with its engine running. She approached and let herself in.

She said, "To the airport."

The ruddy face with a thick mustache said, "Si. Aeroporto." He turned back around and increased the volume of his Italian music station.

Casey stared out the windows and said a mental goodbye to Rome and the wonder it filled her with. She chuckled under her breath when she suspected she would miss Europe more than she would ever miss Jason.

# CHAPTER 28

CASEY ENTERED the coffee shop and trudged up to the counter. "I'll have two double espressos."

The teenaged blonde asked, 'Two shots?"

Casey shook her head. "No. I want two separate dopio espressos—in different cups."

With a blank look, she said, "Okay."

Casey wondered how difficult it was to understand her order. Two double espressos. Two double wasn't like a double negative, it was two orders of double espressos. One for now, one for later.

She had to co-host Kat's bridal shower in under an hour and was working on three hours of sleep. She wasn't sure there was enough coffee in the world to help.

She took her two little paper cups from the counter. She removed the lid from one of them and chugged, followed by a swig from her water bottle. She tossed it in the trash and started the trek to Kat's sister's house.

She knocked on the large, oak door.

Kat's sister, Shelly, grinned. "Casey! You're here. Come on in." Casey wondered if it was a dig at her being twenty minutes late.

She entered the grand living room with floor-to-ceiling

windows looking out at the hills of Mt. Diablo. Casey wondered what it would take to become successful enough she could have that view every day? Her list of things she wanted from life continued to grow. Travel the world. Fancy hotels. House with a view. She thought, *Note to self. Talk to Eddie about career paths.* Her current salary most certainly did not align with her new life goals.

She followed Shelly, a tall, thin model-type with perfect teeth and wide blue eyes, into the kitchen, where she promptly gave Casey a list of her tasks and asked if she had any questions.

Casey said, "No, I think I've got it." She held up a white plastic bag. "Also, here are the decorations I picked up and the outfit for Kat."

She handed Kat's oldest sister the bag.

She smiled. "Cute! I love it." They'd agreed on a Hawaiian theme since that was where Kat and Glenn would be honey-mooning.

Casey began chopping chicken for the salad and asked, "What time is Kat getting in?"

Shelly was bent over, peering into the oven. She called out, "She should be here at eleven or so." Shelly placed a tray of chocolate cupcakes and a tray of vanilla cupcakes on the counter-top. "So tell me about your trip. You got back yesterday, right?"

Casey said, "Yep, last night. I'm a bit jet lagged." Casey went on to tell her about all she saw and what she loved most as they prepared brunch and a homemade boozy punch.

SHELLY PLAYED the perfect host to the arriving guests and relatives Casey didn't know. The only guests Casey actually knew would be Maddy and Kat's mom. She was setting out the props for the first bridal shower game when she heard a chirp of, "Hi! Wow! Everything looks amazing!" Casey glanced over her shoulder and was happy to see Maddy in a red and white hibiscus flower print dress. She put down Bridal Shower Bingo and ran up to her and gave her a hug. "Hi, Maddy!"

"Hey, girl! Good to see you. Wow, some digs, huh?"

Casey smirked. "No kidding, right?"

"What can I help with?"

"We've got everything pretty much covered. May I offer you some party punch?"

Maddy grinned. "Yes, please!"

They headed over to the punch bowl, got their libations, and introduced themselves to the newcomers, mostly childhood friends of Kat. They made small talk until the guest of honor arrived.

Shelly opened the front door in the entry, and Kat sauntered in with her hands waving above her head. "Hey everyone!"

The partygoers cheered. Casey approached with the grass skirt, coconut bra, and glittering tiara she'd purchased for her. She said, "For you, our island princess!" Casey bowed.

Kat pushed back her sandy blonde hair and giggled. "Why thank you! I love it, and you know, I don't think I have a coconut bra *in this color*."

The crowd broke into laughter as Casey helped Kat put her costume over her white tank top and black skinny jeans. Dressed in island princess perfection, Kat went on to greet all of her subjects.

After a round of silly games and plenty of boozy punch, the group gathered in the living room to watch Kat open her gifts. Casey sat perched next to Kat to record the gifts and who they were from for her thank-you cards. Maddy sat on the other side of Casey.

Shelly handed Kat a package wrapped in shiny, silver paper. "First gift, Miss Bride-To-Be."

Kat read the card and faced Casey. "This is from Shelly." Casey made the note. Kat untied the bow and tore back the paper. She slid off the lid of the box and proceeded to turn pink. She lifted the black lace bra and matching panties and giggled nervously. Maddy yelled, "Woo woo! Glenn will love those. Hubba hubba!"

Kat's cheeks went from pink to magenta. She eyed Shelly. "Thank you, darling sister. I'll, uh keep the other items in the box for now—but, I'll be sure to put them to good use."

Shelly smiled devilishly, "You're welcome." She handed Kat a gold gift bag with glitter hearts on the front.

Kat read the tag and grimaced playfully. "It's from Maddy. I'm almost afraid to open it!"

The crowd laughed.

Casey nudged Maddy.

Maddy giggled.

Kat pulled a red lace nightgown from the gift bag and held it up. Kat's cheeks matched the latest gift. "Thank you, Maddy!"

Maddy giggled some more. "You're welcome."

Casey watched Kat as she opened a set of knives followed by a plaque displaying her new last name and a poem about marriage. The cheesy gift reminded her of her own bridal shower. All of the gifts she'd received with her and Jason's name engraved or etched were in a box somewhere. She couldn't remember if she had them or if Jason had won those in the separation. She remembered scanning items with Jason for the gift registry in preparation for the shower. They'd picked out fine china and crystal wine glasses and discussed how they would have everyone over one day to use the newly acquired treasures. They'd never used the china or the wine glasses.

Maddy leaned toward Casey and whispered. "Hey, are you okay?"

Casey suspected Maddy could see the cheer drain from her as she took the trip down memory lane. "Yeah. It's just a little weird for me, but I'm okay."

"I can imagine all the wedding stuff must be a little hard. How's the divorce? Is that a weird thing to ask?"

Casey and Maddy paused to "ooh" and "ahh" over the latest gift.

Casey shrugged. "Every once in a while something trips me up, but I'm good. My time in Europe really opened up my eyes to a whole new world that I would've never seen if I were still married to Jason. I think a life without him is right for me. I don't think I was meant to be a stay-at-home perfect mom and wife. I think I was destined for adventure."

Maddy slid her arm around Casey and squeezed. "I think you were too. But if you ever need a pick-me-up, you've got my number."

Casey nodded. "Thank you. I'm going to be okay, even if I'm not quite 100 percent yet. I'm confident I will be one day."

Maddy winked at her. "I know you will."

They refocused their attention on the gift opening. When it was over, they said their goodbyes. Maddy and Casey exited together and made plans to share a hotel room in Seattle for the wedding. She was excited for the wedding and for visiting Seattle. She loved the city with its vibrant markets and eclectic shops. Now that she'd be rooming with Maddy, she knew there wasn't a chance for a single tear the entire weekend. Thank goodness for Maddy.

ON THE DRIVE from the shower to Jason's, she was a bit melancholy at the idea of leaving a bridal shower in order to go to her estranged husband's house to pick up their shared canine. She snapped out of it when her favorite fluffy ball of cheer greeted her. She knelt down. "Hi, Roxie! I missed you!" Roxie continued to jump and pant until Casey picked her up.

Jason said, "Come on in."

"Thanks." She entered and sat on the living room floor as she calmed Roxie down by throwing her toys. Roxie scampered off to retrieve them.

Jason sat on the sofa. "How was your trip?"

She glanced over at him. Part of her didn't want to share her experience with him, and part of her didn't care enough to make an excuse to not share it with him. Begrudgingly, she responded, "It was great."

"What were your favorite parts?"

Casey went on to tell him all her favorite places and how she couldn't wait to go back.

They discussed his future plans for a trip to Italy with his buddies and shared different tips and things that would be good to see. She knew she had to be cordial for the sake of Roxie. She'd accepted they would remain in each other's lives for the duration of Roxie's life.

Their conversation soon moved on to chit-chat when Jason asked, "How is work? Are you still enjoying it?"

"Yes, it's fine." How much of a conversation were they going to have? She forced herself to be polite. "How is school?"

"It's good. I'm on campus a lot more."

She nodded. "That's great."

"Yeah, it was about time. Hey, I just saw the new Star Wars. It was awesome. Have you seen it?"

She didn't understand why he wanted to continue the conversation. Did he seriously think they'd be friends? She didn't hate him, but it didn't mean they would all of the sudden become best buds. She was content with a friendly relationship, but friends was pushing it too far.

"No, I haven't."

"Oh, you have to. It's so great."

Before she knew it, fifteen minutes had gone by. It was like they were two buddies catching up. She'd felt that way before, but this time she didn't feel any animosity or anger toward him. It was more of an indifference.

She felt almost grateful that he'd ended their relationship that was, frankly, bad for both of them. Since they'd split six months ago, she'd gone on her first European vacation and was already contemplating where she'd go next and beginning to focus on her career. He was in therapy and going to school regularly with a graduation date on the horizon. They were both doing better apart than they ever were together. Had they been holding each other back all these years?

She said. "I should get going. The jet lag has hit me pretty hard."

"I bet."

She rubbed behind Roxie's ears. "You ready, girl?"

She picked up Roxie, gave her another squeeze, and waved as she exited the house. On the drive home, she didn't curse Jason, and she didn't cry. She just drove.

# SUMMER

# CHAPTER 29

THE MORNING of Kat's wedding, while still in bed, Casey chugged an entire bottle of water. She could hear Maddy and Kat snoring on the next bed over. Why had they thought it was a good idea to do a girl's night out? After all the champagne at the spa, they'd gotten it in their heads that after the rehearsal dinner they should have one last single lady dance party. The dance party turned into a tequila shots party. *You'd think we would've known better,* Casey thought.

Casey extended her arm to pick up the hotel phone and proceeded to mumble an order of coffee and breakfast from room service. She hung up the phone and rolled back over. The knock on the door shook her awake. Her heart raced as she slid out of bed to open the door in her pajamas.

She put her finger to her lips when the male room service attendant entered. He slid the cart to the side and handed her the bill to sign. She mouthed, "thank you," and he was gone. She poured herself some coffee and sat herself on the sofa near the window overlooking Seattle. She grinned when she spotted the Space Needle.

She glanced at her watch. Only three hours until the wedding.

She needed to wake up Kat to start getting ready. Kat was getting married! She jumped off the sofa and skipped over to a passed-out Kat. She said, in a loud whisper, "Hey Kat! You're getting married! You need to get up!"

Kat grumbled something indiscernible. Casey tugged at her arm. "Kat! Time to get up!"

Maddy rolled over, pulling the blanket over her head. Kat opened her amber-colored eyes. "Huh?"

Casey chuckled. "You're getting married today—must wake up. There's coffee!"

Kat pushed her straight bob out of her face. "Okay. I'll get up if there's coffee."

She shimmied out of bed and shuffled over to the cart with coffee. From there it was all systems go. Showers. Makeup. The dress. Kat's mom and sisters' arrival to provide moral support and take candid getting-ready photos.

All gowned up and glowing, Kat and the bridal party filled up the stretch SUV and headed for the country club.

---

BEFORE THEM LAY a lush green backdrop surrounded by tall pine trees and a red carpet with white wooden folding chairs on either side. Only Casey and Jonah, Kat, and Kat's father were left to walk down the aisle. Casey forced back the tear starting to form in the corner of her eye and turned to Kat. "This is it."

They hugged, and Kat whispered. "I love you." Casey managed to say, "I love you too," without succumbing to a full-on meltdown.

Casey gave a recurring nod to Kat and stepped toward Jonah, the best man and Glenn's brother.

He said, "You ready?"

With a lump in her throat, she eeked out, "Let's do this."

They strolled down the aisle with nervous smiles as the

photographer and guests snapped photos. Casey took her place next to Shelly and watched as Kat linked arms with her father, and an ever-widening grin spread across her face as she drew closer to Glenn. Casey marveled at the normalcy of it all. Beautiful scenery. A father giving away his daughter. A happy young couple. There was nothing but the air of joy and hope all around.

As she stood next to Kat exchanging her vows with Glenn, Casey made the observation that Kat and Glenn's wedding day was nothing like her wedding day to Jason. For Casey, the wound of his betrayal and subsequent lack of emotion afterward had been too fresh. The only time she and Jason spent time together on their wedding day was for photos and the first dance. The rest of the time Casey latched on to her friends and family. A happy bride she was not. Knowing that Kat's day was nothing like hers, Casey was delighted for her best friend and her new partner.

At the reception, Casey sat with Maddy and a few of the younger folks drinking, eating, and laughing. They paused as the bride and groom took to the dance floor for the first dance, followed by the father-daughter dance to Louis Armstrong's *A Wonderful World*. Casey and Maddy linked arms on the sidelines swaying as they soaked in the sight.

At the end of the song, the music changed to a dance beat. Maddy and Casey strutted toward the dance floor, grabbed Kat, and got their groove on. The dance floor was packed, and the women went crazy as the DJ played *Girls Just Want to Have Fun* by Cyndi Lauper.

After the song, the DJ stopped the music and said, "Okay, ladies, now that we've got your attention." He paused for the laughter that ensued. "It's the time of the day where Kat will toss the bouquet to the next lucky lady to walk down the aisle!"

The event coordinator handed Kat a tossing bouquet made of five white roses tied with a red ribbon and situated her and the single women. Three dramatic drum rolls later, Kat threw the bouquet into the air so high it nearly hit the ceiling. It came down onto the center of the dance floor with a loud, thump. The crowd of women stood back and stared at the bouquet. Casey glanced around at her fellow singles and thought, *Huh. Nobody else wants to get married, either.* The bouquet remained on the floor. The women began exchanging nervous glances. Casey thought, *Was this one of her maid-of-honor duties too?* She shook her head and stepped forward, straight-faced, and picked it up. Maddy grabbed her arm as she almost fell onto the floor laughing. Between fits of laughter Maddy said, "Thanks for taking one for the team!" The group laughed as Casey made her way to Kat and Glenn for photos.

Casey realized now that she was single, she was sort of normal. It was normal for a twenty- five-year old to be single and free, traveling the world, and not wanting to be married. She liked the idea of being a little bit normal. She wasn't sure she was capable of being totally conventional, considering she'd soon be a twenty-six-year old divorcee with shared custody of a Shih Tzu, but a little bit normal was kind of nice. Comforting.

# FALL

CHAPTER 30

A FEW MONTHS LATER, a muffled knock on her cubicle wall caused Casey to swivel around in her desk chair. "Hey, Javi, Seth."

Javier bent over for a quick hug. "Hi." He moved back near Seth. "We just heard about your promotion and wanted to say congratulations! You're such a rock star!"

Seth grinned shyly. "Yeah, uh, congratulations."

Casey smiled. "Thank you. I'm excited about a new challenge and to be on the new project team."

Seth crossed his arms across his chest. "Yeah, I'm on the project, so we'll be working together. "

Casey could feel her cheeks warm. "Cool. Looking forward to it." Casey thought, *Hmm, a promotion with a side of eye-candy. Not too shabby.*

"Are you going to the Town Hall meeting? We figured we could walk over together."

She said, "Yep, I need to send off this email, but then I'll be ready to go. Give me a second." Casey refocused on her computer and tapped out the last few words of a sentence, did a quick proof read, and hit send. "Done!"

She ejected herself from the chair, and the three of them strolled out of the office toward the main building.

Javier said, "So, honey, what else is going on? It's Friday. Any big plans this weekend?"

Casey said, "I'm having a single ladies party at my apartment this weekend!"

Javier said, "I'm so jeal. I wanna go."

"Uh, last time I checked you aren't a single lady. Am I right?"

Javier pouted. "I guess. How's little Roxie?"

Casey frowned, "She's good. I picked her up from Jason last night. She's at home all by herself. It's her least favorite day, I think."

"Still sharing custody?"

Casey scrunched up her face. "Still? It's been less than a year."

Seth stopped walking and faced them. "Wait, are you talking about a human? Or a dog?"

Casey said, "A dog. Roxie."

Seth was new to the company, but she'd assumed Javier would've filled him in. Him and Javier were practically joined at the hip working on a new analytical purification joint project.

Seth cocked his head. "So, you're sharing custody of your dog with your ex?"

Casey replied. "Yep."

His blue eyes widened. "I mean, I share custody of my human son, Riley. I've never heard of joint custody of a dog!" He chuckled. His eyes twinkled as he laughed.

Casey shrugged. "I suppose it's a little unconventional. It works for us." She was beginning to get used to people's surprised and somewhat amused reactions to finding out about their arrangement with Roxie. She had to admit it was a little crazy.

Javier ushered them to keep walking on the cement path between the two large buildings. "I still think he's just trying to keep in contact with you."

Casey said, "I still seriously doubt that!"

Although, ever since her trip to Europe, they had been on pretty friendly terms. It was as if they'd never been married and now were getting divorced. Maybe he really did want to stay friends and knew her well enough that if they didn't share Roxie he'd never see or hear from her again? Is that why he'd stayed with her all of those years—because of how much he valued their friendship? She shimmied off the thought. At this point it was too weird to even think about.

She had already been fretting her reaction to the final divorce papers that would be arriving at her apartment any day. She'd been doing so well, even when their anniversary passed in June, she'd shrugged it off. She understood now that the day had no meaning since it had all been a lie. Now she and Roxie had a good routine going, and she was seeing a lot of her friends and her little sisters. She'd even started planning her next trip with Rachel. She just got promoted. Everything was going well. She didn't want some stupid papers sending her into a fetal position clutching onto a pint of ice cream. Maybe she'd shake them off, too? Fingers crossed.

---

LATER THAT DAY, she entered Eddie's office and sat in the chair across from his desk. Eddie rushed in and said in his thick Mandarin accent, "Sorry. Sorry. Running so late today!"

"Not a problem." Casey had liked Eddie from the first time she met him during her interview all those years ago. He had a positive attitude and always encouraged her initiative, and when she wasn't feeling optimistic, he'd build her back up. Overall, a great boss.

He sat and gave her a warm smile. "Having a good day?"

She nodded.

"Have you had lots of congratulations since I sent the announcement?"

"Yeah, quite a few actually. I'm excited to start on the new project."

Eddie chuckled. "Good, good. Any questions or concerns?"

"Not yet. I'm sure once I get in there I'll have a million. I'm ready to learn!"

Eddie chuckled again. "So enthusiastic. That's good. I think being on a project team will be good for you. I think you'd make a great project manager." He focused on his computer, typed something and swiveled the monitor toward her.

"See her? She's the associate director of project management. You're way smarter than she is! That could be you!" His dark oval eyes twinkled as he grinned.

Casey wasn't sure how to interpret his declaration. She was a scientist, not a project manager. She said, "Oh."

He continued. "Your career opportunities are endless with project management! And you've run projects—like the Amino Acid Assay team you led with interns. And the new ELISA development team you led. And the Process Analytical Technology initiative you took on for the whole company! You'd be running up the career ladder in that field. They wouldn't be able to catch you. You'd just go straight to the top!"

Casey giggled at his colorful explanation, but now she understood. For a scientist without a PhD, the career ladder was limited, and since their last conversation about goals and career paths, he knew she was ambitious.

Sensing she wasn't fully convinced, he said, "I have something I think you'll like."

He scooted toward his bookshelf and pulled out a book. He handed her a thick hardcover book with an old white guy on the cover. Casey accepted it graciously. "Thank you." She stood up and waved as she exited, *Winning* by Jack Welch clutched to her chest.

SATURDAY NIGHT, Casey opened her front door and exclaimed, "Come on in."

Maddy pulled back after their hug. "Hey, did you get some sun?"

Casey nodded. "I went to the pool and decided to read a book while lounging. It was fabulous, but I lost track of time, hence the sunburn."

"Must be a good book?"

"Yeah, I totally got into it—" Before she could close the door behind Maddy, Rachel approached. Casey said, "Oh hey! Come on in."

"Hey girl!"

Casey ushered them both in. "Rachel this is Maddy—Maddy, Rachel."

They exchanged pleasantries while Casey poured the wine. A few minutes later, another knock sounded, and Gina and Natalie arrived with more wine and a tray of brownies. Maddy led the introductions as Casey set out cheese and crackers.

Seated around her dining table, Roxie in Casey's lap, they drank and laughed.

Maddy said, "I'm curious what you've made for dinner."

Casey giggled. "No fear. I've made one of Roxie's favorites. Chicken tenders and rice with broccoli." She gazed down at Roxie. "You like it, right, girl?"

Gina's mouth dropped open. "We're eating dog food?"

Casey laughed. "Yep! Dog food for dinner!"

Maddy said, "Don't worry, Casey, you know we're not friends with you for your culinary skills." She giggled.

"Nice segue. Who is ready for a dog-food dinner?"

Rachel said, "Me!"

Gina shook her head and said, "I guess, I'm ready for dog food," followed by laughter.

Natalie chimed, "Yes, please! I love dog food!"

Maddy said, "Let's eat!"

They all laughed as Casey got up to serve her friends. Over their chicken and rice dinner, Casey asked. "Rachel, what's new with you? Are you so excited about our trip to the south of France, or what?"

Rachel nodded. "Totally. I'm bummed it's still three months away!"

"Me too." They discussed details and got tips from Gina, Maddy, and Natalie, all of whom had visited Nice, Monaco, and Cannes. Casey was a little in awe of how much they'd already traveled, and they were younger than she was! She needed to catch up.

Gina said, "The guys in Nice are so hot!"

Rachel pursed her lips. "Good to know. We'll have to keep an eye out for some French cuties, right, Casey?"

Casey shook her head. "No, thank you! French and cute, or not. I'm officially on break from men. All men! Rachel, more French studs for you!"

Maddy asked, "Seriously? Why?"

"I want to dedicate my energy to my new life goals. Travel, career, and figuring out what to do with my life. Maybe go to business school."

Natalie nodded. "I think you'd love business school. I do! I think it's a great plan, Casey."

Casey tipped her head to Natalie. "Thank you."

Maddy scrunched up her face. "I don't know. I think you can do that and play a little, right?"

Casey shook her head. "I think men are too much of a distraction."

Natalie agreed. "Totally."

Gina retorted, "Coming from someone with a live-in boyfriend!"

Natalie finished her wine. "Yeah, yeah. Peter and I have been together so long now he doesn't count as a distraction. But a new relationship, those are time-suckers."

Gina shrugged. "I hate to admit it, but I think Nat's right. The whole get-to-know you stage takes up a lot of energy."

Casey surveyed her gal pals. "Who wants brownies?"

"I do!"

"Me too!"

"Me three!"

Casey brought back the tray of brownies from the kitchen and an unopened bottle of wine. The women continued on until nearly midnight. A little buzzed and a lot happy, Casey went to sleep with a smile on her face.

<hr />

MONDAY MORNING, she knocked on Eddie's open door. He glanced up and waved her in. She said, "I wanted to return this to you."

Eddie's normal jovial face fell flat. "You didn't like it?"

Casey grinned. "I loved it! I couldn't put it down. I finished it last night!" She'd spent all of Sunday snuggled next to Roxie on the couch reading. It resonated deeply within her. By the time she'd gone to sleep on Sunday, she had decided she wanted to be the next Jack Welch—except young and female without all the golfing. More like a Jackie Welch. She visualized it all. She'd be a titan of industry. CEO. She wouldn't stop until she got to the top.

Eddie broke into full-blown laughter. "Oh. Good. I thought you'd like it."

"I should go, I've got a meeting. Thank you again for lending it to me."

Eddie smiled. "No problem. I'm really glad you enjoyed it."

She waved and exited. She was excited about her future, which was still a bit fuzzy, but hopeful. She knew wherever it led her it, it would be great.

As she walked to the conference room, she shuddered at the memory of her once telling a coworker that her retirement plan was her husband. She wished she could go back and smack twenty-two-year-old Casey right across the face. Why had she ever thought relying on Jason, for anything, was a good idea?

# CHAPTER 31

A FEW WEEKS LATER, Casey approached her front door and paused at the sight of the large white envelope on her welcome mat. She held her breath before kneeling down, picking it up, and tucking it under her arm. She unlocked the door and rushed inside. She threw her bag onto the floor and plopped herself down on the couch. She carefully tore along the top and pulled out the packet of papers. She stared at the first page. It was official. She was twenty-six and divorced. She didn't cry or yell at an empty apartment. She sat, numb, while studying each page. She let out a bit of a laugh in the shared assets section describing joint ownership of "one canine, Shih Tzu, named Roxie." Well, if nothing else, they probably had one of the most unique sets of divorce papers out there.

She was perturbed she didn't feel more or anything, really. She was simply numb. She had been married. She was now divorced. At one time she'd thought it was impossible to ever stop loving Jason. She'd said she loved him and that she always would. At the time, she'd meant it and believed it.

A few years later and she didn't even have any emotion toward their divorce papers? Was love something that faded? Or died? Could someone hurt you so much you stopped loving them? Had she ever really loved Jason? Casey shook her head, hoping the thoughts would dribble out her ears. It was too grim to contemplate.

She walked into her bedroom and tucked the envelope in a box at the back of her closet. She glanced over at Kelly's wedding dress and thought, *Thank goodness the wedding is almost here, so I don't have to keep seeing that every day!* It was as if the dress had moved on from haunting her to taunting her. She imagined the folds of the skirt becoming a mouth and teasing her, "Haha. You're a twenty-six-year-old divorcee with a giant wedding dress in your closet. Na na na na." She said aloud, "Stupid dress," and exited her bedroom.

She didn't feel sad, but she didn't feel great either. She felt kind of icky. The occasion definitely warranted Mint Chocolate Cookie ice cream. She picked up her keys and purse and set out to procure her first pint of Ben and Jerry's as an officially divorced woman.

---

LATER THAT WEEK, she met Jason in the car-park of their shared gym to do the Roxie hand-off. She parked and waited until he arrived. She heard an engine pull up next to her and glanced over her shoulder. She hopped out of her car to grab a wiggling Roxie from his arms. She glanced at Jason. "Hey." She gazed back down to Roxie. "Hi, girl! I missed you!"

Jason said, "How are you?"

"I'm doing well, actually." She smirked. "Got the papers."

Jason nodded. "Yeah, me too. It was kind of a downer."

Casey thought, *Yep, the fact we wasted five years of our lives on each other is a bit of a downer.* She replied, "Yeah. How are things otherwise?"

He said, "Oh, before I forget, I need to give you a check for

Roxie's last vet bill. Hold on." He opened his car door and pulled his checkbook from the glove box and used the car window as a writing surface. He glanced back at her and said with a tinge of irritation in his voice, "Still Pepper?"

Still Pepper? She hadn't even started thinking about changing her name. Probably because she knew it would be a major hassle due to the fact she hadn't planned to go back to using her hyphenated maiden name. Taking Jason's last name was one of the few perks to being married to him. She said, "Yep."

He finished writing out the check and handed it to her.

She said, "Thanks. So all is good with you?"

"Yeah. I actually just ordered my cap and gown for the spring commencement. It makes graduation seem so real."

Casey's eyes widened. "That's amazing! You must be so excited." She suppressed laughter as she realized when he was done with his PhD program he'd be referred to as Dr. Pepper. And he wanted her to change her name? He ought to worry less about her and seriously consider changing his own name.

"Yeah, after all this time, finally about to graduate. I mean, it's a ways off, but I'm confident I'll be finally removing the student status from my resume." He chuckled, nervously.

She said, "That's great."

"How about you, what's new?"

Casey gave a lopsided grin. "Kelly's wedding is coming up so I'm pretty swamped with finalizing bridal showers, bachelorette spa day, and of course getting ready for the actual wedding. It's so much work!"

Jason nodded. "Boy, you've had all the weddings this year."

"Tell me about it. But at least after this one I'll be done for a while, and then Rachel and I will be off to the south of France for a fabulous vacation."

"That's right. I'm jealous. I have to focus on my dissertation. No vacations for me."

She said, "I'm sure it will go by fast. Well, Roxie and I ought to go before she jumps out of my arms. Have a good weekend." She wondered if he was expecting sympathy that although his whole life had basically been a vacation, he wouldn't be able to travel over the next eight months?

He started walking back toward his driver's side, "You too."

Casey plopped Roxie in her carrier and buckled up. She peered over at her and said, "I did almost forget, Roxie. I still haven't changed my name. What should I change it to?" Roxie stared at Casey with her big brown eyes.

"You're not sure either. We'll think about it, okay?"

Roxie cocked her head to the side.

Casey gave her a scratch behind the ears. "Thanks for the help, girl."

She drove off irked by the "Still Pepper?" comment. It was so petty of him to ask her to change her name in the first place, and now she was moving too slow for him? She'd change her name when she was good and ready. She took a deep breath in and told herself to let it go. He wasn't worth her energy. She laughed bitterly as she heard her favorite song, Pink's *Just Like A Pill*, start to play on the radio. She thought, *So fitting for the occasion.* She cranked it up and sang along at the top of her lungs.

SATURDAY NIGHT at Dana and Jerry's, Casey and Roxie seated themselves across from Javier and Ben as Jerry mixed Cosmopolitans and Dana prepared appetizers.

Casey asked, "How have you two been? And little Peanut?"

Ben gave a warm smile. "Peanut is wonderfully feisty but is such a joy. We're good. We just decided to go to Aruba for our anniversary!"

Casey nodded. "Sounds awesome!"

Ben asked, "How about you? Dating anyone new or ..."

Casey said. "Oh, no. No dating. I just received our final

divorce papers, so I'm officially single, but I'm not ready for dating. Next thing for me is to figure out a new last name." She went on to explain the request from Jason and her obvious disdain.

Javier took the cosmo from Jerry and took a sip. "Ooh. That's good." He gazed intently at Casey. "You know what you should do? You should change your name to Jason. That'll teach'm to tell you to change your name!" The table broke into laughter.

Casey said, "I totally should!"

Dana set down the platter of meats and cheeses and took a seat next to Casey. Jerry brought a few more cosmos for the rest of them and sat next to Javier.

He grinned. "What did we miss?" Casey explained the silly recommendation.

Jerry asked, "Why not just go back to your maiden name?" Casey supposed it was a legitimate question, if you didn't know her life history, which most people didn't.

Casey shook her head. "Ugh. Lots of drama associated with it, and it's hyphenated—kind of. Long story short: Since birth I've had five different last name variations due to marriages and divorces—my mom's, now mine. I want a new name that is mine alone. It will be my forever last name, so I must choose wisely. Any suggestions?"

Javier said, "What's your middle name?"

Casey grimaced. "It's Leslie."

Javier tapped his finger to his chin. "You could use your middle name as your last name. Casey Leslie. I think it sounds bold." He paused. "And if you think about it, it's always been your name so it's not some random name you made up."

Casey contemplated his suggestion. Casey Leslie had always been her name and would always be her name. She kind of liked that aspect of it. "Hmm. But then I wouldn't have a middle name. I'd have to come up with something good."

Javier and Ben nodded. "Definitely."

Casey turned to Dana. "So, what's new with you? It's been ages since I've seen you. How are things at the not-so-new-now company?"

Dana said. "It's good. I like it. It's a little crazy, but it keeps me on my toes. How's my replacement doing, Javier?"

Javier glanced at Casey. "He's fitting in well. He's smart and really easygoing." Javier wiggled his brows at Casey. "What do you think of Seth?" He overemphasized the "you."

She turned pink, and it wasn't just from the cosmos. "He seems nice. I haven't worked with him much, but I will be soon on the new project."

Javier teased. "Oh, nice. He seems nice. Nice-looking." He chuckled.

"Yeah, yeah. He's an attractive man, but like I've said, I'm not ready to date. Plus he has a kid, and I'm not sure how I feel about that."

Ben smacked Javier in the arm. "Leave her alone."

Casey was thankful for Ben and the change in topic. She and Roxie enjoyed a home-cooked meal that wasn't chicken and rice and the company that kept her sides aching all night from laughter.

On the drive home, she thought about changing her last name to Leslie. The more she thought about it, the more she liked it. She'd let it marinate for a few days before making a decision, but she was pretty sure it was the right name for her. Now to choose a middle name. She'd want something with pizzazz. With moxie. Like Roxie. She'd love to be more like the pooch: fearless, determined, loyal, loving, and fun to be around. She pulled into her carpark and thought, *Hmm. What if I changed my middle name to Roxie?*

# WINTER

# CHAPTER 32

TWO MONTHS LATER, Casey stood in line at the buffet in Kelly's living room with swirling thoughts of the last two weeks overloading her brain. The cheap polyester dress scratched her skin. She couldn't wait for the day to be over.

Her role as maid-of-honor had expanded over the last few weeks. She hadn't realized it would be her duty to call all of Kelly's friends and relatives to inform them the wedding had been canceled. And of course, she'd received a million questions from the dis-invited guests wanting to know all the dirt. She politely said, "I'm sorry. I don't know all the details. Take care." The truth was she did know all the details. Too many details. Who would've thought that a couple who became a couple when one of them was still married to someone else, would find themselves having family drama as the wedding neared? Hmm. Drama ensued and resulted in Kelly's dream wedding being canceled.

Of course, after all the reservations were canceled, the wedding was back on, which expanded Casey's maid-of-honor role to include emergency backyard wedding planner, wedding officiant, and wedding-cake procurer.

She shook her head. She could not wait to get on that airplane to France.

Her paper plate full of Mexican food, she found a seat at a table of relatives. She gave her best smile and said, "hi."

Her aunt said, "Great job with the ceremony. It was lovely."

"Thanks."

She scarfed down her food to avoid the awkward silences. Through her shoveling, her aunt asked, "So how are you doing with everything?"

She glanced back up at her aunt. "I'm great."

"Divorce final yet?"

"Yep."

"At least you're not alone. Your uncle Max is also going through a divorce."

Like she ever saw or spoke with her uncle. How was that comforting? Was she pointing out she wasn't the only divorcee in the crowd? She knew for a fact every blood member of her family had been divorced.

She replied, "Oh yeah. My mom told me. That's too bad."

She wished she could get out of there, but her duties also included cleanup crew. Therefore she'd have to suffer until the last guest left. She hurried up with the food since she still hadn't gone around with the video camera capturing everyone's well wishes for the bride and groom. She chewed the last bite and said, "Good talking to you. I've got to get back to my duties." She waved as she hurried into the house to get the camera. Camera in hand, she began approaching guests. "Hi! We're making a video for the bride and groom. Do you have something you'd like to say?" By the twentieth guest, her enthusiasm drained.

She approached her grandfather. "Hi, Grandpa. Anything you'd like to say to the bride and groom."

He chuckled. "Congratulations, Kel. Hope you don't get divorced—like some people." He smirked at Casey.

Casey stared in disbelief before she grimaced. "Thanks." She scurried over to Anna. "Hey Anna, can you take over? I need a break. I was almost done. Just need to do those two tables over there."

"Sure."

"Thanks."

Casey walked as slowly as she could back to the house, pretending to be unaffected by her grandfather's cruel remark. Wasn't family supposed to support you when you were down? Thank goodness she had a non-blood-related family and a few blood-related family members that weren't totally judgmental. What would she do without Roxie, Anna, Cara, Mom, Dana, Jerry, Kat, Maddy, Rachel, Javier, Ben, Gina, and Natalie? And all her other friends who did nothing but provide her encouragement and support since her separation and subsequent divorce. Now here was her family who hadn't reached out to her once over the last year, judging her? When they themselves were divorcees too?

After her quiet rage session in the bathroom, she found a quiet spot in the house to relax and eat cookies. She was soon surrounded by Anna, Cara, and Sam.

"Hey, Sam, how have you been?" She hadn't seen her brother since Sam Junior's birthday the year before. It made her a little sad that she only saw her brother one or two times a year and sometimes not even that often. With the arrival of Sam Junior, Sam had started coming around the family more, but when he and Junior's mother split up, Sam had retreated once again.

"Good." He pulled out pictures of Junior and displayed them proudly.

Anna cooed. "He's sooo cute."

Cara and Casey agreed.

Sam said, "What's up with you, Casey? I hear you've changed your name? You're now Casey poodle chihuahua Leslie." He belted out laughter.

Casey unamused said. "Ha. Ha. Yes, I just filed with the courts. My new legal name is Casey Roxie Leslie."

Sam laughed so hard she doubted he heard her. She thought, *Note to self. If I need love and support, avoid all family members.*

Cara grinned. "I love your new name!"

Anna smiled. "Me too."

Casey thought, *Maybe not avoid ALL family members—just most of them.* She brushed off her brother's special brand of humor and avoided anything other than small talk the rest of the afternoon.

She arrived home to a spirited Roxie. She had a crazed look in her eye and was jumping non-stop. She had not been pleased to be left home all day. Casey took her out on a walk and fed her before curling up on the couch and watching reruns of the Golden Girls.

THE NEXT WEEK, she knocked on Jason's front door. He opened with a tight smile. "Hey. Thanks for dropping her off. I'm swamped right now."

"Sure, no problem." She set Roxie down and she hopped into the living room to retrieve a toy from her bin.

He asked, "Excited about your trip?"

Casey nodded. "Yes. I am definitely ready for a vacation."

"You leave tomorrow, right?"

"Yep. I probably ought to finish packing." She chuckled.

It had been difficult to pack with Roxie around, seeing as every time she tried to pack, Roxie either stole her clothes and dragged them into the other room or tried to hop into the suitcase.

Jason leaned against the wall. "Oh, um. I've been talking to my parents. I've decided to give them my half of Roxie once I gradu-ate, since I'll be working and won't be home anymore. They're both retired now so Roxie will have lots of company during the day. And you know how much they love her."

Casey tried to process what he said. He was giving up his half of Roxie to his parents? They love her so much? What happened to he couldn't live without Roxie so he insisted on joint ownership? Was he serious? Her heartbeat quickened, and her blood began to boil. She needed to get out of there.

She fought the urge to strangle him right then and there. She said, "Oh? How would that work exactly? "

Jason said, "Same arrangement, except she'd be with my parents instead of me. I could probably still pick her up or you drop her off at my parents' house."

She really couldn't believe what he was saying to her. He was giving up his half of Roxie to his parents? She was now going to have joint ownership of Roxie with her ex-in-laws? She couldn't hold it in any longer. "I'm not okay with this. Why don't you give her to me? She is my dog. I can take care of her full time."

"I think it's best for Roxie."

"I'm not sure I agree."

Jason shook his head. "We've been over this before. You work. She hates being left alone. My parents are retired and can watch her during the day. It's not up for negotiation. Legally, I can do whatever I want with my half of the ownership."

Casey wondered if this was true and if a legal battle would be worth it to be rid of him and have Roxie full time. Why had she ever married him? Why didn't she fight harder for Roxie before their arrangement was legally binding? Oh right, because her world was falling apart. She had been defeated and didn't have the energy to fight any more battles.

She rolled her eyes. "Whatever. Fine. I guess it is what it is." She went over to Roxie and gave her a hug and kiss on the top of her furry head. "I love you. I'll miss you. Be good, okay?"

She put Roxie back down and scurried toward the door. She left without saying another word to Jason and jogged to her car before she totally lost her cool. She shut her car door and sped off.

On the freeway, she yelled and screamed at an invisible Jason and at herself. Why was she so surprised? He'd done the same thing to her! Told her he loved her and wanted to marry her. Two years later he didn't love her and never did. Six months ago, he said he loved Roxie and couldn't live without her. Now he was giving up his half of her to his parents? To his parents? Who does that? She thanked the Universe they never had human children.

She was so furious she missed the exit to her apartment. She exited the highway and ran into the grocery store for her drug of choice: ice cream. Back on the road, she shouted at Jason once again. At that moment, she wished she'd never met him, let alone married him.

---

SHE DEVOURED her Mint Chocolate Cookie ice cream, took a few shots of tequila, and proceeded to crank up the stereo and finish packing while waiting for Rachel to arrive. The doorbell chimed, and Casey sauntered over to the door and opened it wide. "Bonjour, Rachel!" Casey sang.

Rachel's mouth dropped open. "Bonjour. Am I late to the party?"

Casey chuckled. "Nah. Just in time. Sorry, I needed a little fun juice. Had a day. You want some tequila?"

Rachel shrugged. "Sure. Hey, I'm on vacation!"

Casey grinned. "That's the spirit!" She shuffled into the kitchen and poured Rachel a shot into a glass with an etching of the Eiffel Tower on the side. She handed it to her and poured herself another.

She raised her glass. "To France! And to good friends! And to vacation! Cheers!"

They clanked glasses.

Rachel chugged hers in a single gulp. "Tell me about this day you had."

Casey didn't want to talk about it but realized in all the years she'd known Rachel, Casey had never drunk that much and certainly not alone. She needed to explain and did.

Rachel's green eyes widened. "That's insane. How do you give away half a dog? If anything, he should just give you full ownership. She's your dog!"

"No kidding. It's crazy, right?"

"Totally crazy."

Casey shook her head. "I'm so angry. I just wanted to strangle him. The nerve of him! He says it's his legal right. He's such an asshole!"

Rachel said, "I don't know if it's legal or not, but it's definitely a jerky insensitive prick thing to do."

Casey yelled. "Asshole!" She took a breath and said, "Okay, no more talk about stupid Jason. It's all France now, baby! Another shot?"

They drank and stayed up all night until the airport shuttle arrived at five in the morning. Casey was beyond relieved to be getting out of town. Just when she thought she could be cordial and friendly toward Jason he went and did the one thing left he could to piss her off. The only silver lining of the whole messed-up situation was now that she'd be sharing custody of Roxie with his parents, she'd see a lot less of him.

ONE YEAR LATER

# CHAPTER 33

A FULL YEAR LATER, Casey sat on Betty and Frank's living room floor scratching Roxie's belly, when Betty said, "Oh, before you go," she went under the Christmas tree and grabbed a gift bag with a penguin on the front and handed it to Casey. "This is for you. It's just a little something."

Casey stood up and accepted the bag. She said, "Thank you," and picked up Roxie. She held Roxie in her arms as Betty and Frank said their goodbyes to their grandpuppy. Casey said, "Have a Merry Christmas."

"You too, Casey."

Casey held Roxie close as she walked back to her car. She set Roxie in her carrier and said, "Hi, girl," followed by scratches behind her ears.

She drove off thinking about how much had changed in the last year. Since Jason graduated in May and he'd given "his half" of Roxie to his parents, Casey had barely spoken to him. Instead of the normal weekly pick-up and drop-off of Roxie with her ex-husband, she now did the normal weekly pick-up and drop-off with her ex-in-laws.

There had been perks to the new arrangement. Roxie's grandparents took her to the groomers and the vet while Casey was at work. When she traveled for work or for fun, she had a reliable and caring environment for Roxie to stay in. It was comforting to know Roxie would always be well taken care of. Was it weird to see her ex-in-laws twice a week? A little. Casey simply shook it off like most of the things she didn't have any control over. It was just part of her new normal.

The whole situation was odd, but it didn't bother Casey. Everything else was going great. She'd been focusing on her career and finding new places to travel. She loved living alone and wondered how she'd ever not lived by herself before. She had complete freedom to clean or not. Cook or not. Go to bed. Don't go to bed. Total freedom. And there was so little drama or conflict in her life. She couldn't remember ever feeling so at peace. She began to truly love her life.

She arrived at Dana and Jerry's house and parked across the street for the annual holiday party. She glanced down at Roxie. "You ready for the party, girl?" Big brown eyes stared back at her.

They walked, stopping to sniff every few feet, up to the front door. As they approached, the door opened. Jerry stood in the entry wearing a Santa hat and holding Roxie's ball in his hand. "Merry Christmas, party people and party dog!"

Casey hugged him. "Merry Christmas!"

He then bent down to greet the party dog with her special ball. They entered the dining room and greeted all the usual suspects who were currently enjoying gin cocktails.

They sat at their assigned seats. Casey grabbed the cocktail being handed to her and said, "Thanks."

She glanced across the table at Javier and Ben. "What's going on? Sorry we're late. I had to pick up Roxie across town."

"We just arrived too."

Casey asked, "How was your weekend in Pt. Reyes?"

Ben grinned. "It was perfect. We hiked. We ate. We drank. It was like a little piece of heaven. Have you been?"

"No, I haven't. I should give it a try."

They continued chatting as the other guests arrived, friends of Jerry's Casey saw only once a year at the annual holiday party. Dana and Jerry stood at the end of the table and gave a toast before inviting them all to the kitchen to fill their plates with the roast beef dinner.

While munching on white chocolate cake and sipping a tawny port, Casey said, "Thank you again for having us each year. It's a highlight of the holiday season for Roxie and me."

Jerry said, "You're very welcome. You know you can bring someone next year if you want to."

Casey cocked her head. "Other than Roxie?"

Jerry said, "Yes, a date. It's okay. We've got plenty of room."

Casey didn't know what to say.

Ben smiled brightly, "Casey, are you seeing someone? I hadn't heard."

No, of course not. She was still unsure what to say. Were they really having this conversation?

Javier nudged Ben and frowned. "Casey still isn't dating."

Ben's eyes widened. "What? You're still not dating? How long has it been?"

Casey sighed. "It's been a year or so."

Javier smiled.

Casey said. "Well it's been a bit over a year since my divorce was final and almost two since we separated. I just haven't had the desire to date. I've been focusing on my career, travel, and getting used to my new single life. I'm good. And besides, it's been so long since I dated anyone but Jason. I don't even know what I would do to start dating." She took a sip of port.

She had wondered what it would be like to date again, but it wasn't like there was anyone she wanted to date.

Ben said. "You know online dating is all the rage. I know a ton of people who have met online."

She didn't revel in the idea of dating online or dating at all for that matter, but maybe she should at least try? She asked, "Really?"

Ben gave a reassuring smile. "Yes, really. It could be fun."

Javier winked at her. "Girl, you'd be beating them off with a stick."

Casey wasn't fully convinced of that, but she enjoyed the compliment. She shook her head. "Oh, I don't know. Maybe I'll think about it."

She nodded, smiled, and laughed the rest of the evening, but she couldn't get the idea of dating out of her head. Was it time she at least tries it? She guessed it did sound a bit odd that she hadn't dated in two years. It wasn't like she missed having a man around, but then again, the majority of her romantic history was limited to her time with Jason. She was sure, or at least hoped, not all men were like him. But would a man only complicate her life?

THE NEXT DAY she entered the posh restaurant and waved when she spotted Maddy, Gina, and Natalie seated at the white table clothed four-top. Mimosas had already been served, and she was delighted to see the fourth glass waiting for her.

She grinned as she sat. "Hi, ladies. Merry Christmas!" She handed each of them identical small red gift bags. At her place setting was a small pile of gifts ranging from a small box to a tin of homemade goodies. Oh, how she loved Christmas, especially when she was surrounded by her closest friends.

They clinked mimosas before ordering a scrumptious brunch of crab Benedicts, Belgian waffles, and blueberry ricotta pancakes.

Gina asked, "Hey Natalie, what did you get Peter for Christmas?"

Natalie said, "A football jersey and a few little things. Nothing major. What did you get your new guy, what's his name again?"

Gina smirked. "Jeff, and he's not *that* new. Mostly clothes and some cologne he likes."

Maddy grinned and raised her glass. "Casey, cheers to not having to buy men Christmas gifts!"

Casey smiled. "I'll toast to that!" It was refreshing to be around people not trying to force her to date. She said, "Actually, I was kind of thinking of… maybe… considering dating."

Maddy almost spit out her bubbly juice. "What? Really?"

Gina said, "Do tell!"

"Calm down. I was just thinking about it. I was at Jerry and Dana's party last night and we got to talking about online dating. I'm kind of curious what dating would be like."

Gina said, "I think you totally should. I've been online dating for a while. It can be fun."

Maddy added, "I agree. I could even help you set up a profile if you want."

Casey thought, *Wow. They think I'm so hopeless they offer assistance!*

She took a bite of Dungeness crab, savored it and swallowed. "What site do you recommend?" She thought, *Am I really doing this?*

Gina said, "Well it depends on what you're looking for. I'm guessing you don't want just a hook-up. There's eharmony.com and match.com. Either are okay. Match is the cheapest, I think, and the easiest to set up. At eHarmony they make you answer a bunch of questions before you can start connecting with anyone —it's a little more serious. If you want quick and easy, Match would be good." She giggled. "I personally like quick and easy."

They laughed as the waiter approached asking if they'd like a refill on their mimosas. They responded in unison. "Yes, please!"

Natalie, with a stern hand on the table said, "Back to business. Casey, are you going to do it?"

She shrugged. "I don't know. Maybe? I think so."

Maddy clapped her hands excitedly. "Yeah! I'm excited for you."

Casey wasn't sure why she was excited for her. Was it that big of a deal? She took a deep inhale and exhale. "I'm going to do it. But I'll wait until after the holidays. After New Year's."

Gina nodded. "I think that is reasonable. Good plan."

Natalie said. "I agree."

Maddy screeched. "Me too."

Casey took a long sip of her mimosa. She was doing it. She was going to start dating. Watch out new year, Casey Roxie Leslie was jumping into the dating pool.

They moved on to fun holiday chit-chat about family and boyfriend plans before opening their gifts and saying their goodbyes.

On the drive home, she called Kat to tell her about her new plan for dating. Kat responded similarly to the brunch gals. There was squealing and "I'm so happy for you." Casey was surprised how excited all of her friends were about her dating. They weren't that excited when she'd gotten promoted or went on an amazing trip—both of which Casey was considerably happier about than the idea of dating. Dating made her nervous and twitchy. What if she met a psycho or she met someone she actually liked, but they didn't like her? It had been nearly seven years since she dated anyone new, but she recalled a distinct dislike for the whole dating process.

CHAPTER 34

A FEW WEEKS into the New Year, tucked into bed with her laptop balanced on her thighs and Roxie snuggled by her side, Casey stared at the profile of her first love interest from match.com. He was thirty-four, was an engineer, and liked to hike. His profile picture was a bit blurry, but from what she could make out he had dirty blond hair, blue eyes, and a nervous smile. Casey thought, *Hmm. He doesn't look like a serial killer.* But then again, how many serial killers looked like serial killers? She continued to study the profile before deciding whether she should email him, Ruben, back. What would she say? She hadn't anticipated getting email from anyone within the first twenty-four hours. It all seemed to be happening fast. Too fast.

She closed out of his profile and clicked on the next guy who had contacted her. She saw his picture and thought, *Yikes.* She'd set the cutoff age to thirty-nine, but this guy had to be at least fifty, and that was being generous. She closed out. She wasn't looking for a father figure. No, just a normal guy would do. Ruben looked better already.

Next profile. She opened up the third of her potential connections and began to read. She shook her head and thought, *seri-*

*ously?* This is what was out there? Not that she didn't think unemployed ex-convicts with three kids didn't deserve love, but come on. Was it too much to ask for a guy to have a job and be able to take care of himself?

Is that all she needed? What did she want from a partner? He definitely should have a job. No graduate students, please and thank you. It would be nice if he knew how to cook, considering she herself was hopeless in the kitchen. What else? Ah. No room-mates. She did not want some guy still living with his old frat house brothers. No, thank you. What else was important to her? Obviously, her ideal mate would love to travel and support her ambition. Was she looking for a life partner? She thought, *Hmm. Let's focus on getting a date before making lifestyle decisions.* She'd simplify. Three criteria for a potential date: must have a job, must know how to cook, and must not have roommates. Should be easy, right?

She returned to Ruben's profile. It made her nervous to dive into his life as if he could be watching her contemplating an email reply. It was silly. Nobody was watching her. Dating was already making her paranoid! Maybe she was overthinking it. She decided she'd do it. She'd email him back. Was it too soon to email the same day he emailed? Was there a rule? She didn't want to come off as desperate. Screw it. She would email him. What was the worst thing that could happen?

She tapped it out.

*Hi Ruben,*
*Thank you for reaching out. Yes, I do like to hike and travel. What are your favorite places to go? I like the Pleasanton Ridge. I'm a dork.*

SHE THOUGHT, *Thank you for reaching out? What, was he a potential hiring manager?* She shook her head and deleted the message. Why was this difficult? She took a breath and started again.

*Hi Ruben!*
*Yes, I do like to hike and travel. I just got back from a fun trip to New*
*York to visit a friend from high school. What a great city—so alive and*
*full of energy. What are your favorite places to go? Are you familiar*
*with the Pleasanton Ridge? It's a pretty cool trail that my friends and I*
*like to hike when the weather is nice.*
*Have a great night,*
*Casey*

That's probably okay, right? Less formal? Her fingertips
vibrated over the keys. Why was she nervous? It was just a
freaking email. She told herself, *Come on, Casey, stop being a wimp*
*and just do it*. She held her breath and clicked send.

THE NEXT MORNING she sprang out of bed to grab her laptop. She
picked it up off the floor and climbed back into bed. She opened
the lid and opened her email. She said, "wow!" Not only had
Ruben emailed her back, but she had three more emails from
new matches. Ben was right. This could be kind of fun.

She opened up the reply from Ruben.

*Hi Casey,*
*That's cool you went to New York. I've never been. I like to hike, too, but*
*I don't go very often. If you're not too busy, would you like to meet*
*for lunch?*
*Bye,*
*Ruben*

It was a little dry and not very inspiring. Not funny or interesting. However, it wasn't creepy, and no alarms went off in her
gut. Maybe it was the medium? It was difficult to convey emotion
and personality in an email, right? She sent him a quick email

back telling him she was open for meeting for lunch. She pressed send, and her heart raced. She was going to have her first date since Jason. Why was she nervous already?

To distract herself, she read the email from one of her next potential suitors. She grimaced before deleting the email. No, she didn't want to hook up tonight for a night of passion. Gross. She was almost afraid to look at the next one.

She opened the next email and read.

*Hey Casey,*
*Your dog is too cute, both of you look really happy. Dogs are better than most humans, am I right? I personally love animals and have two dogs myself. I'm also a wild-life photographer. I've attached a photo from my latest trip to Africa. Hope you enjoy!*
*Have a great week,*
*Steve*

She chuckled. "Ain't that the truth." She opened the attachment and cracked up at the picture of a zebra with its tongue sticking out. She closed the email and went to his profile. Not bad-looking, although a bit older, at thirty-six. His profile photo's backdrop was of the Grand Canyon. She thought, *He travels, that's a plus.* She continued to read. He definitely had a sense of humor. She grinned as she emailed him back. This was fun! Was it possible she might actually find someone she was compatible with? Someone to have fun with and travel with? She was warming to the whole idea of dating. Maybe it wasn't as bad as she had remembered.

She opened the next email and read it three times before deleting it. She wasn't 100 percent sure she understood what he was asking, but she decided to err on the side of caution. She wasn't into three-way sexual encounters or bondage or fake kidnappings or whatever it was he implied. Yikes. She went into the dating website and blocked Mr. Roberto.

At least she had two potential non-psycho dates. Not bad for two days of online dating, right? Optimistic for her dating future, Casey shut her laptop and turned to Roxie who was snoring softly. She said, "Good morning," and began to scratch her belly as Roxie stretched and rolled around digging into the pillow. Roxie popped on to all fours and ran down the stairs. Casey hopped off the bed, threw on her jacket, and chased Roxie to the door, where she slipped on her harness for a brisk Sunday morning walk.

THE FOLLOWING SATURDAY MORNING, Casey stood in front of the mirror checking out her outfit. After a week of studying profiles, blocking weirdos, and corresponding with a few potentials, she was getting ready for her first date. She wasn't super-excited about meeting Ruben. His emails hadn't gotten more interesting, but she was giving him the benefit of the doubt. What she was looking forward to was getting her first date in seven years out of the way. She refocused on her clothing choice. Was she too casual in skinny jeans, boots, and a sweater? It was just lunch. It was lunch-worthy, right? Unsure, she called Maddy. "Hi Maddy, it's Casey."

"Hey. What's up?"

"I'm getting ready for my lunch date with Ruben. Are jeans, boots and a sweater too casual?"

"Where are you going?

"The Elephant Bar."

"Really? Whose idea was that?"

Casey thought about it. "His."

"Oh."

Casey gritted her teeth. "Is that bad? The food is okay."

"I wouldn't call it romantic or fun or somewhere people under sixty went on a date. He could've picked so many better places."

Casey could hear Maddy's signature chuckle. Casey said, "It's not that bad."

Maddy said, "I'm only teasing. It'll be fine. Call me after to tell me all about it, okay?"

Casey said, "Will do."

Casey wasn't sure she'd been teasing. Maddy had a point, with all the non-chain options, why had he chosen Elephant Bar? Maybe he didn't have a lot of money? It was an economical choice and a safe choice too, given that the menu had something for everyone. Maybe he was practical? Practical wasn't a bad thing.

She hung up with Maddy and studied her reflection again. She fluffed her hair and put on some glittery lip gloss. She thought, *Here goes.*

SHE APPROACHED the entrance of the giant restaurant and pulled open the heavy door. With butterflies in her stomach, she checked the two benches for someone resembling Ruben. She glanced over near the hostess podium and spotted a medium-height man wearing a pair of khaki pants and a white polo shirt. He turned around and studied her. She thought, *Could it be Ruben?* If it was, that photo was blurrier than she'd realized. He began to approach her. She casually smiled. "Are you Ruben?"

He grinned flashing a row of tiny straight teeth. "Yes, Casey?" He extended his hand.

She thought, *No immediate physical attraction, but looks aren't everything.* She shook his clammy hand. "Nice to meet you."

"You too. Shall we get a table?"

She gave a reassuring smile. "Sure."

She followed him back to the podium and thanked the universe they were able to be seated immediately. There was already an awkward vibe between the two of them. Maybe he was just nervous. She had been nervous until she met him. Now she had an overwhelming desire to bolt. With the emails plus the dorky outfit and lack of attraction, her gut told her it would be a painfully dull lunch. She convinced herself that if nothing else, it would be good practice for when she went out with someone she may actually want to spend time with. It wasn't a complete waste.

Seated, she smiled. "So, tell me more about you, Ruben." She tried to maintain eye contact and to not be distracted by his severe case of adult acne.

He remained straight-faced. "I grew up in Washington and moved to the Bay Area after college." He stopped talking and stared at her.

Was that it? That was the whole story?

She said, "Oh. Cool. I was born and raised in the Bay Area. What do you like to do for fun?"

He responded. "I like to hike and play video games." He paused. "And going out with friends."

She wasn't sure she believed he had friends. He studied his menu, not looking at her or asking any more questions. She thought, *Boy he is really putting my conversation skills to the test.*

The uncomfortable silence was broken when the waitress approached. "What can I get you two?"

Casey rattled off her order in record time. She wouldn't let this thing go on longer than it needed to. Thankfully, Ruben had been ready with his order too. The waitress left, and they were once again alone.

He sat and stared at her. Was she wrong about him not being creepy?

Casey asked, "So where in Washington are you from? I have a friend in Seattle."

He responded, "Tacoma."

"Oh, I've never been. I do love Seattle though. My friend graduated from the University of Washington last year with a PhD in Biochemistry." She went on to tell him about their entire friendship to fill the time. He was giving her nothing to work with! No wonder this poor guy was single.

Thrilled to get her fettuccini, she immediately dug in. They ate in silence. A few minutes later, the waitress returned. "How does everything taste?"

Casey had already scarfed down half her meal. She said, "It's great. Thank you."

The plucky middle-aged woman said. "Glad to hear it. No rush—you two take all the time you need." She winked and scurried off.

Based on her encouragement for them to take their time, she must have realized they were on a date and for some reason thought it was going well. Talk about lack of intuition. Casey didn't want to take any additional time and continued to shovel pasta in her mouth. Mid-bite, Ruben asked, "What do you like to do for fun?"

She thought, *Seriously? Now you ask?* She swallowed. "I like to travel. I go out a lot with my girlfriends or have them over at my place for a party to celebrate whatever we can think to celebrate." She chuckled. "A few weeks ago, I had a Christmas tree un-decorating party. It was really fun, and my Christmas tree is now packed away! Two birds. One stone."

He gave a gargoyle-type grin. "Sounds fun."

He continued to stare with that weird look on his face. She was almost sure he was harmless, but she had the sudden urge to say she had to use the restroom and sneak out the back of the restaurant. She was conflicted about her thoughts. Who does that? It would be cruel. Why was she plotting her escape? She wasn't that girl. Was she that girl now? She wondered how long it would take for him to realize she wasn't coming back. She forced herself to stay seated long enough to finish her lunch.

He asked, "Should we get dessert?"

She snapped, "No." She realized she was rather abrupt. "I

mean. I'm diabetic and can't have a lot of sugar." She knew it was inconsistent with a pasta lunch, but maybe he wouldn't notice.

"Oh, okay."

The waitress returned. "Any dessert?"

Casey said, "No, thank you. Just the check."

"No problem." She slid it from her apron and placed it on the table. She said, "Take your time," and winked at Casey.

Casey thought, *What the heck was that?* She shook her head and pulled out her wallet.

Across the table, Ruben said, "Oh no, please my treat."

She felt guilty she'd contemplated ditching him. The poor guy was inflicted with no personality and social awkwardness, but he was polite-ish. Not a psycho. Maybe one day he'd meet his boring match, but today was not that day. She thanked him and smiled.

They sat and waited for the waitress to come back to get his credit card. She should have insisted on paying in cash, so they could just leave. Five painful minutes later their transaction was done. She said, "Thank you for lunch. Talk to you later." She didn't wait for his response. She slid out of her chair and hurried out of the restaurant to her car.

---

SHE CHANGED into a pair of sweatpants, curled up on the couch with Roxie, and called Maddy. "Hi Maddy."

"Hey, girl. How was it?"

"Oh my gosh, Maddy. It was awful. I felt like I was on a date with a wax statue—an unattractive one at that."

"Oh no. It was that bad?"

"The conversation was like pulling teeth. Is this what online dating is like?"

"How were his emails?"

Casey thought, *consistent.* "Boring. I guess I should've known."

"Yeah. That sucks. I'm sorry. I wished your first date back out there would be better. How about that other guy you've emailed?"

Casey perked up. "He's funny and smart. I really like emailing him, but it's been over a week and he hasn't asked me out yet. I'm not sure what to make of that."

"Maybe he wants to get to know you a little more before investing in an actual date. Think about it, if he'd asked you out after one email like Mr. Boring did, maybe it would turn out just as bad."

Casey thought it was a fair point. She really did like emailing Steve. He had a witty sense of humor and sent her cool pictures from his job as a wildlife photographer. She actually wanted to meet him more than anyone else she was communicating with.

She said, "I guess you're right. I'll be patient."

Maddy said, "Or...you could ask him out?"

Casey did not like that idea at all. After her last relationship, the guy needed to like her enough to ask her out. She didn't need a Jason 2.0. "That's a firm no. If he wants to go out with me, he'll have to ask."

"Okay, just putting it out there. Anyone else pique your interest?"

Casey shrugged. "There's another guy that seems okay— Mario. I think it could lead to a date. He's semi-interesting and funny. He did ask for my number to call me. I guess in online dating, that is the progression? Email. Phone. Lunch?"

Maddy said, "Yeah, sometimes. Sounds promising."

"We'll see." She thought, *Maybe online dating was a numbers game?* If it was, how much stamina did she have?

Maddy said, "Hang in there."

"Thanks. Talk to you later."

Casey hung up, deflated. She hoped her other dates went better. She ignored her laptop and switched on the TV for an evening with the Golden Girls and ice cream.

# CHAPTER 35

CASEY STARED across the table at the rather large, doughy-faced man in front of her. She thought, *Does anyone use a current photo in their online dating profile?* Luckily, the plan for the date was just coffee and a movie. She could handle that. She said, "So, Mario, where did you grow up?"

He chuckled. She didn't understand why. It wasn't a funny question. He grinned. "Not far from here! I went to Amador Valley High right here in Pleasanton. My parents still live here, in the house I grew up in. Actually, before meeting you, I was at my parents' house visiting. I usually visit at least once or twice a week."

Red flag.

Casey replied, "Oh, that's nice."

He took a sip of his coffee. "You know, I think my mom would really like you."

What the heck? His mom would like her? Who says that within an hour of meeting someone? Someone who doesn't know her, that's for sure. Casey asked, "Do you still live around here?"

More laughter. Why did he think her questions were funny? They weren't funny or even that interesting. After composing himself, he said, "Yep. I just bought my first house a few blocks from my parents. It's nice to be close. It'll be especially nice, once I have kids of my own. Mom definitely wants grandkids." He winked at her.

Casey was stunned and had no idea how to respond to that.

He continued, "Yeah, I'm thinking maybe three or four little rug rats. How about you? How many kids do you want?"

Casey, semi-recovered from his bold declarations, said, "Uh, I don't know." She glanced at her watch. "Should we get going, so that we aren't late to the movie?"

He gave her a sly smile. "Punctual. I like that. Yeah, let's go."

Casey thought, *Oh boy. I need to do a much better job at screening potential dates.*

Casey stared at the big screen while nausea spread through her stomach. It was their first date. Why would he be holding her hand? And why did he say his mother would like her? Who says that on a first date? Her feelings of bolting from the theater were in full effect. It would be so easy to say she needed to go to the ladies' room and never come back. Would it really be that terrible of her? He kind of deserved it. He looked nothing like his photo, and now he was trying to fast-forward to some weird relationship where she was meeting his mother. He hadn't seemed deranged in their emails or on the phone. She wanted to run. She wanted to hide. She needed to get out of there.

She leaned over. "I have to use the restroom. I'll be right back."

He smiled and nodded. She unlocked her hand from his moist sausage-like fingers. She rushed out to the lobby and went into the ladies' room. She stood in the corner trying to decide what to do. Should she call Maddy and find out if she was being totally crazy? Yes, that was it. She'd call Maddy.

She put the phone up to her ear. It rang and rang until it

reached voicemail. Shoot. It was decision time. Was she really going to be that person who runs out on their date? Would he realize she'd run out? She gasped. "That's it." She concocted a plan to text him as soon as she was in the safety of her car and drive away right after. He wouldn't have to wait the whole time wondering if she'd be back. She could even say that she was sick to spare his feelings. She thought, *Yes, great plan*.

She jogged out to her car and climbed in. She turned the key and tapped out a quick text. "Not feeling well. Going home. Sorry." She pressed send and drove off as if her life depended on it. She wasn't proud of running out, but it was too much, too fast. She wasn't attracted to him, and she certainly wasn't ready to meet anyone's mother. She'd thought Mario had potential. Oh jeez. What if her date with Steve would be just as bad?

She glanced at her phone on the passenger seat. Mario was calling. She was not answering. She turned up the stereo and focused on the road. She didn't want to think about the last hour and a half.

She entered her apartment and sat on the floor and played with Roxie. Her phone in her pocket buzzed. She shook her head. It was Mario again. He clearly lacked the ability to read a situation. She heard herself and thought, *Who have I become?* The poor guy was probably lonely. He wasn't mean or stupid. Why had she had such an aversion to his presence and holding his hand? It wasn't like he had pulled out a knife and said, "Hold my hand or I'll cut you!" What was wrong with her? She sighed and thought, *Maybe I'm just damaged beyond repair.*

She knew better than to give up after two bad dates. Her friends would be all over her if she said, "Yeah, I went out with two guys. I'm done now." She was meeting Steve tomorrow. She liked him. She liked his sense of humor and thoughtfulness. She convinced herself to keep at it. The first two just weren't a match. She had felt bad about leaving Mario at the theater. She decided she'd apologize to him and explain why she left so he'd be able to move on. She wasn't a total monster.

She moved over to the sofa and opened her laptop to craft an email to him.

*Hi Mario,*
*I'm sorry I left abruptly at the theater. I left because it made me uncomfortable when you talked about your mother and children and held my hand. I freaked out and had to leave. I'm just not ready for that. I don't think you and I have a future, but I wish you the best.*
*Casey*

She evaluated the message. It wasn't exactly nice, but it was honest. Cruel to be kind? She pressed send and hoped he didn't take her awful departure personally.

Her phone buzzed. She answered. "Hi, Maddy."

"Hey girl. What's up? I saw I missed your call. I thought you were on a date?"

Casey gritted her teeth. "I was. I left him at the theater." She went on to explain the situation.

Maddy cracked up. "Oh, Casey. That is classic."

"Am I awful?"

She was still laughing. "No. You at least texted and came clean with him later. You could've just never returned his calls and emails. That would have been significantly worse."

Casey began to feel a little less guilty. "I guess you're right."

Maddy asked, "So, the big date with Steve is tomorrow, right?"

"Yep."

"You already pick out your outfit?"

Casey felt her mouth turn upward. "Yes. I actually bought a new outfit."

"You excited?"

"Kind of, yeah. I like this guy."

Maddy asked, "Where are you meeting him?"

"In Palo Alto at some courtyard."

She said, "At least it's not some chain restaurant! That's a plus."

"True. He said we could meet in the courtyard and then pick from a few really cool restaurants nearby."

"Definitely a step up!"

Maddy's enthusiasm cheered her up. Casey said, "I think so."

"Well, I have a good feeling about this one. I want all the details tomorrow!"

Casey smiled. "Alright. Talk to you later. Bye."

She put the phone back on the arm of her sofa. She was excited to meet Steve. They'd been messaging for two weeks and now she would meet him in person. She sank back into the sofa and turned on the TV.

THE NEXT DAY, Casey, relieved to finally find parking at the far end of University Avenue, climbed out of her car, wrapped her scarf around her neck, and quickly stuck her hands back into her pockets. It was freezing out. The idea of meeting outside now seemed a little odd.

She strolled down the busy street and found the outside seating. Not surprisingly, there were plenty of seats available. She opted to stand near one of the tables, too nervous to sit. She kept an eye open for Steve.

She jumped when a man wearing a ratty sweatshirt and jeans tapped her on the shoulder, "Casey?"

She was near speechless. "Yes. Are you Steve?" She felt ridiculous for buying a new outfit when he wore an old gray sweatshirt with tiny holes in it. Was it really him? He mostly looked like his picture, but she guessed the photo had to have been from fifteen years ago. He still had a headful of dark hair, but the lines on his face made her wonder if he was older than the thirty-six years he claimed. She deflated before reminding herself of all the funny and thoughtful emails. She convinced herself to ignore his physical appearance. Maybe she'd learn to be attracted to him?

He extended his tiny hand. "Nice to meet you."

She shook. "Nice to meet you too."

He said, "Sorry I'm a little off today. I had a lot going on earlier. You ready for lunch?"

"Yeah. Sounds good." She was dumbfounded. Was it really him?

"How does Italian sound? There's this great place just across the way."

"Sounds good."

He powered down the street, and she quickened her pace to keep up. So many thoughts ran around in her head. She thought there would be sparks and he would be dressed nicely—not like he was going to paint a house after their date. Her disappointment was crippling.

Seated at the crowded restaurant, she studied the menu. He said, "Get anything you want—it's on me."

She glanced up, stunned. "Okay, thank you." Who says that? Who were these people she kept going out with? Had she missed the part where online dating was only for the socially inept? She wanted to cry.

She ordered comfort food and a glass of red wine. She thought, *Dating is making me a day drinker.*

He asked, "How was your week?"

She thought, *At least he's asking me questions, unlike Ruben.*

She said, "Good. Work has been pretty busy. I have a big presentation in a few weeks I've been preparing for. How about you? Any cool photo locations this week?"

He smirked. "Nah. Just a lot of planning for next week's location and putting together a layout from my trip to Africa last year. I took two thousand pictures! It's challenging to narrow it down to about a dozen. I swear I can't help myself!" He chuckled before continuing to talk about his trip to Africa.

Casey said. "That's fascinating. I'd love to go to Africa one day and go on safari."

"It was amazing. What do you have planned for the rest of the day?"

Casey said, "I have a dinner with friends tonight and then home early because I have work tomorrow."

"Busy weekend for you!"

She grinned. "Yes, I usually do keep busy on the weekend. Normally I have a few social events per weekend. I'm trying to cut down to one event per day. I'm pretty tuckered out by Sunday night!"

She realized it was true. She always had something going on. Rarely did she have a day where she had nothing planned.

She asked, "How about you? Do you have an active social life?"

"Not nearly as much as you. I usually go out once a week or so."

She wondered how true that was. The way he dressed, she couldn't imagine what kind of social events he would be attending. Maybe he was having an off day, like he'd said. The rest of their conversation was easy and comfortable.

She found him charming in a sarcastic kind of way. He definitely could hold a conversation, and his stories were interesting. He didn't mention his mother or try to hold her hand. When the lunch ended, he offered to walk her to her car and gave a friendly hug after they reached it. He received points for gentlemanly behavior.

She waved as she opened her door. She sat in the driver's seat and although disappointed there wasn't more of a spark between them, she was thankful it was better than her last two dates.

"So...Casey how were this weekend's dates? Tell us everything," Javier demanded with a fist under his chin.

Casey grimaced. "Saturday's was not great, and I didn't respond to it well." She gulped her wine before explaining her exit from the movie theater.

The table found the story hysterical. Jerry said, "That is the funniest thing I've ever heard." He continued to laugh. She was glad someone was amused by her dating woes. She certainly wasn't.

Javier asked, "Didn't you have a date earlier today too?"

Casey grimaced again, and Jerry said, "Oh no! Did you ditch this one also?"

Casey shook her head. "No. It was fine, but I wasn't attracted to him. These guys just don't match their profile photos. Real life is definitely a letdown—at least for the ones I've been going out with."

Ben, the only one not laughing at her pathetic dating life, said, "I'm sorry Casey. That must be a little disappointing. I'm sure the right one is out there. Hang in there."

More than a little. It was zapping all of her energy and draining the hope she had for finding a suitable partner. "Thanks."

Jerry said, "Yeah, hang in there. We need more stories! We're old and married. We have to live vicariously through you."

"I'll do my best!"

She was thankful for the conversation to switch over to the latest drama at Dana's workplace. Her coworkers, according to her, were crazy, and based on her stories, it seemed to be a fair assessment.

At the end of the evening she said her goodbyes. She couldn't wait to go home and get in bed. It had been a long day.

Before sleep, she decided to check her email. She was surprised to see an email from Steve. He told her he'd had a great time and wanted to get together again. She wasn't sure if a second date was right for her. She wasn't attracted to him. She wished she was. That wasn't likely to change, which frustrated her because she really liked his personality. Maybe she ought to give it one more shot? If he really was having an off day, maybe he would be properly dressed for their next date? His face and body wouldn't change though. Maybe her feelings would change?

# SPRING

## CHAPTER 36

THE FOLLOWING SUNDAY, Casey shut the front door to her apartment and tossed her purse on the living room floor. What a day. She could've strangled Kelly for telling everyone she had to leave Olivia's birthday party to meet up with her "future brother-in-law." Casey had shaken her head and explained to her relatives she was in fact going on a second date and there were no wedding bells ringing anytime soon. Did Kelly think she was being funny? It didn't feel funny to Casey. It felt like unnecessary pressure to be married again.

To add insult to injury, she went on the second date with Steve, and it had gone as she suspected, dead on arrival. He showed up in another old sweatshirt and jeans. She couldn't fathom how anyone thought that was appropriate dating attire. It was like he wasn't trying to impress her at all. And how many holy sweatshirts does one person have anyway?

They clearly weren't a match. Casey didn't think it was just the clothes. There was the eight-year age difference and the realization that they didn't have much in common. Oh, and that small little annoying detail—they had absolutely no chemistry. She still thought he was a good guy and there was likely a woman for him somewhere, but it wasn't her. It was unfortunate, but she knew she and Steve were going to have to move on. Casey wasn't sure Steve realized it yet.

She thought, *man, dating sucks.* She had her third strike, did that mean she was out? She had been perfectly happy before she attempted to date again. She was pretty sure she didn't want anything serious. What was the point? She'd tried it. She didn't like it. It was becoming more trouble than it was worth. Maybe it was time to deactivate her online dating account? The headache and pressure from friends and family was too much too. Why couldn't people accept that you don't have to be in a relationship to be happy?

She plopped on the sofa and went on to her Match page with intentions of closing her account. She perused her latest messages. Pervert. Loser. She paused. Huh. One of the men, Terrance, was actually pretty good-looking. She read the message.

*Hey Casey,*
*I like your profile. You seem like a great gal. Hope we can talk soon.*
*Terrance*

It was kind of generic, but harmless. Should she give it another go? Maybe she would at least be physically attracted to this one. She emailed back a breezy message.

*Hi Terrance,*
*Nice to meet you! I'm glad you reached out. It's been a busy week with work and social engagements. Looking forward to a lazy Sunday. What are you up to the rest of the weekend?*
*Cheers!*
*Casey*

It was lame, but not more lame than his message. She was

about to shut the computer lid when she saw a message come through.

*Hey Casey,*
*Just chillin' this weekend with my dog. A beautiful woman like yourself must have a busy social calendar. If you could spare an evening, I'd love to take you to dinner. Hope to hear from you soon.*
*Terrance*

Casey's first thought was, who still says "chillin'"? And the "beautiful woman" comment was straight-up cheesy. She could barely fathom the idea of another bad date let alone summon the energy to go on another bad or boring date. Those dates had sucked the life out of her. Maybe she ought to go with her gut and close her account. She was supposed to be listening to her gut. It had yet to lead her astray.

Against her better judgment she replied.

*Hi Terrance,*
*Wow! Speedy reply. Sure, I'd be up for dinner. I'm free tomorrow night or next Wednesday night. Let me know when you're free.*
*Cheers!*
*Casey*

She figured at this point she didn't have much to lose. She was willing to give it one last shot.

---

THE FOLLOWING WEDNESDAY NIGHT, fifteen minutes late, Casey hurried toward the restaurant in downtown Walnut Creek. She saw him down the alley next to the restaurant with a phone to his ear. He slid it in his pocket as she neared. He was medium height with dark hair and sparkling blue eyes. She asked, "Terrance?"

He said, "Yep. Casey?"

She gave a nervous smile. "In the flesh."

"Wow, you're a lot better-looking in person."

She knew it was a compliment, but something about it felt slimy. "Thanks. Sorry I'm late. Between traffic and parking, I'm surprised I made it all."

"Glad you did. Shall we?"

She nodded and followed him into the restaurant.

Seated with wine, they sipped and chatted about the weather, where they lived, and what they did for work.

When their entrees arrived, he said a sarcastic, "Bon appetit," in a fake French accident that seemed condescending. There was an air about him that said, "you're lucky to be out with me," that she found off-putting. He was physically attractive but personality-wise not so much. Casey was mid-bite when he said, "On your profile it says you're divorced."

"Yep." Why would he bring that up?

"What happened? Why did you get divorced?"

She thought, *Who asks that on a first date?* She said. "I'd rather not talk about it."

"Well, it's on your profile. What do you have to hide?"

She arched her brows. "I don't have anything to hide. Things didn't work out. Can we talk about something else?" She thought, *This guy is a jerk and probably a drunk.* He was already on his third glass of wine.

He said, "Well I can tell you about why my last relationship ended, because I have nothing to hide."

Why would she want to talk about why his last relationship ended? What was this guy's deal? It was as if he was trying to pick an argument. She was exhausted, and they hadn't even gotten to dessert.

She said, "If you want to talk about it, go ahead." She focused on her chicken skewers and rice pilaf.

She started contemplating ditching scenarios, but the outdoor seating would prove it to be a difficult endeavor. She told herself, just get through dinner, and then you can go home and delete your match.com account. Put a fork in her, she was done.

He went on to talk about some girlfriend he'd had. She wasn't paying close enough attention to know what the deal was.

When the meal was over, she thought she'd be free of him, but she was surprised when he asked, "Can I walk you to your car?"

She hadn't seen that coming. "Oh, sure. I guess," Casey replied. She placed her napkin on the table and scooted her chair back. She walked around the table, and he followed alongside her.

As they reached her car, he said, "I had a good time tonight."

"Oh. Really?" Casey asked.

His face neared as he leaned in to kiss her. She didn't stop him. His lips were wet and tasted like barbecued chicken. It wasn't bad, but it wasn't great either. He pulled away after a minute. He gazed into her eyes, "Have a good night."

Flushed, she replied in a hushed tone. "You too."

In her car, she thought, *Did that just happen?* Did she have a crappy date and then make out with the guy? On the drive home, she wondered if seeing him again would be worth it to experience more post-divorce firsts.

---

THE NEXT MORNING, she woke up to her alarm clock. She glanced at her laptop on the nightstand and contemplated the fate of her online dating. She knew in her gut it was over. Like she had known it was over with Jason those fateful weeks before their wedding. She thought, *Lesson learned, Casey. Know when to cut your losses. You know this is the right decision.* She grabbed the computer and opened the lid. She went directly to her online dating profile, ignored the multiple new matches and messages, and canceled her membership. She shut the lid of the laptop and let out a sigh of relief.

For years, she had envisioned she'd end up as a crazy cat lady, but it never fully made sense to her. Not the part about never finding a life partner, that she understood. The puzzling part was that she wasn't really a cat person, so why would she spend her life surrounded by cats? And then, it hit her like a ton of bricks. Her vision wasn't wrong, it was just a little blurry—the small furry creatures weren't cats. They were fluffy Shih Tzu's the size of cats! It all made so much sense now. She was going to be a crazy dog lady, and she was good with that.

Satisfied with her most recent life decision she got ready for work with a spring in her step.

Later, she strolled into the office and slid onto her chair. She was reading emails when she heard a familiar, "Hey girl."

She swiveled around and grinned. "Hey, Javi. How goes it?"

Javier raised his brows. "Someone's in a good mood. I've got a feeling someone had a good date last night. Dish!"

She threw her head back and giggled. "No. It was terrible. He was a total jerk. However, he did inspire me to quit online dating. So, it wasn't a total loss. I'm officially done. Canceled my membership this morning. Say hello to the new non-dating Casey!" She looked him dead in the eye. "I'm done."

Javier's mouth dropped open. "What? Are you giving up already? It's only been a few months."

She shook her head. "Yeah, a few months I'll never get back. I know in my gut this is right for me. Dating took up so much of my energy. Energy I can use for focusing on my career and travel. I'm even thinking about finally researching business schools to pursue my MBA."

Javier pleaded, "But. A good partner can bring so much to your life."

"I can have a full life without a man. I have a full social life, travel, work, and Roxie."

Javier deflated. "I suppose you're right. You do have one of the busiest social calendars of anyone I know. Okay, if this is what you really want."

She said, "It is." She paused. "Now what's going on with you? You excited about your upcoming trip to Hawaii?"

She listened as Javier described his weeklong plan for fun in the sun. After he went off to a meeting, she wondered if she would have to defend her latest decision to all of her friends and family too.

She hadn't considered the reaction from her friends and family when she'd made the decision to swear off dating. Most of them had always supported her other decisions, she hoped they would support this one too. She knew in the core of her being that prioritizing herself and what she wanted to accomplish in her life was absolutely the right decision. She'd never been surer of anything in her whole life.

LATER THAT EVENING, Casey sung, "Hey, ladies," as she joined Maddy, Gina, and Natalie at one of their favorite Cuban restaurants in downtown Walnut Creek.

Maddy said, "We just ordered a pitcher of mojitos."

"Awesome."

Casey asked, "How are you guys?"

They nodded and muttered a chorus of "good." Gina said, "More importantly how are you doing?"

Casey grinned. "I'm great!"

Gina smirked. "Oooh. Give us the deets! Maddy says you were out last night with a hunky man. I suspect it's related to your chipper mood."

Casey beamed as she explained her epiphany and new life prioritization. They all sat stunned before launching into similar arguments as Javier. The noise from their pleas to reconsider hurt her brain.

Casey shook her head and lifted her hands in protest. "No. I'm serious about this, and I'm happy about my decision. You're not going to change my mind. Can we please change the subject?"

She knew she sounded harsher than she would've liked, but she needed them to stop. It was her life.

She couldn't believe how much they opposed her plan. Why were people always pushing singles into coupledom? It wasn't the end-all. It wasn't her life goal to be married now or maybe ever. Why was it so difficult for them to understand? Was it conditioning from their families, the media, and society? If this was how her close friends who had supported and comforted her through the darkest times reacted, she didn't even want to think how her family would react.

Happy hour ended peacefully and with laughter, typical for the foursome. Casey was glad they were able to move on and enjoy the night, but she was increasingly worried about future conversations she would have with others.

It was her life, and they could either support her or not be around her. It was as simple as that.

# SUMMER

# CHAPTER 37

A FEW MONTHS LATER, sitting on the sofa with Roxie by her side, Casey researched business schools on her laptop. There were a lot to choose from. She was reading about the Haas Business School when her phone buzzed.

She flatly said, "Hi."

"Hi, sister, just calling to make sure you're still alive."

Casey rolled her eyes. She wasn't sure if Kelly thought she was being humorous when she called to make sure she was alive or if she truly believed Casey would die in her apartment alone and nobody would find her body until the odor was so bad they had to break down her door.

She said, "Still alive."

Kelly giggled. "Oh, good. I was just thinking of you. I think I have someone to set you up with."

Casey shook her head. "No, thanks, for the zillionth time."

"No seriously. Paul's brother is single. You may hit it off."

Casey was dumbfounded by her sister's ridiculous notion that she would date Kelly's husband's alcoholic brother.

"First of all, I don't date family members, and second, no. Stop trying to set me up. I've told you on multiple occasions to not set me up. If you can't accept that, I'm not talking to you anymore."

Casey was ready to hit "end" on her phone. She had barely spoken to Kelly since she'd given some random guy her email, without her permission, thinking she was doing her a favor despite Casey's continued explanation she didn't want to be set up.

Kelly paused before saying, "Oh. Okay. I'm just worried about you. You have nothing in your life. No husband and no kids."

Was she joking?

Casey said, "Excuse me? I have a full life with friends, a career, travel, and Roxie." She knew her sister couldn't possibly understand her life since she hadn't ever left the Bay Area and didn't have a career. All she ever knew was having kids and, more recently, being married. She didn't understand that someone could be happy without those things.

Kelly retorted, "You know Roxie is going to die one day, and then you'll be all alone."

Casey thought, *Who says that?* Did she think Casey was some delusional woman who thought dogs lived forever? Her patience had evaporated.

She said, "When you can respect my life choices, we can talk, but until then, goodbye," and she hung up.

She'd had it with Kelly and her obvious lack of respect for her and her choices. She exhaled and thought, *You can't choose your family.*

She shook off the phone conversation and returned to her laptop. She was blown away by the cost of UC Berkeley's MBA program—it was a public school, so why was the program six figures? She quickly moved on to the Saint Mary's site. She was shocked again when she saw the MBA program at Saint Mary's was half the cost of UC Berkeley's, and it was a private school. Maybe she'd learn why that was during her studies?

She read through the different programs Saint Mary's offered and continued to learn more about entrance requirements and the GMAT.

Next she visited the Cal State East Bay website and studied the details of their MBA program based on a recommendation from Natalie. Natalie graduated from Cal State East Bay with her MBA and said she mostly liked it. Her only complaints had been the large class sizes and lack of access to professors during non-class hours. The cost was comparable to Saint Mary's, but the campus was much further away from her apartment and work.

Her thoughts drifted back to Saint Mary's. The idea of returning to her alma mater was enticing. She had loved her time at Saint Mary's, strolling through campus while friendly strangers waved and said hello in the halls. The professors who bent over backward to help the students. It was a no brainer. Saint Mary's would be her top choice.

She realized she must look like a crazy person sitting on her couch with her dog, grinning at a computer screen.

———

A FEW WEEKS LATER, Casey sat in the lunchroom with Javier and Seth. During lunch, Javier told Casey about a position at Dana's company she was trying to fill. Javier said, "Casey, I actually think she wants to recruit you."

"Really? I have no experience in Quality. I don't think I'm qualified."

Javier waved her off. "Please, you could learn it easy. I think it would be a good fit for you, and it's a good opportunity. You could go far in that field—like to the top."

She said, "I don't know."

Casey wasn't sure she wanted to leave BayArea BioPharma. She liked her job, her coworkers, and her boss. Although, she knew if she really wanted to be in the C-suite she'd need to be in a different position—out of the lab.

Javier said, "You should talk to Dana."

"I was planning to invite her and Jerry over for a poker party next week—that reminds me, you and Ben are invited too." She glanced over at Seth. "You should come too! It'll be fun. We are going to play Texas Hold'em and eat enchiladas—my specialty." And when she said specialty, she had meant she'd made them once before.

Seth smiled, and his ocean blue eyes twinkled. "When is it?"

Casey said, "Next Saturday night."

Seth's smile faded. "Oh maybe not, I've got Riley."

Riley was Seth's infamous ten-year-old son. Casey hadn't spent much time with Seth since he'd started at BayArea BioPharma, more than a year ago. Their conversations had been limited to greetings in the hallway, chit-chat in the lab or after a project meeting, and the occasional lunch with Javier, but Casey didn't miss that in nearly every conversation he had talked about Riley. It was like Riley was his mini-me. They played soccer and video games as well as cooked and went camping together. Casey had never known a more involved or proud father.

She shrugged. "Bring him! It's family-friendly. We don't dance naked or rave or anything crazy. Just poker, dinner, and spirits. My little sisters may be coming over too."

She'd never seen Seth outside of work and hadn't planned on inviting him, but he was there, and it would have been awkward not to invite him. Not that she didn't want him there. He was nice, smart, and funny. Maybe he would be fun to hang out with outside of work? It didn't hurt that he was easy on the eyes.

Seth said, "Sure. Let me talk to Riley about it."

Casey grinned. "Great. How about you and Ben?" She found herself hoping Seth would be attending. What was that about?

Javier said, "I think we're free, but let me double check with Ben. We love a good poker party!"

"Cool."

Javier said, "So you start your class tonight?"

"Yep. Accounting 1A, Summer Session, here I come!"

Javier said, "Accounting sounds exciting. Not." He chuckled. "Don't you forget us when you're a rich and a powerful CEO. Promise?"

Casey was excited about starting the pre-requisite courses for the MBA program at Saint Mary's at the local junior college. Due to the fact that her bachelor's degree was in chemistry, she didn't have any of the foundation courses she needed for a master's degree in business. Saint Mary's offered the classes she needed, but she had found out from the admissions counselor that she could take the classes at the junior college and save a ton of money.

She laughed. "Oh, Javi. I'd never forget you. I may act like I don't know you, but I won't forget you."

Javier and Seth laughed. Casey watched Seth for a moment before she realized what she was doing and quickly looked away.

THE FOLLOWING SATURDAY, Casey hauled the new table and chair set through her front door. Why did she think inviting twelve people over to her one-bedroom apartment was a good idea? It was going to be cozy.

She unpacked the folding table and popped out the legs. She carried it to the dining room and lined it up with her dining table. Perfect match. She threw on the red table cloths she normally used during the holidays, making it look like one seamless table. She tucked the chairs under the tables and stood back to admire her handiwork.

From her closet, she pulled out the heavy metal case filled with cards and poker chips and set it at the center of the table. She appeared poker-ready.

She took the cardboard packing materials out to the dumpster and hurried back into the apartment to avoid a Roxie freak out.

She pulled her hair up in a ponytail and entered the kitchen for an afternoon of cooking homemade enchiladas and guacamole. Hours later, she cleaned up the kitchen and set up the bar on her kitchen counter.

She was a shower away from party-ready. She stepped out of the bathroom and perused her closet for a poker-party outfit. She tugged on a pair of black jeans and a white flowing blouse. She slipped on a long gold and multi-colored stone necklace to complete the ensemble. It was her favorite look, "celebrity on her day off." Stylish but effortless.

She glanced at her chunky timepiece. Guests would start arriving in an hour. She took Roxie on one last walk to release some energy and ensure there would be no excitement-induced accidents. Back inside, she checked on the enchiladas in the oven and set out the appetizers. It was party time.

Roxie barked at the knock on the door. Casey opened the door. "Welcome! Come on in."

Maddy and Gina entered the apartment. "Hey, Casey." Maddy paused to greet a jumping Roxie. "Oh, hi, Roxie. You wanna play?" Maddy threw a toy into the living room, and Roxie ran off to retrieve it.

Gina said, "How's it going? Where should I put this bottle of wine?"

"By the bar, also known as the kitchen counter, will be perfect."

Gina asked, "So I hear a new friend is coming tonight."

Casey failed to fight the smile forming on her face. "Oh, he's just a coworker."

Gina said, "Uh-huh. I hear ya. Just a coworker. If you say so." She giggled.

Casey admitted she may have a little crush on Seth, but it was nothing more than that. She was sure it would pass.

Another knock. Casey opened the door. "Hey, Javier! Ben! Come on in."

She made introductions among the girls and her work bestie and his partner. She realized tonight was going to be monumental because all of her worlds would be colliding. Family. Friends. Coworkers. They all knew of each other, but now they would all meet.

Another knock. Maddy yelled out, "I'll get it!"

She heard a familiar voice. "Hey, Natalie!"

Within twenty minutes, nine people milled around the dining table. Two people hadn't yet arrived: Seth and Riley.

Casey tried to not think about them while standing in the kitchen chatting with Dana about the new position she was trying to fill. Dana insisted. "I'm telling you Casey, you'd be perfect for the role. And, my company does education reimbursement. They'd probably pay for your MBA program."

Casey cocked her head. "Hmm. That would be nice. What is the environment like? From the way you've talked about it, it sounds a little crazy?"

Dana sipped her wine. "Oh, it's not that bad. You can handle it. I wouldn't recruit you if I didn't think you'd be able to deal with it."

Casey thought the company sounded a little dicey, but the idea of being in a position where she could climb the corporate latter and with a company that would pay for an MBA sounded pretty nice. She'd have to give it some serious thought.

She said. "Okay, email me the job description, and I'll consider it."

Dana said, "Okay, but I recommend you make a decision soon, and send me your most current resume ASAP."

She heard a door knock, and her heart beat faster.

She said to Dana. "I'll work on it this week." She felt an arm around her shoulder. Javier put his lips to her ear. "Hey, girl. Seth is here."

She turned around. "Okay. Thanks." Javier wiggled his eyebrows. She playfully slapped him on the arm. She spotted Seth's six-foot frame in the entry talking to Maddy. She approached. "Hi, Seth. Glad you made it. No Riley?"

"He wanted to go to his best friend's house instead. Kids." He gave a shy smile. From behind him, she saw a wide grin and an approving nod from Maddy. She thought, *Oh boy.*

Casey smiled. "Can I get you a drink? Jerry's making cocktails, but we also have wine, beer, and water." She realized it was a good thing Riley hadn't shown up, the only non-alcoholic beverages she had to offer was water and a cocktail mixer Jerry brought.

Seth asked, "What kind of cocktails?"

Standing close to Seth, butterflies filled Casey's stomach. She said, "I'm not sure. I'll introduce you to Jerry and well, everyone, and he can let us know what he's mixing tonight!"

Flushed, she made her way to the kitchen. Jerry shook a metal cocktail shaker when they approached.

She said, "Hey, Jerry and Dana, this is Seth. Seth, this is Jerry and Dana. Funny story, Dana—Seth is your replacement, actually."

Dana extended her hand. "Nice to meet you Seth." She gave a suspicious grin to Casey.

He shook and said, "You too."

Jerry put down the shaker and said, "Nice to meet you. I'm making Manhattans. Can I get you one?"

Seth said, "Sounds great."

Jerry gave Casey a wink and said, "Coming right up." He laughed.

Casey wondered if Javier had been starting rumors about her and Seth or if he was trying to set them up. She recalled when Seth had been interviewing a few years before, Javier had tried to be a matchmaker and she'd told him she wasn't ready yet. She wasn't. She had been in the middle of a divorce, and her whole world was falling apart. Her world was so different now. It was so much better.

She continued to introduce her guests and Seth when the oven timer went off. She exclaimed, "Enchilada time!"

Maddy asked, "Do you want us all to sit at the table?"

She chimed, "Yes please!"

She hurried to the kitchen as Maddy corralled the crowd. She set the trays of enchiladas onto the range. The cheese was melted; they were done. She brought plates and silverware over to the table where Gina and Natalie helped pass them around. She grabbed the first tray and carefully placed it on the table. Before she could go back for the second, Seth asked, "Anything I can help with?"

Casey grinned. "No, I think we're good. Does anyone need another drink before we eat?"

The group had various responses indicating they had everything they needed. She set the last tray on the table before picking up Roxie and taking a seat next to Anna.

Jerry said, "Before we eat—a toast to the hostess with the mostest!"

She surveyed the table. Jerry. Dana. Javier. Ben. Maddy. Gina. Natalie. Rachel. Seth. Anna. Cara. Roxie.

All the humans raised their glasses. Jerry continued, "To Casey. Thank you for your generous hospitality and great company!" He peered at Seth and back at her. He wiggled his eyebrows and exclaimed, "Cheers!"

Shouts of cheers and the sounds of glass clanking filled the space. Casey said, "Now we eat!"

She watched her closest friends, and her new friend, and was filled with what could only be described as joy. These were the people who pulled her from the darkness and supported her as she created a new life for herself. A life better than she'd ever imagined. She was thrilled to be pursuing a master's degree, intrigued by a new job prospect, and couldn't wait for her trip to Switzerland with Kat and Maddy in the fall. She couldn't remember ever being as content and at peace in her entire life. She'd listened to her gut, and it hadn't been wrong. She was right where she was supposed to be.

# PLEASE LEAVE A REVIEW!

Thank you for reading *Where I'm Supposed to Be*! I hope you enjoyed reading it as much as I loved writing it. If you did, I would greatly appreciate if you could post a short review.

Reviews are crucial for any author and can make a huge difference in visibility of current and future works. Reviews allow us to continue doing what we love, *writing stories.* Not to mention, I would be forever grateful!

To leave a review, please go to the Amazon page for *Where I'm Supposed To Be* and scroll down to the bottom of the Amazon page to the review section. It will read, "Share your thoughts with other customers," with a button below that reads, "Write a customer review." Click the "Write a customer review" button and write away!

Thank you!

"I couldn't put it down. Such a heartfelt story.. Heartwarming, touching, honest, raw & emotional. Very well written." - 5 STARS *Amazon reviewer*

"It definitely was a heart wrenching tale, but also a wonderful story of encouragement, and the title sums it all up perfectly." - 5 STARS *Amazon reviewer*

"Absolutely gripping story, tragic along the way, but heartwarming conclusion. I enjoyed reading it, and it held my interest 100%" - 5 STARS *Amazon reviewer*

"All families have some difficult times to overcome but usually it is not a matter of actually trying to survive. In We Can't Be Broken author H.K. Christie spins a story about pain, shame, tragedy, outstanding endurance, love and overcoming the odds. Well written and edited, overall a very good first novel." - *5 STARS Amazon reviewer*

# ABOUT THE AUTHOR

H.K. Christie is the author of *We Can't Be Broken*, a novel inspired by her own family's battle with childhood cancer as well as the follow up novel, *Where I'm Supposed to Be*. She found her passion for writing when she embarked on a one-woman habit breaking experiment. Although she didn't break her habit she did rediscover a love of writing and has been at it ever since.

She is a native and current resident of the San Francisco Bay Area and a two time graduate of Saint Mary's College of California. Before becoming a writer, she worked in the Biotech industry in various roles ranging from scientist to project manager. She currently lives in the Bay Area and is working on her next set of novels, a series of stories about the adult lives of Casey and Anna.

www.authorhkchristie.com

# JOIN MY NEWSLETTER CLUB

Join my newsletter club to be the first to hear about upcoming novels, new releases, giveaways, promotions, and more!

It's completely free to sign up and you'll never be spammed by me, you can opt out easily at any time.

Sign up by going to
www.authorhkchristie.com

# ACKNOWLEDGMENTS

This is a work of fiction. However, like my first novel, *We Can't Be Broken*, it was inspired by my own life.

Like Casey, my life was forever changed when a sweet and *incredibly* feisty Shih Tzu named Kiki entered my world. She brought love, laughter, and comfort for more than fifteen years - not only to me, but to all of her family (If you are wondering how powerful the love for Kiki was - like Casey, I too shared my Shih Tzu with my ex-husband's parents for over *fourteen years*.). She was so very loved and cherished by all of us who were lucky enough to know her.

Our Kiki passed away two months prior to publication of this book, at fifteen-and-a-half years old, due to a very aggressive form of mast cell cancer. At the end we were lucky to have found a loving hospice doctor, Dr. Helen, at Restful Paws. She made Kiki and our comfort a top priority until the day we had to say good-bye. I will be forever grateful to have found Dr. Helen and Restful Paws when we did. My most sincere thank you to Dr. Helen.

I'd like to thank all of my family and friends who have supported me on this project. Especially my husband, Jon, who agreed to postpone our anniversary celebration at the last minute so that I could meet my editing deadline. Thank you, darling!

I'd like to thank my amazing developmental editor, Dawn Husted. I'm so delighted to have found you! You've helped improve my craft by leaps and bounds. Thank you!

I'd like to thank my SUPER beta readers: Juliann Brown, Barbara Carson, Jennifer Jarrett, Dusty Fox, and Kaitlyn Cornell. You guys were with me from the beginning! I don't know if you'll ever realize how much it has meant to me that you've joined this journey with me. Your feedback has been invaluable. I'm lucky to have all of you in my life. Thank you!

I'd like to thank Ashley Strosnider for the detailed and humorous comments and explanations that accompanied her copyedit. They were extremely helpful. Thank you!

I'd like to thank Suzana Stankovic who designed the beautiful cover. You totally nailed it and as you know, I absolutely love it. Thank you!

Last, but certainly not least, I'd like to thank my sweet angel, Kiki, for so much love and comfort throughout some of the toughest times in my life. I will always love you, miss you, and never forget you. Not that I could even if I tried - considering my middle name has been Kiki for more than a decade. I hope you are somewhere out there sniffing to your heart's content and letting that big green frog know who's the boss. I know, I know. I'm bugging you. I'll stop for now, since I know you don't like to be bothered while you're resting.

Made in the USA
San Bernardino, CA
06 September 2019